I0641476

BLIND TRAILS AT TONTO
THE COMPLETE TALES OF
SHERIFF HENRY, VOLUME 8

BLIND TRAILS AT TONTO

THE COMPLETE TALES OF SHERIFF HENRY, VOLUME 8

W.C. TUTTLE

PRIMARY ILLUSTRATOR
PETE KUHLHOFF

COVER BY
RAY QUIGLEY

POPULAR PUBLICATIONS · 2025

TABLE OF CONTENTS

HENRY THE SILENT

*According to one theory it was the slackness
of the sheriff that was turning Wild Horse
Valley into a counterfeiter's paradise*

1

THERE WAS NO road, not even a trail, yet the two men on that dilapidated buckboard threaded their way around Joshua-palm and mesquite as nonchalantly as though they were on a wide highway. The two men were Frijole Bill Cullison, cook at the JHC Ranch, and Slim Pickins, a cow waddie from the same spread.

Frijole Bill was past sixty, so small and lean that he would not weigh over a hundred pounds, soaking wet. His lean face was adorned by a large mustache, a red nose and a pair of searching blue eyes. Slim Pickins was well over six feet, lean as a hound, buck-toothed, and with a long, lean nose. On the back of the buckboard was a home-made box, about half-filled with mesquite-roots, used for fuel in the desert country.

"I'd shore admire to live where they burn coal," said Slim. "This here idy of diggin' for wood don't appeal to me none."

Frijole spat dryly. "It reminds me of a Irishman which lived down in Mexico," he said. "His spring was a hundred feet up a hill from his shack. He said, 'Curse any country, where yuh climb to get water, dig to get wood, and call a jackass a bureau.'"

"It's burro—not bureau," corrected Slim patiently.

"Pearls before swine," sighed Frijole.

"Huh?"

"Mebbe it's the sun."

"Anyway a jackass ain't no bureau. We had a bureau in our house."

"After the jackass went away," sighed Frijole. He stopped the buckboard in the shade of a mesquite, rolled a cigarette and handed Slim the makin's.

Slim accepted, yawned heavily and then drooped a little.

"I never hired out to be no root digger, Frijole," he said. "Fact of the matter is, this ain't no job for the best cowpuncher in Wild Horse Valley, and the man who is prob'ly the best cook."

"I don't exactly like that 'prob'ly', Slim," said Frijole, "and I ain't exactly noddin' my head at yore statement about the best cowpuncher in this valley. But we ain't exactly t' blame for the present predicament.

"When Thunder and Lightnin' went down into Mexico

to celebrate *Cinco de Mayo,* nobody thought they'd be gone for a week."

"Henry should have knowed that," said Slim.

"Henry! How'd he know it? He ain't no mind-reader."

"Reads mine," said Slim.

"Yore head is a open book, Slim. I can read yore mind, and never even put on my glasses. Why, I can even tell what yo're *goin'* to think about."

Frijole reached under the seat and lifted out an old, gallon jug. He removed the wooden cork, shook the jug carefully and tilted it up to his lips, balancing the jug on one elbow. Slim's eyebrows lifted slightly as he appeared to count the number of convulsive jerks of Frijole's Adams-apple. Then he accepted the jug and drank deeply.

Slim's eyes were full of tears and he panted like a man who had run a long distance, as he handed the jug back to Frijole.

"Yo're actin' delicate this mornin'," observed Frijole.

"You shore put plenty horse-liniment in that last batch," said Slim.

"Jist enough to flavor it. Henry and Judge liked it."

"Yeah-a-ah. But they've got a stummick—and I ain't."

In addition to being the cook at the JHC Ranch, Frijole Bill spent much of his time distilling a rather deadly sort of liquor from prunes and any other handy ingredient. But no matter what he added to the prunes, the finished article was closely related to a depth-bomb.

Slim elevated his well-worn high-heel boots to the top of the dashboard, sighed deeply and glanced down at the ground. After several moments he slowly shoved his sombrero back from his brow, but did not take his eyes off the object near the front wheel. Frijole looked at him quizzically, as he said quietly, "That stuff didn't *set* yuh, did it?"

Slim did not move nor reply. Frijole said:

"It can't ossify yuh that quick, I know that."

"Huh!" grunted Slim. He started to turn, but jerked back, still staring at the ground.

"Where do yuh feel the worst, Slimmie?" queried Frijole.

"Yuh know," observed Slim quietly, "I've drunk a lot of different kinds of liquor. I've sampled everythin' from pulque to cognac brandy, but I'll be damned if anythin' I ever drank before would make a curled-up leaf look like a twenty-dollar bill."

"Yore eyes," remarked Frijole," need more fixin' than I thought. Hold 'em tight shut for a minute, and then you'll see the leaf. Mebbe you've got money on yore mind, Slim. Turn around and let me read yuh."

Slim followed Frijole's prescription, grunted quietly,

took off his hat and began fanning himself. It was about a hundred and fifteen in the shade, but the fanning annoyed Frijole.

"It ain't yore eyes—it's the heat," he said.

"Somethin' is wrong," agreed Slim. "Damn it, I still see that twenty!"

"If it's that good, mebbe we can spend it," suggested Frijole.

Slowly Slim got off the seat and hunched beside the wheel.

"Looks different, eh?" queried Frijole.

"Yeah," whispered Slim. "It ain't no twenty—it's a fifty!"

The effect was almost electrical. Frijole went off that seat and landed on his heels beside Slim. There in the heat they crouched shoulder to shoulder, examining the piece of currency. It was a fifty-dollar bill, worn and torn.

"My Gawd!" breathed Frijole. "Must be five miles to any road, and there ain't even a trail through here. Imagine that—right here in the desert!"

"Yuh don't suppose they're growin' out here, do yuh?" asked Slim.

"If I did, I'd shore take me up a piece of land," breathed Frijole. "Fifty dollars of coin of the realm."

"It ain't coin—it's currency," said Slim.

"Twenty-five dollars apiece."

"What do yuh mean—apiece? I found it."

"I know; I read yore mind before yuh spoke. We'll ask around and mebbe we can find out who lost it. Yuh see, when a man's as stingy—"

Frijole's statement died away. His eyes were glued to a creosote bush about six feet away. Suddenly he dived forward in a sprawling slide and made a quick grab. Slim went forward on his hands and knees, staring at Frijole.

"A—a twenty!" yelped Frijole. "Hung up in that sticker-bush!"

"They—they're growin' on bushes!" gasped Slim.

FRIJOLE GOT TO his feet and looked around quickly, as though he expected someone to step from the brush and take the money away from him.

"Whatcha starin' around for?" asked Slim nervously.

"I'm trying to figure out which way most of the wind comes from down here."

"Money on the bushes, and you worry about the wind."

"That money," declared Frijole, "blowed here."

Slim wrinkled his long nose, as he sniffed the slight breeze.

"I smell somethin'," he declared.

"Same here," agreed Frijole, "and it ain't money. C'mon."

Like a pair of pointers they began working against the slight breeze, weaving in and out through cactus and mesquite. Suddenly Slim leaped aside, as though a rattler had buzzed at him, and began backing up.

"What's eatin' yuh?" asked Frijole.

"C'mere and take a look, will yuh?" replied Slim. "It's about seven-eights skillington, and the rest ain't much."

"Skillington?" queried Frijole, picking his way through a cactus patch.

"Yeah."

"Yuh mean skeleton, don'tcha? Oh-h-h-oh!" Frijole halted sharply and studied the remains. "Dead, huh?"

"Well," drawled Slim, "if he ain't he's shore got a wonderful constitution."

"Died with one boot off," remarked Frijole quietly.

"Yeah—and the foot's still in it, Frijole."

Frijole squatted on his heels, ten feet away and studied the remains. Slim's fingers shook a little, as he rolled a cigarette.

"Buzzards shore find everythin'," observed Slim.

"Well," said Frijole, "we better look closer."

"Hop to it," said Slim. "Personally, I can see from here."

Frijole gingerly approached the remains. There was no chance of identification. What clothing remained had been torn to shreds by buzzards. The boots were about all that remained.

"Might trace him through them boots," said Slim. "Look kinda new."

Frijole poked at a boot with a stick. He turned it over and peered inside, a puzzled expression in his eyes. Slowly he took a large claspknife from his pocket and began sawing at something inside the boot.

"What didja find?" asked Slim curiously.

"I dunno—yet," replied Frijole jerkily. "First damn time I ever seen a pocket in a boot. If I can—Gawd'lmighty!"

Frijole dropped the knife, grabbed the boot and began tugging at something inside. Slim forgot his aversion to dead men, and came over. Inside the boot was a flat pocket, and from that pocket Frijole had taken a number of pieces of currency. To be exact, there were six bills, hardly discolored. Slowly Frijole separated the six pieces of currency and held them fan-wise between his fingers. Neither Frijole nor Slim said anything. Slim licked his lips and scratched the back of his right hand. Frijole drew several deep breaths and tried to spit, but his lips merely squeaked.

"Yuh know," observed Slim quietly, "a feller hadn't orto drink that prune whiskey, Frijole. If yuh drink too much and too long, you'll see snakes and little red devils, with tin hats on their peaked heads. But if yuh stay with it as long as me and you have—look what yuh see."

"Yeah," agreed Frijole. "Yeah, that's right. In the first place, they don't make 'em that big."

"Uh-h-h-h, Frijole," said Slim thoughtfully, "jist what size bills do you see?"

"Me? Oh, I dunno. Mebbe it's my eyes. Yuh know they don't make thousand-dollar bills, Slim. You know that as well as I do."

"The hell they don't!" snorted Slim. "Do you see that same amount? Shucks, we couldn't both be wrong. Frijole, we've got a fortune!"

They examined the other boot, but that one had no pocket.

"Six thousand dollars!" exclaimed Frijole. "Three thousand apiece. Wait a minute."

Frijole produced a piece of old envelope and a short pencil. After a lot of figuring he said:

"Slim, at forty a month, it would take yuh six years and three months to make that much money. Yessir, and if yuh acted normal in every respect, it would take yuh seven hundred years to save that much."

"All right," nodded Slim. "We'll cache this money. There ain't no earthly reason to tell Henry and Judge about this feller. Nobody on earth will ever find him. What do yuh say, Frijole?"

"Suits me right down to an ant's antenny," agreed Frijole. "But we've got to hide this money, until we're ready to pull out of Wild Horse Valley. If they ever found that money on us, we'd shore have a lot of lyin' to do."

"Oh, shore. Let's get goin'."

They went back to the buckboard and pulled the jug from under the seat. Slim drank heavily, leaned against a wheel and held his head, until the paroxysm passed.

"The minute yuh get rich, yuh start gettin' delicate," said Frijole.

"I've allus had a particular stummick," said Slim. "I was borned to eat doughnuts and drink champagne—not prune juice and horse-liniment."

They climbed into the buckboard and Frijole turned the team around. They only had a halfload, but sudden riches drove all thoughts of fuel out of their minds.

"Tell me somethin', Frijole," said Slim soberly. "What the hell is a flesh pot?"

"I've done wondered that m'self," replied Frijole. "Mebbe, when we go away to become idlin' rich, we can find a couple of 'em for ourselves."

"They don't sound so awful good."

"No, but they might taste better than they sound, Slim."

2

IT WAS HOT in the sheriff's office at Tonto City that afternoon. Henry Harrison Conroy, the sheriff, and owner of the JHC spread, was tilted back in his old swivel chair, his booted feet on top of his desk, his sombrero covering more than half of his florid face. It had been no simple task for Henry to get his feet on that desk top, because Henry was not designed by nature to put his feet higher than his head.

Henry was five feet, eight inches in height, almost that big around the waist, and was past fifty years of age. His head was nearly bald, his face round and moonlike, surmounted by the largest and reddest nose in the whole state of Arizona. As an Arizona sheriff, Henry Conroy did not fit into the picture. As a matter of fact, up to three years ago, Henry Harrison Conroy's only impression of the West was gained through seeing a single performance of the "Squaw Man."

Henry had been born of the theater. For years he traveled over the best vaudeville circuits, a headliner, featuring a red nose. Improvident, and with a thirst, vaudeville waned, contract cancelled, leaving Henry Harrison Conroy stranded for the moment. Hardly knowing that he had a living relative, he was notified that his uncle had died and left him the JHC ranch in Wild Horse Valley.

Grasping at this last straw, Henry came to Arizona. And

Arizona marveled. Never had they seen anything exactly like Henry. Dove-gray, tailored suits, fancy vests, pearl-colored derby hat, spats, and a gold-headed cane. And that nose! Arizona chuckled. Some had paroxysms of mirth. But they took Henry to their bosom.

When the county election time came along, some joker whispered that he would write Henry's name on the ballot for sheriff. The word spread swiftly. Wild Horse Valley played a huge joke on Henry; they elected him sheriff. Henry realized what had been done. If Wild Horse Valley liked a joke; so did Henry Harrison Conroy. So he appointed Judge Van Treece, a once brilliant lawyer, but who had succumbed to liquor, and was almost a derelict, as his deputy. Adding to that, Henry appointed Oscar Johnson, a giant Swede cowboy, as the jailer. Oscar was huge, powerful, unreliable, with a bland countenance, tiny blue eyes, a button-like nose, and a love for personal encounter.

Judge Van Treece was sixty, six feet three inches tall, skinny, and with the general demeanor of a tragedian. His face was long and thin, sad eyes, heavily pouched, hooked nose and a wide, severe mouth. The Judge invariably dressed in rusty black, which fitted his sonorous voice.

Just now Judge was tilted back in a chair against the wall near a fly-specked window, as he read thoughtfully from a dog-eared copy of Shakespeare. At times he made appropriate gestures.

There were the usual street noises. Tonto City was the county seat, and was also the shopping point for cattlemen and miners. Tonto City had certain virtues, but it also had certain vices. A mining and cattle town draws a certain number of undesirables, and Tonto City had her share.

Henry Harrison Conroy was not comfortable. He shoved his hat back and squinted at Judge Van Treece, who was moving his lips, as he read passages from the Bard of Avon, making finger and wrist gestures.

"There's matter in these sighs; these profund heaves. You must translate:'t is fit we understand them," quoted Henry easily.

Judge carefully marked the place with a bony finger and looked up.

"Eh?" he grunted. "Oh, yes. Awake, eh? Grunting and groaning in your sleep, like a porpoise with a bellyache."

"Sir," replied Henry, "I would have you know that I was not asleep. I but closed my eyes, meditating on the sins of Tonto.'T was a big order."

Judge closed his book and placed it aside.

"What in the devil do you suppose became of Oscar?" he asked.

"Oscar," replied Henry, "borrowed enough money from me to hire a buggy and horse at the livery stable. He desired to squire Josephine to another of those muggy balls at Scorpion Bend. They have not come back as yet. They dance late at Scorpion Bend, Judge."

JOSEPHINE SWENSEN, OSCAR'S light o'love, was maid at the Tonto Hotel, a huge, two-fisted Swedish lady, who wore queer hats of her own manufacture and who would fight at the drop of one of them—and drop it herself.

Judge looked at his watch. "Almost stage time," he said.

As he spoke they heard the clump of heavy boots on the wooden sidewalk. It was Oscar Johnson, his Sunday suit wrinkled, dusty, but with his celluloid collar bravely shining in the sunlight.

He came in, spoke to no one, and sat down on the end of a cot, where he proceeded to remove his boots and collar. Then he sighed deeply.

"Exhaustion in every line," breathed Judge.

"Ay am yust a little bit tired," admitted Oscar. "It vars owful dosty on de stage."

"On the stage?" queried Henry. "Did you not take a livery rig, Oscar?"

"Yah, su-ure. But Ay come back on the stage."

"Oh, I see—your buggy broke down."

Oscar shook his head slowly. "It vars not de boggy."

"Surely not the horse."

"It vars Yosephine."

"My God! You do not mean to say that Josephine broke down."

"Yosephine," said Oscar, "is no lady."

"I see," murmured Henry thoughtfully. "But where is the horse and buggy?"

Oscar shrugged dismally. "Yosephine leaved me."

"You mean—she came home alone?"

Oscar nodded. "Ay had to come home on de stage."

"But what on earth happened?" queried Judge. Oscar wiggled his sore toes and rubbed his neck, where the tight collar had galled him.

"It vars all over Yulius Yornstead."

"And just who is Julius Jornstead?" asked Henry. "The name is not familiar. Do we know the gentleman, Oscar?"

"Yentleman? Va'al, Ay got in poker game and Ay lose t'ree dollar and sax-bits de fiorst pot. Ay have to stay and get even, you bat you. Va'al, ven Ay vent up to de dance hall everybody is giggling, and dere is Yosephine and das

Yulius on the floor, and he is learning her to yig. Ay took von look and Ay vent out dere and Ay says, 'Yulius, das is going too far. Yosephine is not a yigger.'"

"Go on," begged Henry.

"Va'al, Yulius say, 'Who in de ha'al are you to say?' Ay says, 'Val, Ay brought her here and Ay knows she is not a yigger.' Ay says to him, 'Take your hands off her, before Ay bost you vone in the nose.'"

Oscar shook his head sadly. Judge said:

"And you took your eyes off Josephine."

"Yah, su-ure," sighed Oscar.

"And she hit you with her fist?" asked Henry.

"Vit a chair, Henry. Ay voke up and Ay said to myself, 'Ay am t'rough vit vimmin.' So Ay went down to get my hurse and boggy, but it is gone. Yosephine pulled out and left me. She is no lady, Ay can tell you that."

"The evidence is rather conclusive," said Judge. "Were there any other passengers on the stage today, Oscar?"

"Yust von," replied Oscar wearily. "A young girl."

"How young?" asked Judge.

"Ay vars too much of a yentleman to ask her, Yudge."

Tommy Roper, a stuttering young cowboy, who had charge of the livery stable, came into the office.

"Gug-gug—"

"Good afternoon, Tommy," said Henry.

"Th-thank you. Oscar, wh-wh-where is my huh-huh-horse and bug-bug-bug—"

"Buggy," said Henry. "Where is your horse and buggy."

"Uhuh-huh."

Oscar squinted at Tommy thoughtfully. "Yosephine brought it back," he replied.

Tommy shook his head violently.

"You mean—it hasn't come back?" queried Henry. Tommy nodded. Judge said, "More complications, I suppose."

Oscar rubbed his nose violently, trying to figure out just why Josephine had failed to return the horse and buggy.

"Yudas!" he exclaimed. "Do you suppose she vent into de canyon?"

"Perhaps she eloped with Julius," suggested Henry.

"Yulius," said Oscar soberly, "is in de horspital."

"My goodness!" exclaimed Henry.

"Wha-wha-wha—" began Tommy.

"Be calm, Tommy," advised Henry. "We shall locate your equipage. Now, Oscar, just where did you leave that horse and buggy in Scorpion Bend?"

Oscar squinted thoughtfully. "Ay left de hurse tied to the—Ay left de hurse—oh, my gudeness! Oh, my! Yosephine didn't—oh, my gudeness!"

Oscar jumped to his feet and fairly ran outside, where he headed for their stable at the rear of the jail.

"It seems, sir," remarked Judge, "that you awakened a memory in the mind of the Vitrified Viking."

Henry sighed and shook his head.

"I suspect," he sighed, "that Oscar left the horse and buggy at the livery stable at Scorpion Bend, forgot it entirely and, because he did not find it at a hitch-rack, blamed Josephine for leaving him flat."

"Th-that will cuk-cuk-cost him two dud-dud-dud—"

"Two dollars extra," prompted Henry. "Thank you, Tommy."

Tommy Roper nodded and went back to his job. Henry

yawned and relaxed again. Judge picked up his Shakespeare and thumbed the pages thoughtfully.

"I do not see why you keep Oscar," said Judge. "He has never done anything right. As far as that goes, why do you keep Thunder and Lightning? A week ago they went to celebrate *Cinco de Mayo,* and they are not back yet. Frijole and Slim were complaining—"

"Have done, my friend," interrupted Henry. "Oscar pleases me very much. I detest efficiency. As for Thunder and Lightning and their fiesta, it comes but once a year. And as for the complaints of Frijole Bill and Slim Pickins, those two are too lazy to even wash their own faces."

"You condone inefficiency, sir?" queried Judge severely.

"Judge," replied Henry soberly, "when people live in glass houses—"

"I stand rebuked, sir."

"By the way," remarked Henry, "I seem to remember that Frijole Bill brought in a jug of something from the ranch last eve."

"Of *something*," agreed Judge. "When Frijole kept to his original recipe for making prune whiskey, all was well. But now he uses everything that will ferment, and colors it with horse-liniment. Hair-oil, horse-liniment, pain-killer, it is all the same to Frijole."

"Is there anything particularly obnoxious about this last batch?" asked Henry.

"Not obnoxious, Henry, merely damnable. I tried a drink of it last night, and I give you my word my teeth lifted a quarter of an inch."

"Mine," said Henry, "have always been a mite too short. Bring in the cups with you, my friend."

Henry yawned and looked around. A girl was standing in the doorway, looking at him. She was both young and very pretty.

"I would like to see the sheriff," she said.

Henry sagged back a little and managed to get his feet off the top of the desk. Judge came to the doorway, carrying the jug and cups.

"Ah, yes," said Henry. "The sheriff. My dear young lady, I am the sheriff."

"Oh," she said quietly. "May I speak with you?"

"Why, certainly. Judge, place a chair for the young lady. Nice weather we are having. Thank you, Judge."

"I know little about the weather," she said.

"Who does?" smiled Henry. "But no matter. You came to see me?"

"Yes. I came on the stage this afternoon, and they told me at the hotel that I should see you."

"Officially, or—well, as sort of an attraction?" asked Henry soberly.

"Officially, I suppose," she replied. "My name is Mary MacLean and I am from San Francisco."

"Market Street, the Embarcadero, Fisherman's Wharf," muttered Henry. "I can see it all now, with the fog drifting in over the Twin Peaks—"

"You have lived there?" she asked quickly.

"For a week at a time. But pardon me—I think out loud at times. You were saying—"

"That I am Mary McLean, from San Francisco. Last January—the 26th, to be exact—my father, James McLean, drew eight thousand dollars from a bank and came here to buy an interest in a mine. I have never seen nor heard from him since."

"My goodness!" exclaimed Henry. Judge shoved the jug and cups aside and came over by the desk.

"I have never known a James McLean around here," he said.

"And you came here to try and find him," said Henry.

"Yes," nodded Mary, "I want to find him."

"That should not be difficult," said Henry. "He left San Francisco on the twenty-sixth of January. This is the twelfth of May. Have you any idea what mine he was interested in?"

Mary shook her head. "He only told me it was a mine."

"Is your father a mining man?" asked Judge.

"No, he isn't. In fact, I don't believe he knows anything about it."

"Just what was his business?" asked Henry.

"He has owned an engraving shop for a long time. But business was bad, and his eyes needed a long rest; so I guess he wanted to get into something else."

"You worked with him?" asked Judge.

"No—I am just a department store clerk," she replied.

"You are staying at the Tonto Hotel?"

"Yes."

"Well, my dear, I shall make every effort to find your father. If he has been here as long as you say, someone should know him. There are a number of mines, of course, and it may take a little time to trace him."

"I—I hope it will not take too long," she said. "You see, I am not financially able to stay here very long. I gave up my job to come here."

"Yes, I can understand. However, we shall do our best, Miss McLean."

"Thank you both very much."

Henry rubbed his red nose, sighed heavily and looked at Judge.

"Bring on the dynamite, sir."

THEY FILLED THEIR cups and bowed solemnly to each other.

"To Miss McLean?" queried Judge.

"No, Judge; to her father. It is customary to drink to a friendship, beauty or brains, but this time let us drink to a man who was fool enough to draw all his life savings and come down here to buy into a mine. Sir, I give you the biggest fool I have heard about since I went to Arizona."

They bowed gravely, lifted their cups and drank deeply. Judge shuddered, as he placed his cup on the desk, blinked violently and shook his head.

"Your toast missed fire, sir," he said soberly. "It should have been to the two men who just drank Frijole's whiskey."

Henry blinked tearfully. "It has a certain air of authority, I grant you, sir," he said huskily. "Have another, Judge?"

"Not until that cupful has demonstrated its explosive qualities. I am still young enough to cherish thoughts of a more advanced age, sir."

"Perhaps you are right," said Henry thoughtfully. "It has an after-taste much like a combination of shoe polish and vinegar, but withal it hath a glow."

"It hath," agreed Judge dryly. He walked over to the doorway and glanced across the street. "Those Mexican prodigals are back," he said.

They came across the street, hesitated at the doorway,

but came in, weary but smiling broadly. Thunder and Lightning Mendoza were brothers, about five feet, five inches in height, fairly broad of girth, and their I.Q. was not over six and seven-eighths. Their paternal ancestry showed mixtures of Mexican, Yaqui Indian and some allied tribes. Both of them took great pleasure in talking a certain brand of English, which, at times, needed interpretation.

"How am I, you hope and trust?" queried Lightning, smiling broadly.

"And the same to you," added Thunder. "Ees that so?"

HENRY LOOKED THEM over severely. "So you came back," he said quietly. "I let you off for a celebration of *Cinco de Mayo*, and you stay an extra week. What have you to say for yourselves?"

"I cross my heart, you hope I died," replied Lightning soberly. "All you can say for me ees that I never keel heem."

"You never killed who?" asked Judge.

"Those died man," said Thunder. "You know heem, Jodge?"

"Pause a moment," suggested Henry. "There is a dead man?"

"I geeve us your words," declared Lightning solemnly. "Those man ees jus' so dead as—as—"

"Hell," prompted Thunder.

"Sure," grinned Lightning. *"Mucho gracias*, my leetle brodder."

"I see," nodded Henry. "That is settled. There is a dead man."

"Who is he—what does he look like?" asked Judge anxiously.

"Who he is?" queried Lightning. *"Ouien sabe?* Wat he ees look like? W'at you think, Thunder?"

"Pretty damn bad for looking," replied Thunder.

"Merely a skeleton?" asked Henry.

"W'at ees skelimton?" asked Lightning.

"The bony framework of a body."

Lightning took this under advisement, scowling heavily, as he tried to repeat Henry's statement. Finally he smiled broadly.

"I theenk so, too," he agreed. "Plenty bone—not *mucho* skeen left."

"W'at ees fram'works?" asked Thunder.

"Have done!" snorted Judge. "Where is this dead man?"

Lightning shrugged his shoulders. *"Quien sabe?* I theenk I can fin' heem—I hope. My leetle brodder and me lose our mule; so we have for walking home from Agua Frio. Pretty dam hot, eh?"

"Yes, yes; proceed."

"We fin' those dead man on the ground."

"How far from here?" asked Henry.

"Oh, seven mile, I theenk but not much more than seex."

"At least ten, as the crow flies," remarked Judge.

"No crow," said Lightning, "jus' bozzards."

"Well," sighed Henry, "I suppose we must investigate, Judge."

"In all this heat?"

"Remember your oath of office, Judge."

"I never took any oath. The only oath I ever swore in regards to this office was, 'Damn such a job.'"

"Amen," said Henry wearily. "Shall I sound 'Boots and

Saddles' or do you feel capable of saddling your horse without any inspirational music?"

"That is not funny," declared Judge. "In this heat—and my rheumatism—"

"I believe," interrupted Henry, "we may as well call Doctor Knowles. Lightning, can we reach that spot in a wagon or buggy?"

"Spot?" queried the Mexican.

"The place where you found the dead man."

"Sure, I theenk so. Boggy track pretty close to heem."

"Is that so? Hm-m-m-m. Well, Judge, will you engage an equipage from Tommy Roper while I discover the whereabouts of the good doctor?"

"Gladly," replied Judge. "I hanker not for the creaking saddle and the feel of an equine between my rheumatic knees."

While they were waiting for Tommy Roper to hitch up a team Slim and Frijole Bill came to town. The money was already burning holes in their pockets. They tied their horses in front of Henry's office, where Thunder and Lightning waited in the shade.

"Where have you Colorado-maduro mavericks been?" demanded Slim.

"Hello, Sleem," grinned Lightning. "I look good, eh?"

"Yeah? It's about time yuh came back. Whatsa idea of takin' a week more than we allowed yuh. You ort to be fired—both of yuh."

"Nice wedder," said Thunder.

Frijole Bill wiped his brow with his sleeve and glared at Thunder.

"Nice weather! Nice for what?"

"Quien sabe?"

"I guess yuh *don't* know. Where's Henry and Judge?"

AT THAT MOMENT Judge drove out of the livery stable, and over to the front of the office. Henry and Doctor Knowles were coming down the sidewalk toward them. Slim said:

"What's goin' on, anyway, Judge?"

"It seems," replied Judge, "that Thunder and Lightning, walking back from Agua Frio, discovered the remains of a dead man."

"The fram'works of a skelimton," corrected Lightning.

"I'll be a liar!" whispered Frijole.

"Where-at?" queried Slim.

Lightning pointed vaguely in a general southerly direction. Henry and the coroner climbed into the light wagon, and the equipage headed for the old road to Agua Frio.

Frijole and Slim stood together on the sidewalk and watched the departure of the law. Frijole said bitterly:

"With a hundred miles of open country on each side, them two damn *Mejicanos* had to find that corpse."

"What if they did?" queried Slim. "It can't hurt us, Frijole."

"Mebbe not. But Henry is no fool. If he finds them buckboard tracks near there—and our tracks. Hell, they can track that buckboard back to the ranch."

"You paint a terrible picture," sighed Slim. "You almost make me wish we hadn't found the money—almost. C'mon, let's buy a drink."

3

ACTING UNDER LIGHTNING'S direction, Judge drove out toward the JHC ranch, turned right on the old road to Agua Frio, and went south.

"I hope you know where you are going," said Judge.

"Going weeth you," stated Lightning blandly.

"For a ride," added Judge. "I do not believe you have the slightest idea of where you found the dead man—if you found one."

"See those beeg patch ocotillo on those heel?"

"Yes, I see the patch of ocotillo on the hill."

"That ees not the place," said Thunder.

"Get together on this, please," said Henry.

"I theenk," said Lightning, "that from those dead man I can see those patch from ocotillo."

"Brilliant reasoning," said Judge. "Why you can see that patch of ocotillo from Agua Frio."

"Nice patch, eh?" said Lightning.

"Look!" exclaimed Thunder. "Those buckboard tracks turn off."

Judge drew up the team and they considered the buckboard tracks.

"If we follow those tracks, do you suppose we will find the man?" asked Henry.

"You mean, those man who ees drive those bockboard?"

"No, no!" rasped Judge.

"No, I don' theenk so," said Lightning.

"Follow the tracks," suggested Henry. "This heat is damnable."

Obligingly Judge turned off and followed the tracks of the buckboard, which wound from mesquite patch to mesquite patch. Doctor Knowles sighed deeply and fanned himself with his hat.

"I am afraid it is a wild-goose chase, Henry," he said.

"You theenk he ees a goose?" queried Lightning.

"Have done!" snorted Judge.

"Whoa!" yelled Lightning, and the horses stopped short. Henry slid off the seat and bumped his head on the back of the front seat.

"Theese ees the places!" exclaimed Lightning.

They climbed out of the light-wagon and Lightning led the way over to the remains of the dead man.

"Damnably gruesome," complained Judge. Thunder and Lightning, their duty over, squatted in the shade of a mesquite and rolled cigarettes, while Henry and the doctor examined the remains. Henry was particularly interested in the pocket in the boot, the leather of which had been recently cut with a knife.

"There is little left for identification," sighed the doctor. "In fact, there is nothing to indicate the manner of death. It could have been from natural causes—thirst—perhaps."

"Ah!" exclaimed Henry. "A ring, Doc! Third finger, left hand."

It was a peculiar ring, too. In fact, the entire ring, including the setting, was a snake, the head resting in the middle of the coil, its tiny, garnet eyes flashing in the sun.

Henry examined what was left of the hand, while the doctor and Judge examined the ring.

Then they placed the remains on a large piece of canvas, rolled it carefully and placed it in the back of the wagon. None of them relished the job, but it had to be done. Henry was very thoughtful.

"You are thinking of that girl's father?" said Judge.

Henry rubbed his red nose and looked at the doctor.

"Doc, would a man look like that—after two or three months—out here?"

Doctor Knowles, an old range practitioner, squinted thoughtfully at a pair of circling buzzards far up in the sky, nodded his head sadly and climbed into the wagon.

"The ring should settle the matter," said Judge.

"That man ees pretty dead, all right," said Lightning.

"Yes," agreed Henry quietly, "we may depend on that much."

"CASINO" EVANS, OWNER and boss gambler of the King's Castle Saloon, Gambling Palace and Refined Honkatonk, had only been in Tonto City about six months. He was tall, handsome, well-dressed, possibly forty years of age. Casino Evans was not a talkative person, and he had cold, calculating, greenish-gray eyes, which seemed slightly tilted at the outer edges.

Henry was alone in his office, when Evans came in. It was the first time that the gambler had ever been in the office.

"I heard the boys talking about that girl and her father," he said.

"Yes?" replied Henry. "Rather a bad situation, Mr. Evans."

The gambler nodded. "I understand she identified her father by a ring."

"Outside of that there was no chance of identification."

Casino Evans nodded. "Any evidence as to how the man met his death?" he asked.

"Impossible to determine the cause."

"I suppose that is true. And I understand that it leaves the girl in bad financial shape, Mr. Conroy."

"As I understand the situation," replied Henry, "this man drew out his savings and came here to buy a mine. Naturally, the girl has no money."

"That's hard luck," said the gambler. "Of course, we can take up a collection and pay her way back home. I'd be willing—"

Casino Evans stopped, as footsteps came up to the doorway. It was Mary McLean, the object of their discussion.

"Come right in, Miss McLean," invited Henry, as she hesitated at the doorway. "Miss McLean, may I present Mr. Evans."

"How do you do," said Casino Evans quietly. "I was very sorry to hear about your father, Miss McLean."

"Thank you," she said. "Everyone has been most kind to me here."

"Won't you sit down?" invited Henry. Mary sat down. It was an awkward situation, because no one seemed to know just what to say. There was a long pause, before Mary said:

"It was about the—er—funeral," she said. "I—I mean the expense will—"

"There will be no expense to you," assured Henry quickly.

"We will do our share," offered Casino Evans.

"But don't you see," said Maty, "I—I can't accept charity."

"Suppose we call it friendship," suggested Henry.

"But about yourself, Miss McLean," said Evans. "What are your plans?"

"I haven't any, Mr. Evans. Of course, I cannot secure employment here."

"If you could only sing—or something," he ended lamely. Mary shook her head.

"I'm afraid I cannot sing," she said. "I can play a violin."

"You can?" he queried eagerly. "But can you—I mean, can you play well?"

"I have studied ever since I was six years of age."

Casino Evans' gray eyes studied the girl. She was pretty and had a nice figure. He said finally:

"I might—Miss McLean, it isn't much of an offer, but I could use you in my show. I could pay you twenty-five a week—possibly more—if they liked your music."

"In your show?" she asked quickly. "I—I didn't know you had a show."

"Well, it may not be the finest show on earth," smiled Evans. "Out here we call it a honkatonk. You might not like it at all. You think over my offer, Miss McLean. The job is yours, if you want it. If you don't—nobody is hurt. Let me know later."

Mary thanked him, and he walked out. Henry rubbed his nose thoughtfully, as he looked at her.

"What kind of a show is it, Mr. Conroy?" she asked finally.

"My dear, it is the worst possible kind of a show. The girls are not your kind, and the men are not exponents of any sort of virtue. The jokes are very, very bad, the songs worse. I believe the piano player is a cocaine addict, and the drummer smokes marijuana. But—and you may take this as mere belief on my part—if Evans wants you as an attraction in his show, and will give his orders to the others, you will be as safe in there as you would be in a church."

"In other words," she said, "I do not have to be like the others."

"God forbid."

"And you think I can trust Mr. Evans?"

"My dear," replied Henry earnestly, "have you ever read the inscription on a silver dollar? It says, 'In God We Trust'."

"I believe I know what you mean, Mr. Conroy. But I need a job."

HENRY SAT THERE for a long time, deep in thought, after Mary had gone. Judge came in and sat down. It was nearly dark.

"The young lady came to see you?" asked Judge.

"Yes, Judge. She has an offer of work from Casino Evans."

"From Casino Evans? From that tinhorn? Why, Henry—"

"Please, Judge—protect your blood pressure. He wants her to play her violin in the honkatonk."

"But—but, Henry! In that place? A charming, unsophisticated, innocent little girl—in that place. Damme, it is unthinkable!"

"It was kind of him to offer the job, don't you think, Judge?"

"Kind? Casino Evans—kind. Why—little Red Riding Hood and the wolf."

"And no grandmother to guide her," sighed Henry. "Well, it may not be as bad as it looks."

"Hell!" said Judge quietly. "I do not like the idea a bit."

"Rather depressing," admitted Henry. "We might have another try at Frijole's jug. After supper I want to ride out to the ranch and see Frijole and Slim."

"Why?" asked Judge.

"You saw those buckboard tracks, and you saw the marks of high heels around the body. Those were the tracks of the ranch buckboard."

"You believe they discovered the body and did not report it, Henry?"

Henry smiled and rubbed his nose. "Get the jug, please," he replied. "I need inspiration."

As Judge started back to get the jug, Nick Borden, owner and manager of the Shoshone Chief Mine, came in. Borden was tall and muscular, just a bit gray at the temples, and had been a professional gambler, before he became a mine owner. The Shoshone Chief was the largest producer in Wild Horse Valley, and the stock was listed at five dollars a share.

"You are just in time, my friend," smiled Henry. "Judge is just in the act of getting the jug. Sit down, Nick."

"Not if it is some of Frijole's prune juice," said Borden quickly. "Once was enough, Henry. I took a test tube of it and tried it on some concentrates out at the mine."

"What was the reaction, if I may ask?" queried Henry.

"It ate the bottom out of the test tube," said Borden dryly. "Thank you for the invitation, anyway. Henry, I have a rather peculiar letter from a man who seems to own some Shoshone Chief stock. It means that he owns certificate number five two seven nine, five five eight one and six two to six five, each for five thousand shares. He complains that he has never received a dividend, while an acquaintance has received two dividends. Naturally, he wants to know why."

"It sounds like a reasonable query, Nick," said Henry.

"Except," said Borden, "the fact that no certificates of that number have ever been sold; they are still in the stock book."

"My goodness!" exclaimed Henry. "Not sold? And each one for five thousand shares. At the market price that would be seventy-five thousand dollars."

"And," added Judge, "if those numbers up to over six thousand were sold, someone netted a neat profit."

"If this letter is true," said Borden, "someone has counterfeited stock certificates of the Shoshone Chief. Henry, that is a hell of a situation."

"Does the man say where he bought them?" asked Henry.

"From a broker in San Francisco."

Judge whistled sharply. "Counterfeited certificates and a crooked broker. Why, Borden, with that stock in demand for months, imagine what a cleanup has been made!"

"I've been thinking about that," replied Borden dryly. "For about four months that stock has never been listed below four dollars and fifty cents a share. Even before that it was above three dollars."

"How long ago did you receive that letter, Nick?" asked Henry.

"About three weeks ago."

"And you have said nothing?" asked Judge quickly.

"It is not a situation to be handled by county peace officers," replied Borden. "I don't know what action has been taken, but I wanted you to know. Wild Horse Valley may not be connected in it in any way. Possibly the counterfeits are made far away from here."

"No doubt," nodded Henry soberly. "You may secure the jug, Judge."

"And I'll be going," laughed Borden. "I don't even want to be around, when it is uncorked."

4

IT WAS NEARLY dark, when Oscar Johnson rode into Scorpion Bend. Through lack of memory as to where he had left his horse and buggy, he had deserted Josephine Swensen, and just now he did not want to meet her. So he went to a saloon across the street from the Scorpion Bend hotel, and proceeded to imbibe a few glasses of courage. After a sufficient number of drinks he would feel more capable of taking care of himself.

Josephine had been there all day, getting madder every moment, and she saw Oscar from a hotel window. There was nothing wrong with her memory. She knew that the horse and buggy were at the livery stable, but Josephine, in spite of her fighting ability, was a bit timid of driving a horse over those grades to Tonto City. But the fact that Oscar came back and went straight to a saloon, without making any inquiries about her, was the last straw. Yanking her plumed hat down over one eye she headed for the livery stable, determined to go home alone.

"Ay vill show that yigger," she muttered aloud, as she strode down the dusty street.

The stable-keeper harnessed the horse for her. He asked about Oscar, but Josephine ignored the question. A man came through a side doorway and stood there, watching the man hitch up the horse. When the horse was hitched the stableman said to Josephine:

"Goin' back alone?"

"Yah—alone," she nodded.

He handed her the lines. "It's a long ride alone—at night," he said.

"Pardon me," said the stranger quietly. "I was going to hire a rig to drive to Tonto City, but if the lady could use a driver—?"

Josephine hesitated. The light from the stable lantern was none too bright. The man said:

"I am a very good driver—and I must go to Tonto City."

"Yump in," invited Josephine. "Ve might as vell get storted."

It was about an hour later when Oscar Johnson, lilting a Swedish tune, came to the stable. Oscar was not drunk, but full of courage.

"Ay vant my hurse and boggy," he announced.

"Your girl got it over an hour ago, Oscar," replied the stableman.

"Yosephine got it? You mean to stood there and tell me that Yosephine drove that hurse avay—alone?"

"Not alone—she had a man with her."

"Ay vill yust be damned!" snorted Oscar. "Yulius! Ay vill fix him."

Then Oscar went back to get his saddle horse.

5

THINGS WERE RATHER sad out at the JHC ranch house. Frijole Bill, his thin face nicked from a dull razor, stood in the middle of the main room and tried to admire himself in a cracked mirror over the fireplace. Frijole was dressed up. He was wearing a pair of white flannel pants, which Henry had given him, and an ancient cutaway coat, which he had owned for years. The pants were over forty inches around the waist, while Frijole was barely twenty-seven. Ensued many and sundry tucks. They were also too long, necessitating a six-inch cuff.

A red and white stripped shirt, topped by a bat-wing collar, much too large and with many smudgy thumb-prints, was encircled by a bright green necktie, while on his feet were a pair of yellow shoes with elastic sides. That is, they once had elastic sides. And the color was rather jaundiced.

"How do I look, feller?" asked Frijole. After a long pause he asked the question again. Slim Pickins sighed.

"I'm gropin' for the right word," replied Slim. "Lookin' at yuh from the back side, yuh look a hell of a lot like a beetle that had got his hind legs in white paint. But, lookin' at yuh front view, Frijole, you look like one of them pitchers the medicine show feller had, showin' the effects of alcohol on yore kidneys."

Slim got to his feet, none too steadily, and walked around Frijole. Slim was clad in a tight-fitting, store-made suit of bilious green. He had purchased it by mail two years ago, but never wore it, except on state occasions. His shirt was pink, while his tie was white and blue.

"Well?" queried Frijole, when Slim sank back into a chair.

"I can't think of the word, Frijole," he admitted. "It could be stoopend-ous—but it ain't."

Frijole took the jug and poured out two more drinks.

"'Course," he said, "I don't aim to keep duded up all the time, but I thought it'd be nice to dress up to say good-by."

Slim downed his cupful of prune whiskey and waved the cup jerkily.

"Tha's the worst of it," he sighed. "Here's me and you—leavin' home. Jist a-walkin' out on everythin' that's near and dear to our hearts. It's a awful step, Frijole. What'll Henry say? What'll Judge say? It'll break their hearts, I tell yuh."

Frijole poured another drink.

"Breakin' home ties," muttered Slim. "Couple damn traitors."

They drank gustily. Frijole said, "Don't forget that six thousand dollars, Slim."

Slim nodded, dangling the cup in his hand. "Money's broke up happy homes before," he said. Frijole fought his collar. The tie kept pulling under the collar and annoyed him.

"I've been here a long time," he said. "Let's have another drink."

"We'll be drunk before we get to Tonto City," said Slim.

"Yeah," agreed Frijole.

Slim sighed and stretched his long legs.

"What'll we do after we git to Scorpion Bend?" he asked.

"I'll git me a new collar," said Frijole. "Then we'll git us a couple good see-gars, and then we'll buy a couple tickets on the train. Say, Slim, where the hell are we goin', anyway?"

They drank again. Slim said:

"I've allus hankered for them South Seas, where yuh don't have nothin' to do, except set in the shade and wait for a cocoanut to drop into yore lap. And a couple them sireens dancin' for yuh in grass skirts."

"Why?" asked Frijole.

"Oh, jist to dance, I reckon. They're purty, too."

"What's a sireen, Slim?"

"Hell, I dunno—it's jist their names, I reckon."

"I never knowed any sireens."

"I knowed a Ireen oncet, but she didn't have no grass

skirt. Hell, she wasn't even a good dancer. And what's the idea of waitin' for a cocoanut to drop in yore lap?"

"I dunno—they jist do. Not if yore standin' up, of course. Have you got yore war-sack packed yet?"

Somewhere a rooster crowed. Frijole jerked around and looked at Slim.

"William Shakespeare!" he exclaimed. "I plumb forgot Old Bill."

"He'll miss yuh," said Slim. "He'll miss eatin' mash. I wouldn't be a bit surprised if he'd die—him bein' so used to eatin' that whiskey mash."

"Yeah," agreed Frijole. "Hell, I forgot Bill Shakespeare."

"That's what too much money does to yuh," said Slim solemnly.

"I think we need another drink, Slim."

"We'll be plumb stiff before we get to Tonto."

"I want to be stiff, when I tell Henry that we're quittin'."

"I'm gettin' kinda numb already," said Slim, "but I'll have one more."

"Thish may cripple yuh, but it won't kill," stated Frijole. "Here's over the lips and through the gums; look out, intestines, here she comes."

SLIM DRANK AND cleared his throat raspingly. "You better tell Old Bill good-by, Frijole," he said thickly.

"Tell'm good-by—hell! I'm takin' him with me."

"You can't take no rooshter with yuh, Frijole."

"Izzatso? Can't? You watch me. You hitch up the horsh, while I get Old Bill. My Gawd, you don' think I'd leave'm here, do yuh? My ol' rooshter? Slimmie, I'm 'shamed of yuh. Take that jug and put it in the back of the buggy—we might get thirs'y on the way."

Slim shrugged drunkenly, missed the front door by a comfortable margin, grinned foolishly, felt his way out and then fell off the porch. He heard a commotion near the back door.

"Who the hell moved that pump?" said Frijole. "Whoa! Wait a minute, will yuh? All right, I'll wait'll yuh get pasht. Jus' take yore time—don' hurry. Stop that! My Gawd, I give yuh all the room there is—and yuh run into me again. All right, jus' hold still—I'll make it. That's fine."

"Didja get 'way from it?" asked Slim seriously.

"Yeah, I got 'way all right. Which way is the hen housh from here?"

"Which way you lookin'?" asked Slim.

"I dunno. Oh, yeah, I can see the Big Dipper."

"I think the hen housh is right unner it, Frijole."

"Mush obliged. Have a nice time, Slimmie. Send me a poshtal card, will yuh. Oh-h-h-h, Old Man Lute was a gol darn brute, and he couldn't get his cattle up the gol darned chute, comea ty yi yippi ay aye, aye ay-y-y!"

Crash! After a period of silence Slim said:

"Found it, eh, Frijole?"

"Your di-rections was perfec', par'ner," replied Frijole.

"Hit the ol' door dead chenter, eh?" chuckled Slim, as he did a bow-legged stagger in the darkness toward the stable.

"Nosir," denied Frijole, "but I made a new one."

LATE THAT AFTERNOON Casino Evans called together his gamblers, bartenders and honkatonk girls. When they were assembled he said:

"I've hired a girl named Mary McLean. You all heard about her father. She's broke and won't take charity. She plays a violin—and that's all she's supposed to do in here.

I hope you all understand what I mean. As for you men—hands off. And when I say that—I mean it. Treat her right. That's all."

Henry and Judge were at the honkatonk that evening and heard Mary play her violin. Casino Evans came to Henry after her first performance.

"What do you think of her?" he asked. "Did you ever hear better?"

"I never have—in a honkatonk," replied Henry.

"A hell of a place for a young artist to make her debut," growled Judge.

"I know what you mean," said Evans. "But I gave everybody orders regarding her. She's perfectly safe in here, Judge. I'll see to that personally."

"Grandma, what big teeth you have," said Judge quietly.

"What was that?" asked Evans.

"Just thinking out loud," said Judge.

"I sincerely hope your orders will be obeyed, sir," said Henry.

"They better," replied Casino Evans. "I never give an order twice."

Frijole Bill and Slim Pickins, with six thousand dollars between them, came to Tonto City. Slim did the driving, while Frijole, his finery slightly disheveled, held William Shakespeare, the old rooster, on his lap. They were undeniably drunk, but very serious. Slim made several ineffectual attempts to tie the horse to the King's Castle hitch-rack, but finally threw the tie-rope aside in disgust.

Then he got together with Frijole, who was having difficulty with the rooster, and inquired as to just what to do next.

"Jus' where-at are we goin'?" asked Frijole.

"Cooba," replied Slim thickly. "You remem'er, do you not?"

"Where-at's Cooba?"

"Some'ers in the Shouth Sheas," replied Slim, making gestures in the dark. "Long ways ona boat."

"Oh, tha's right. Hm-m-m. Where's boat, Schlimmie?"

"We've got to fin' one. Mus' be one some'ers, Frijole. It stands t' reashon, don'tcha know it?"

"Yeah, it schtands all right. Quit pickin' at me, Bill, or I'll pull yore lasht tail-feather out. Then how'll yuh look? Ter-'ble, eh? Damn right."

"Why don'tcha throw that damn he-hen away?" asked Slim. "They won't letcha take him on a ship. 'F I was you—"

" 'F you was me, eh? How lovely. How exceed'ngly lovely. Throw away my ol' par'ner, eh? Damn you, Bill, if you don't quit pickin' at me—"

"Ol' par'ner—pickin' at yuh. Fine par'ner, he is. I'd jussasoon have a snake. 'S a fact. Rather—mebbe. Well, are yuh goin' to stan' there and argue with a he-hen, or are we goin' to do shomethin' else?"

"Wha's to be done?" asked Frijole blankly.

"I need a drink," said Slim. "Can't think 'thout a drink. Tie up that he-hen and put him in the buggy. You make me nervous. Where's buggy?"

"Where'd yuh leave it?" asked Frijole.

"Tha's the trouble with you," complained Slim. "I've done everythin' else for yuh, and now I've gotta do yore thinkin' for yuh. Well, all right, Misser Cullison, I'll do it for yuh. What do yuh want to know?"

"I dunno," admitted Frijole Bill. "Don' you remember, Misser Pickins?"

"Lemme shee. We're goin' to find a boat, and then—"

"Where?"

"Scorpion Bend, 'f I 'member right."

"Then anshwer me thish—what'r we doin' here?"

"My goo'ness!" exclaimed Slim. "Imagine thish, will yuh? Stoppin' at the wrong place. C'mon."

They managed to find the buggy, where they drank deeply from the jug, climbed in and backed the horse away from the hitch-rack. They had forgotten that they were going to notify Henry Conroy that they had quit the ranch. They made a wide circle of the street and headed for Scorpion Bend, with William Shakespeare sitting on the dashboard.

"Wha's the name of the ship?" asked Frijole.

"Who gives a damn, jus' so it floats?" queried Slim.

THE ROAD TO Scorpion Bend was one to tax the driving ability of a sober man, and the horse they drove was not exactly a trustworthy animal, but Slim Pickins was unafraid. In fact, after another drink or two, Slim Pickins was unanything. He drove in a mental haze, arguing with the hazy Frijole, regardless of road conditions.

After they were on the long, dangerous grades, Frijole said:

"Gotta hurry. Sim'ly gotta hurry."

"What for?" asked Slim.

"That boat might be gone."

"Goo'ness me!" grunted Slim. "I never thought of that. Git up!"

Slim grasped the buggy-whip, took a mighty slash at the

indistinct rump of the horse, and they went faster. In fact, they were going much too fast. Suddenly the horse tried to stop, shied wildly against the cliff side of the grade, and then came a mighty crash in the dark.

After an undetermined length of time, Frijole Cullison discovered that he was sitting on the ground. Something had gone decidedly wrong, but Frijole was unable to understand just what it was. He managed to get to his feet, unsteady, it was true, but still upright. After awhile he dimly remembered that he and Slim had been in a buggy. Where was Slim?

Frijole began walking slowly around, much like a pup trying to find a place to lie down, and he bumped into the rear end of a buggy. After an investigation he discovered that there was a horse hitched to the buggy. He leaned against a wheel and tried to remember.

"That's right," he said aloud. "Me and Slim was in the buggy, when somethin' happened. My Gawd, I wonder if Slim went into the canyon?"

The idea was appalling. He called Slim's name, but there was no response, except an echo. Even the jug was not on the seat of the buggy. Then Frijole decided to see if the horse was all right, and fell over a body. His pawing hands was all the evidence he needed. Here was Slim.

"Ol' Slimmie's dead," he told the world. "Deader'n a door-knob. Poor ol' Slimmie. Bes' feller on earth—and he's a goner. I'll betcha he's settin' on a cloud right now, playin' a harp. Poor ol' Slimmie."

The soliloquy over, Frijole proceeded to get his hands around the deceased, and, after several mighty efforts, to get the body into the buggy, where he propped it up. Then he got in beside it. The horse limped, and it seemed that every wheel on the buggy was out of line. From the sounds, it seemed that many spokes were missing. But Frijole did not mind.

"I don't even give a damn which way I'm goin'," he told the darkness.

6

IT WAS PAST midnight in Tonto City. Henry and Judge had been in bed for an hour or more. Henry was snoring lustily, but Judge was propped up on his pillow, reading by lamplight. Judge was wearing a faded nightshirt and on his white hair was perched a skull-cap. With his glasses on the end of his hooked nose, he looked like an old and very wise owl.

He heard a horse and buggy stop in front of the hotel, and wondered if Oscar Johnson had finally brought Josephine back to Tonto. His musings were interrupted as heavy footsteps came down the uncarpeted hallway, and a heavy hand banged loudly on their door. In fact, it was so loud that Henry sat up, blinking sleepily.

"Enter," called Judge. The door opened and they stared at the apparition, which had a face very much like Frijole Bill Cullison, but the rest of it was—well, the shirt-front was entirely out, with only the back of the collar fastened. The white pants, white no longer, were shy one leg, and the old cutaway coat had split all the way up the back, and it was threatening to come off in front.

"My God!" exclaimed Henry. "Frijole, you look terrible!"

"I am," replied Frijole shakily. "I've been through hell."

"In that make-up? How on earth did you get away?"

"Slim's dead," said Frijole, parrot-like. "He's deader than hell."

"Slim Pickins? What are you talking about?"

"Slim's dead," insisted Frijole. "I brought him home in the buggy."

Judge and Henry crawled out of bed and began pawing around for clothes, while Frijole, catching sight of himself in their bureau mirror, recoiled sharply.

"I shore tore m' pants, too," he said. "And this here coat."

"Was Slim shot?" asked Judge.

"Shot? I dunno. I didn't hear any shots."

"What killed him?" asked Henry, panting a little.

"Wear and tear, I reckon. We hit some-thin'."

"You sure did. Where did you hit something?"

Frijole waved his right arm in an indefinite gesture, and almost lost that side of his coat.

"You better stand quietly, or you will be undressed," advised Judge.

They finished dressing and followed Frijole down through the empty hotel office, and outside. The horse and buggy were near the front of the hotel. Both Henry and Judge lighted matches. The body had fallen over on the seat. Frijole craned in close and looked, too.

"That," he said huskily, "ain't Slim Pickins."

"It decidedly is not," agreed Henry, "but unless his appearances are deceitful, this man is just as dead as you thought Slim was, Frijole. We better get Doctor Knowles. Have you ever seen that man before, Judge?"

"I do not believe so, sir. I shall arouse the doctor."

"But where-at is Slim?" complained Frijole. "I and him started for—wait a minute! This is Tonto City!"

"Surprising, perhaps, but true," agreed Henry. Frijole limped around and looked at the horse. The light from the hotel window was dim, but sufficient to disclose a bay animal.

"That," declared Frijole, "ain't the right horse either."

"Wrong man, wrong horse," said Henry dryly. "Are you sure about yourself, Frijole?"

"Not now, I ain't."

"Just where were you and Slim going?"

"Slim said it was some'ers down in the South Seas, I remember that."

"In a buggy?"

"We was figgerin' on gittin' a ship at Scorpion Bend."

"I see. At least eight hundred miles from enough water to wet your feet."

"I thought it was funny m'self."

"I think you are still drunk, Frijole."

"I hope it ain't no worse'n that, Henry. I've had a awful night."

Frijole sat down on the edge of the board sidewalk. Tommy Roper, the stuttering stable-keeper, came across the street.

"Gug-gug-got bub-back, huh?" he observed, eyeing the equipage.

"Who?" asked Henry.

"Ah-Oscar."

"Is that the horse and buggy that Oscar rented?"

"Uh-huh. Sus-sus-say, that bub-buggy's been bus-bus-busted!"

"My goodness!" exclaimed Henry. "If that is the horse and buggy Oscar rented—where is Oscar? As for that, where is Josephine? Frijole, where on earth did you get this horse and buggy?"

"It must have been where I lost Slim Pickins," sighed Frijole.

"On your way to Scorpion Bend?"

"I reckon so."

"Who—who's the mum-man in the bub-bub-buggy?" asked Tommy.

"That man is dead, I believe," replied Henry quietly.

"Oh, my gug-gug-gosh! Half the sp-sp-spokes are gone."

"Feller," sighed Frijole, "yo're lucky to git the harness back."

Judge came back with the doctor, who pronounced the man dead, and then they led the horse down to the doctor's home, where they put the body. The man was about forty years of age, well dressed, but with empty pockets. Not a coin nor a scrap of paper. Two pockets had been turned inside out, attesting to the fact that the killer or killers had also robbed him.

Henry and Judge took Frijole up to their room, where they tried to get a coherent statement. But Frijole's memory was very bad, except that he was sure Slim and the horse and buggy had gone into the canyon.

"Why," asked Henry, "were you two going to Scorpion Bend?"

"Like I told yuh twenty times, we was goin' to the South Seas," replied Frijole.

"In a ship—from Scorpion Bend," added Judge.

"I reckon we was pretty drunk," admitted Frijole. "It shore seemed all right. But where-at is Slim? Ain't somebody goin' to find him?"

"Why were you and Slim going to the South Seas?" asked Henry.

"Well, Slim wanted to set under a tree and let a cocoanut drop onto his lap."

"In other words, you were quitting the JHC, without telling me."

Frijole squirmed in his chair. "I wish I knowed where Slim was at."

"And," continued Henry, ignoring Frijole's wish, "you took a horse and buggy from the ranch, without permission, started for Scorpion Bend and the South Seas, without ever telling me. Is that any way to act?"

"It seemed all right, at that time, Henry."

"Yes, I suppose it did," sighed Henry. "Now that we don't know any more about the situation than we did before, I suppose we should do a little worrying about Oscar and Josephine."

"What about Slim Pickens?" queried Frijole. "I'll betcha forty dollars that he's in the bottom of the canyon."

"You didn't shove him over, did you?" asked Judge soberly.

"My Gawd, Judge!"

"Any time you would risk forty dollars—"

Henry sighed and rubbed his nose. "Well, our duty is plain, Judge. We will saddle the steeds and proceed to Scorpion Bend."

"With my rheumatism the way it is?"

"I suppose you will be obliged to take it along, sir."

"But, Henry—at this time of night—"

"Time, my dear Judge, has nothing to do with rheumatism. Get on your boots immediately."

"If I had a horse—" faltered Frijole.

"If you had a horse, I would send you home," said Henry. "As it is, you get into bed here and sleep off that overdose of liquid dynamite."

"He might be able to—er—show you where it happened," suggested Judge. "He could ride my horse and—"

"He has no idea where it happened, Judge. Please do not try to avoid your duty."

Judge groaned and pulled on his boots. He detested riding on a horse, especially at night. As far as that was concerned, Henry did, too. Frijole sat down on the edge of the bed and took off his coat from the front.

"I shore must have been hit hard to bust 'er thataway," he remarked. "I'm either awful lucky or awful tough."

"Make it 'awful drunk'," suggested Judge. "Going to sail on a ship from Scorpion Bend!"

"Uh-huh," nodded Frijole. "I think Slim said her name was the *Flyin' Cloud*. Somethin' like that, anyway."

"That is likely where he is right now—on a flying cloud," said Judge.

"Playin' a harp," added Frijole sadly. "And poor old Slim didn't have no ear for music. Couldn't sing a lick on earth. Prob'ly never seen a harp in his life. Makes it awful hard for a feller like that."

"Maybe he got a shovel instead of a harp," suggested Judge.

"He'd do better," said Frijole. "But Slim never liked a shovel. 'Bout the only thing he ever liked that had a handle on it was a beer mug."

Henry groaned, as he buckled on his belt.

"Why carry a gun?" asked Judge. "Slim is very likely dead. I am not going to take mine."

"I shall ride easier, if you do not, Judge," replied Henry. "Frijole, you get into bed and I will blow out the lamp. In your condition, I would not trust you to even do that; you might burn up the hotel."

"And take off your boots!" growled Judge. "This is no bunk-house."

Someone was coming down the hallway, halted at their door and knocked heavily. Henry called:

"Come in!"

It was Slim Pickins, even in a more disheveled condition than Frijole was, if such a thing was possible. In one hand he had the long legs of William Shakespeare, and William was trying to peck him on the knee.

"My Gawd, it's Slim's ghost!" gasped Frijole.

SLIM DREW BACK and flung the squawking rooster straight at Frijole. The gallant bird landed on Frijole's head, squawked shrilly and tried to fly on feather-less wings to the top of the dresser, but hit the side and landed on the floor, where it stood up and gawped around.

"I've nursed that damn he-hen long enough," declared Slim.

"Where did you come from, Slim?" asked Henry.

"Ask Frijole. Dang his hide, he left me out there on the grades. Never even asked if I was dead or not. Took the horse—wait a minute. No, he didn't take the horse. I rode that horse back here. Frijole, how in hell did you get here?"

"He came here in a buggy, with a dead man," said Judge.

"With a—huh! That accounts for it."

"Accounts for what?" asked Henry.

"Josephine's crazy story. She says she was goin' to run away from Oscar in Scorpion Bend. A feller asked to ride down with her and do the drivin'. Then they was stuck up by a couple fellers, and they made her get out of the buggy. Then Oscar came along later and picked her up on his horse. They found me and the buggy horse, and we all came back together. Hell, I thought Frijole was down in the canyon."

"What a night!" gasped Judge. "Look at Frijole—he's asleep!"

"So is William Shakespeare," added Henry. "Slim, you climb in with Frijole, and Judge and I will secure another room. But first, we must see Josephine and Oscar."

They found Josephine and Oscar in the hotel lobby. Josephine's story was the same as told by Slim Pickins.

"Those two men yust stuck a gun in my face," she said, "and one of them said 'You get to ha'al out of ha'ar'."

"And what did you do, my dear?" asked Henry.

"Ay joist got," she said soberly.

"Naturally. Did the man with you have anything to say to them?"

Josephine shook her head. "Ay vars too far avay to hear anyt'ing. Dey yust drove on."

"Have you any idea who those two men were?"

"No, sir; and Ay did not ask dem."

"Free-holey must be dead," said Oscar. "Ve never found him."

"Frijole is asleep in our room," said Henry. "He brought the dead man to town."

Oscar scratched his head, started to speak, but hesitated. Finally he said, "Ay t'ink Ay need a drink vorse den anyt'ing."

"It is rather confusing," agreed Henry. "Good night, Miss Swensen."

"Ay am glad you t'ink so," she said. "Ay certainly don't."

7

TONTO CITY WAS interested in this newest "man for breakfast." They came from far and wide, seeking to identify him. Casino Evans summoned all his gamblers, bartenders and honkatonk girls, and paraded them past the remains. Henry watched each face, as they glanced at the dead man. He noted that Casino Evans was doing the same thing. Mary McLean was the last person past the bier, and Henry thought he detected a decidedly thoughtful expression in her eyes, as she walked on to join the others.

Henry had sent a general description of the man to the Scorpion Bend *Clarion,* asking that the newspaper assist in an identification.

"Help us!" snorted Judge. "Do you think for a moment that James Wadsworth Longfellow Pelly will do anything to assist this office? He will write a scathing denunciation of us and our ability, and crow over the fact that we asked him to help us."

"But we do need help, Judge," said Henry meekly.

"I must admit that, sir. We know that this one was a murder, but we are not so sure about McLean."

"McLean was not murdered," said Henry quietly.

"Not murdered? How do you know that, sir?"

"At least," said Henry, "Doctor Knowles doubts that the

man was murdered. Doctor Knowles has made some tests, which he says has convinced him that the man died from tuberculosis."

"Tuber—why, Henry, that girl never mentioned it!"

"No one asked her, as far as I know."

"H-m-m-m-m. Why do we not get her over here and find out?"

"I would much rather let it go—for the present, Judge."

"Why—uh—" Judge hesitated, looking closely at Henry. "Have you some motive, if I may ask, sir?"

"Only a queer feeling, Judge."

"Queer feeling, eh? Where did Frijole and Slim go this morning?"

"They went out to try and locate what might be left of my buggy."

"I see. Henry, does there seem anything queer about those two starting out to see the Seven Seas, without saying a word, and without drawing their pay—however little it may be?"

Henry rubbed his red nose thoughtfully. "It could be the effects of that prune whiskey," he said.

"You do not believe that, sir."

"It might do strange things," chuckled Henry. "I distinctly remember of one night, when you got out of bed and started to dress. I asked you where you were going and you said to see Teddy Roosevelt about a commission in his Rough Riders. Please do not blame those two irresponsible souls for heading south."

"I had a nightmare," said Judge.

"Induced by at least a quart of prune whiskey."

Jeff Ort and Pete Halley, two of the three owners of

the Doubloon Mine, dropped in at the office. Together
with Dave Miller they bought out the Doubloon property
about a year ago for a small sum, and since then had done
very well with a property which everyone considered all
worked out.

"We heard about the murder," said Ort, "so Pete and I
went down to take a look at the man. Have you got any
line on him at all?"

"Not a thing," admitted Henry. "He did not have on a
single thing to identify him, Jeff."

Ort nodded. "It certainly was a queer thing—being
killed like that."

"Nothing queer about it," said Judge. "They merely
robbed him, took away any identification, and then shot
the poor devil in cold blood."

Ort nodded. "Yeah, I guess that was it."

"Of course that was it," growled Judge. "Then they
propped him up in the seat, turned the horse loose and
headed it for Tonto City."

"All we need now is the names of the men who
killed him," said Henry quietly. "How are things at the
Doubloon?"

"Going along all right," replied Pete Halley. "It's kinda
hard, when you haven't the money to spend for machinery.
Right now, we are drivin' a new tunnel, and it keeps the
three of us busy. But if we can crosscut the vein, we'll make
money. If we don't—we'll have muscles and experience to
show for our work."

After they were gone, Judge said, "I would bet on the
muscle and experience. That old mine has been experted
too many times to ever make me believe it would be a

producer. All they have is a lot of old buildings, a few thousand feet of tunnel and some old shafts."

"I am not a mining expert," said Henry, "and neither are you."

"Having been properly rebuked, I shall proceed to eat a meal," sighed Judge.

THE AFTERNOON REHEARSAL of the show at the King's Castle was over. Three of the girls, Mazie, Dolores and Aileen were sprawled in chairs on the bare stage. Joe Mills, the piano player, was sitting on top of the old upright, smoking a cigarette, while Larry Steel, a gambler, and Whitey Miles, a night bartender, sat on the edge of the stage.

"What was the idea of Casino dragging us all down to the morgue to look at a stiff?" asked Steel complainingly. "You'd think it was his brother, and he was proud of him."

"And me scared stiff of even a dead drunk," said Dolores, shuddering a little. "I only looked with one eye."

"Scared of the dead, eh?" sneered Joe Mills.

"Aw, you didn't stop and study him, Joe," said Whitey.

"Why should I? Hell, I never seen him before."

"It gave me the creeps," said Aileen. "I'm glad I didn't know him."

"The new girl took a good look," said Larry Steel. "She sure looked him over real good. There's a girl with a great deal of nerve."

"Yeah—curiosity," sneered Dolores. "Nerve!"

"What do you think of that new girl, Joe?" asked Mazie.

"Her?" Joe looked up slowly. "All right, I guess."

"You guess?"

"All right, all right—she's damn good—if you want it that way."

"Joe thinks she's damn good," laughed Aileen.

"Too good for this place," said Joe. "I could make somethin' out of her."

"Yes—a bum," said Steel. Color flamed to Joe's pasty cheeks, but he said nothing.

"That's the first time I ever seen Joe get mad," laughed Aileen.

"I didn't get mad," said Joe quietly. "When you get kicked by an ass, you just consider the source. I meant that Mary is too good for a honkatonk show—too good an artist. If I had her in New York—"

Joe left it unfinished. Larry Steel said, "She don't sound nor act like a girl who had never worked in public before. If this is her first job on a stage, I'm a Chinese marine."

"Trying to make a mystery girl out of her, eh?" said Mazie. "The poor kid came down here, looking for her old man. Used up every cent she had, and was forced to get a job. Suppose she has played before? Is that any of our business? Maybe she is too good for the job—what of it? She's making an honest living."

"Sh-h-h-h!" hissed Whitey, as Henry Harrison Conroy came in from the gambling room.

"Howdy, Sheriff," smiled Mazie.

"A greeting to you, my dear," smiled Henry, "and to all of you thespians, a greeting."

"We were discussing the new girl," said Mazie.

"Ah, yes. A very sweet girl and a talented performer."

"Larry don't think this is her first stage job, Henry."

"Possibly not."

"Casino said it was," said Larry.

"I do not know," said Henry. "But what is the difference? The public seems to like her playing."

"What was the idea of taking all of us down to look at the dead man?" asked Dolores.

"That was entirely Casino's idea," replied Henry. "Perhaps he merely wished to cooperate with the law."

Joe Mills laughed shortly, but did not lock up.

"Is that funny?" asked Larry Steel.

"I laugh at things sometimes that are not funny," replied Joe.

"I'm going to fold up a couple hours sleep," yawned Larry, as he got off the stage. The girls went off stage the other direction, and Henry walked back into the saloon, wondering just why Joe Mills had laughed. It might have been the *marijuana* they said Joe put in his cigarettes.

JOE MILLS CAME with Casino Evans to Tonto City. Evans paid cash for the King's Castle Saloon, but Henry knew nothing about Evans' background. He seemed all right, and Wild Horse Valley was not in the habit of prying into a man's past life. As far as Henry was able to determine, Casino Evans' games were honestly conducted. But why did Joe Mills laugh when Henry suggested that Casino Evans was trying to cooperate with the law?

Henry went back to the office, where he found Judge and Oscar. The big Swede was still weary over his trips to Tonto City.

"Ay am t'rough vit vimmin," he told Henry soberly.

"I have heard you say that many times, Oscar," smiled Henry.

"Ay am all t'rough," insisted Oscar.

"Until the next dance at Scorpion Bend," remarked Judge.

"Ay have to pay seventeen dollar for that boggy and hurse. No voman is vort seventeen dollar."

"I will wager that Josephine was glad to see you, when you came along after she had been forced out of the buggy."

OSCAR CHUCKLED. "AY t'ought she vars a ghost, Yudge. She had a vite dress on, and she vars vaving both arms in the moonlight, yust like a ghost."

"Angels and ministers of grace defend us," quoted Henry. "Be thou a spirit of health or goblin damned, bring with thee airs from heaven or blast from hell?"

"Blasts from ha'al," replied Oscar.

"What," choked Henry, "did she say, Oscar?"

"She said, 'Where in ha'al have you been, you big knot-headed Svede'?"

"And what did you say?" whispered Judge.

"Ay yust said, 'Ay have been looking for you, sveetheart'."

"Swedish soft-soap, Judge," choked Henry.

"Yah, su-ure," grinned Oscar. "Ay am ladies' man, you bat you. She said she vars too much of a lady to ride straddle; so Ay let her sit sideways behind me. Everyt'ing vars all right, until ve ran into Slim, who vars pushing a boggy veel along de road. Then de hurse got scared and Yosephine fell off. Ay asked Slim what he vars going to do vit de veel, and he said he vars tired of valking. Ay t'ink Slim vars cookoo. Den ve found the boggy hurse and Slim rode him to town."

"Was Josephine hurt, when she fell off?" asked Henry huskily.

"Vell, she vars yalling like hell that she vars hurt so bad

she can't see anyt'ing, so Ay vent over and took her hat off her face. Ay t'ink de back of her lap vars hurt some."

Henry held his head in his hands for a few moments. Finally he looked up.

"Did Slim say anything about where he and Frijole were going, Oscar?"

"He said somet'ing about having a cocoanut in his lap."

"That seems to have been the lodestone," said Henry. "But where did William Shakespeare come from?"

"Villiam vars vit Slim. That rooster is a tough yigger, Henry."

"That seems to clear up everything—except who killed the stranger—and why," remarked Judge.

Far out on the grades Frijole and Slim bobbed along on their horses. They had seen parts of their buggy hanging to a manzanita snag on the sheer side of the canyon, and were going back to report to Henry.

"Next time we start out on a voyage," said Slim, "you keep that damn jug hid. If we'd been sober, this wouldn't have happened."

"Sober and poor," amended Frijole. "Yuh know, I've allus heard that bein' rich makes yuh unhappy. With forty dollars in m' pocket, I'm a mockin'-bird. With three thousand— look at me! Full of trials, tribulations and some cactus spines. And look at you! You've got more black-and-blue spots than a coach dog. Yuh lost a tooth, and yuh ain't got no skin left on yore right knuckles. Cowboy, how do yuh like riches?"

"Let's me and you forget bein' rich," suggested Slim meekly. "I wasn't cut out to spend over three dollars and six-bits a week. This mornin', when Henry says, 'Slim, why didn't you and Frijole draw yore pay, before yuh quit the JHC—or are yuh so damn rich yuh don't need twenty dollars?' Frijole, I didn't have nothin' to say. I admitted that we got drunk and forgot that yuh have to have money to take a boat ride. Bein' rich must have done somethin' to me. Hell, I couldn't even think up a good lie. When I get in that shape, I better reform."

"Yuh know," said Frijole thoughtfully, "they was a-tellin' me this mornin' about the daughter of the man we found. He drawed all their money out of the bank, leavin' her flatter'n a boiled shirt bosom. She dug up money enough to come a-lookin' for him. Now she's got a job in the King's Castle honkatonk, tryin' to make money enough to git back home."

"Meanin'," said Slim painfully, "that we've got her money?"

"Now don't go off half-cocked," begged Frijole. "We don't *know* that this is the same money. Yuh see, it might be entirely different money, as far as we're concerned. Anyway, yuh can't identify money, Slim."

"Mebbe this stuff has got a curse on it," suggested Slim. "Takin' it off a skilington thataway. It shore ain't brought us no good luck."

"We drank too damn much, that's what went wrong."

"Somethin' shore was a joner," agreed Slim.

8

SEVERAL DAYS PASSED without incident, and it seemed as though Tonto City had forgotten those two mysterious deaths, when an issue of the Scorpion Bend *Clarion* caused Judge to hurry from the post-office to find Henry, half-asleep in the office.

"Read that!" he exclaimed, slapping the open page on the desk. Henry yawned and looked up at Judge.

"So our friend James Wadsworth Longfellow Pelly is at it again, eh?" he remarked. "Hot oil and vitriol, I presume. Ah, well, the boy must use his imagination, I suppose. I suspect—ah-ha, what have we here?"

Spread across the front page in large block letters was the heading:

COUNTERFEITER'S PARADISE

While the sub-head proclaimed:

BAD MONEY PLENTIFUL. COUNTERFEIT SHOSHONE CHIEF STOCK FLOODS THE MINING MARTS.

The two-column story of the counterfeit money was mostly quoted from an interview with John Marshall, President of the Cattlemen's Bank of Scorpion Bend, while an interview with Nick Borden furnished the material for the story about the counterfeit mining stock. James Wadsworth Longfellow Pelly wrote that perhaps millions of dollars worth of worthless Shoshone Chief stock had been foisted upon the public.

There was nothing exciting about the counterfeit money angle, except that the bank held over two thousand dollars' worth, and that the officers, searching for the origin of the spurious money, believed that it was being made in that part of Arizona. Just how they knew this, the editor did not divulge.

"Counterfeiter's Paradise!" rasped Judge.

"He doesn't say where it is located, Judge," said Henry mildly.

"He means Wild Horse Valley. That little snipe-faced rat."

Henry smiled. "An entirely new species, Judge. Still, the poor boy has so little to write about, we must excuse his enthusiasm."

"Turn over to the editorial, sir."

"Ah, yes, the editorial. Hm-m-m-m. Editorial."

Henry blinked thoughtfully at the heavy headline, which read:

WHILE THE SHAME OF ARIZONA SLEEPS

"Not a bad heading," observed Henry. "Mind if I read it aloud?"

"If you can stand it—I can, sir."

"Very good, sir. It reads as follows:

"While it is not this paper's policy to criticize the normal functions of our public offices, we feel, at the moment, that our readers should be fully advised of conditions in Wild Horse Valley. Naturally, the riff-raff of creation follow the big mining strikes, like the buzzards follow the kill. And why shouldn't they go to Tonto City? Big strikes, big gambling in a wide-open town, and a sheriff's office so sound asleep that not even murder will awaken it.

"And now, with the country flooded with counterfeit money and fake mining stocks—what is being done? Exactly nothing, my dear reader. A man comes here with money to buy mining property. He is robbed, murdered and left in the desert hills. Another man is brutally murdered in a buggy, and taken to Tonto City. What is being done about these murders? Exactly nothing, my dear reader.

"Mr. Conroy, ex red-nosed comedian, now sheriff, and his rheumatic, baggy-eyed deputy, Mr. Van Treece, merely shrug their shoulders. It is nothing to them—two murders. They are too sleepy to know or care. They eat, sleep and act merry, ignoring the terrible conditions that exist. Isn't it about time for real men to change such a situation? It has prevailed too long. Let us do something about it."

"What do you think of that?" growled Judge.

"I am disappointed," sighed Henry. "That makes exactly three times he has said that you have rheumatism and baggy eyes."

"Damn him, I shall give him baggy eyes!"

"Be calm, my friend. You bruise easily—too easily. Look at me."

"Look at your nose, sir. By gad, it is seven shades brighter than it was before you read that editorial."

"Seven shades, indeed! As for the editorial, it is only a fair sample of what the man can do. In fact, I am more interested in this tale of bogus money. Surely, we of Wild Horse Valley would not stoop to the manufacture of currency. Why, why—it is illegal, Judge!"

"That fool on the *Clarion* knows that the money is not made here. He merely wants to be sensational."

"How," suggested Henry quietly, "would he *know*, Judge?"

"Yes, I see your point, sir. But—why, it doesn't fit with the country."

"You mean to imply that we haven't sufficient talent to issue bad money; that we are but a lot of clumsy-handed oafs. Pish and tush, Judge. You overlook the fact that we have the riff-raff of civilization in Tonto City."

"And one, possibly two, unsolved murders, Henry."

"Gad, yes! We must gird our loins, Judge."

"And after we have girded them—what?" queried Judge.

"Well—at least we will have them girded. How does one gird a loin?"

"I am sure I do not know, never having been girded—nor seen one."

John Campbell, the big bluff prosecuting attorney, dropped in. He had read the *Clarion*, and had also talked with John Marshall, the Scorpion Bend banker. Campbell was grave over the situation.

"Federal officers have been trying to trace the source of this money for some time," he said. "It is mostly fives and tens, and so well made that it passes well. They say it looks like the work of a man named Ormsby, who was, at one time, connected with the Bureau of Engraving. They lost track of him several years ago."

"John, do you suppose the same people made those fake stock certificates?" asked Henry.

"Possibly. That would be more profitable than making money, as long as it was undiscovered. For instance, one certificate for five thousand shares would be worth twenty-five thousand dollars. As near as we can find out, a mining broker handled the whole crooked issue—and cleaned up a tidy fortune. Of course, the mining broker quit the business. Those fake certificates were bought and sold all up and down the Pacific Coast."

"Have you seen any of the certificates or money?" asked Henry.

"I saw several pieces of the money at Scorpion Bend. They looked good to me. And just for your own information, a lot of it comes out of the valley."

"Perhaps James Wadsworth Longfellow Pelly is not so far wrong," remarked Judge dryly.

"I believe there is work to do," said Henry.

"Federal officers will handle that, I believe," said Campbell. "That sort of work is never handled by the local officers. Is there anything new on the murder, Henry? I mean, have you any inkling as to who he was?"

"Not a single link," replied Henry. "Baffling, I would say, John."

"It may be possible that he is connected in some way with the counterfeiting angle."

"If so," said Judge dryly, "he is a very, very silent partner, John."

The lawyer looked quizzically at Henry. "Folks are saying

that you are not doing a thing to try and clear up this latest killing, Henry. It is always the same hue and cry, when you—well, do not seem active. But you haven't done badly in the past, and it seems that when you seem to be doing the least, you do the most."

"I thank you, John," said Henry gravely. "You are very kind."

After Campbell left the office Judge considered Henry gravely.

"Henry the Silent," remarked Judge quietly.

"Do not be an ass, Judge," said Henry. "Go get the jug."

Before Judge could get up from his chair Nick Borden came in.

"I can tell you something about the dead man in the buggy," he said. "His name was Ed Ward, a private detective."

"How did you find this out, Nick?" asked Henry quickly.

"Because I hired him."

"You—er—hired him, Nick?"

"I asked a private detective bureau to send me their best man. Today I received a letter from them saying that Ed Ward had been sent. They say he has done a lot of investigation work on counterfeit cases, and is rated a good man. The letter describes him."

"It seems," said Judge dryly, "that the *Clarion* is right."

"Never mind the *Clarion*," said Henry. "Give me that address, Nick. They can give us a disposition of the body. We will hold the inquest at once."

9

IT WAS FIVE days later when Henry and Judge rode over the grades to Scorpion Bend in a buggy. Judge drove with one long leg hanging over the side of the buggy, the foot almost scraping the ground. Buggies were not constructed for men of Judge's length. Henry nodded, his hands clasped around his girth, his big sombrero pulled low over his eyes.

Occasionally they had to pull out to allow a freight wagon to pass on the narrow grades. It was hot and dusty along the side of the canyon. In fact, it was nearly always hot in Wild Horse Valley. Henry yawned widely.

"Eat, sleep and act merry," said Judge, quoting the editorial in the *Clarion*.

"There is a sarcastic note in your melodious voice, my dear Judge," remarked Henry. "After all, what else is there in life?"

"An unsolved murder," suggested Judge.

"True enough, sir; and there always will be unsolved murders."

"The people," said Judge, "are beginning to complain to each other. When two men meet they compare currency— if either has some. They shy from a new, or nearly-new, bill as though it had fangs. And, damme, they seem to blame us, Henry. They say that what they need is a new sheriff."

"Exactly," nodded Henry sleepily.

"You do not seem perturbed."

"Over them getting a new sheriff? No, Judge. In fact, it might be a good idea."

"Are you going to have a talk with James Wadsworth Longfellow Pelly?"

Henry shook his head. "The man has no sense of humor, Judge. He is the Destiny who tries to shape our ends. He cries 'Fie upon them,' when he should make people laugh at us. Why, Judge, he almost makes me feel serious— almost, but not quite."

They reached Scorpion Bend, where they had a few drinks and discussed local conditions with the bartender of the Scorpion Bend Saloon. After a meal, they talked with John Marshall of the bank, who assured them that the counterfeit money situation was worse than ever. He showed them specimens of some counterfeiter's art, which would easily pass anyone not an expert in the matter of detecting bogus money.

They were back at the saloon, having another drink, when James Wadsworth Longfellow Pelly sauntered in. The editor of the *Clarion* would have avoided them, but being slightly near-sighted, missed the opportunity.

Henry shook hands with him heartily and congratulated him on his efforts to clean out crime and criminals in Wild Horse Valley.

Pelly started to mumble some sort of an apology for his editorial, but Henry stopped him.

"It was magnificent," declared Henry. "A masterpiece. Such things will do a lot of good. It causes people to think."

"Think what?" asked Pelly.

"That either you or I are unmitigated asses, Pelly."

"I?" queried Pelly. "Why, I—you see, I—"

"Please do not apologize," begged Henry. "Nearly every-one I have spoken to about the editorial has said that you were slightly cracked. In fact, they have gone further than that, Pelly. But I feel that with experience and age you may write something real good—some day. Have a drink?"

"Slightly cracked?" said Pelly. "Why, I would have you—"

"I agree with you—they were a bit delicate," said Judge. "But one must be careful what one says about an editor—shouldn't one?"

Pelly drew a deep breath, coughed slightly and said:

"I do not want any drink. I feel you are trying to insult me."

"If you are not sure," said Judge quietly, "we will will-ingly go over it again. We want you to be perfectly satis-fied, Mr. Pelly."

"Just a small drink, Mr. Pelly," suggested Henry.

"Damn you and your drinks!" snorted Pelly, and walked out.

"There," remarked Henry quietly, "is a sample of your lack of diplomacy, Judge. You insulted the gentleman."

"I?" snorted Judge. "I, indeed! I will leave it to the bartender to decide."

"Not me," said the bartender. "I would not know an insult if I met it face to face in a bright light."

"Suppose we shake dice for it?" suggested Henry. "We both tried to insult him, Judge."

"I think you both did," grinned the bartender. "He acted like it."

"Then," decided Henry, "we will split the honor and have a drink."

They were both in a mellow mood by supper time. After a hearty meal they were going back to Tonto City, and on their way to their vehicle they met Nick Borden, owner of the Shoshone Chief mine. Borden was carrying a package under his arm.

"If you are going back to Tonto, I wonder if you could take this package back with you?" asked Borden. "I don't like to carry it on a horse."

"It will be a pleasure, Nick," assured Henry, and accepted the package.

"I'll call for it in the morning," said Nick. "Much obliged."

Henry placed it on the seat between the Judge and himself, and drove out of Scorpion Bend in the darkness. It was a long, lonesome drive from Scorpion Bend to Tonto City at night. The long, winding road across the mesa, down to the narrow, twisting grades which wound for miles along the depths of the canyon. Moonlight high-lighted the canyon walls, but most of the grade was in darkness.

Judge drove slowly. The conversation was only enough to keep them both awake. Judge said:

"When I drive this at night, Henry, and note the moon-light on those mighty peaks, and the mysterious depths of the canyon, I realize the insignificance of man."

"True, sir," agreed Henry, "but while you steep your soul in realizations you might stoop to consider that every time those wheels get close to the edge of the grade the insig-nificance of two certain men grows smaller and smaller."

"I pride myself on my ability to drive a horse," declared Judge.

"Your pride, sir, is of little interest when they start pick-ing up little pieces of Henry Harrison Conroy at the bottom of that five-hundred-foot drop."

"Timid soul," muttered Judge.

"Careful soul," corrected Henry.

THEY TRAVELED UP a long incline, where the road made a sharp left-hand turn, now bathed in bright moonlight. As the horse started into the turn, two men stepped full into the middle of the road, moonlight flashing on their guns. They were both masked, with hats pulled low over the upper part of their faces.

Judge instinctively drew back on the lines, but Henry leaned forward, jerked the whip from its socket, and slashed the horse across the rump. The startled animal leaped forward, straight at the two men. Two guns flashed, as the two masked men flung themselves aside, but the horse went down with a crash, throwing Judge clear of the buggy. Henry fell forward against the dash, the breath nearly knocked from his body, but he grasped Nick Borden's package and flung it as far as he could out over the rim of the canyon.

A few moments later, as Henry tried to pump air into his tortured lungs, a gun was shoved into his face, and a harsh voice said:

"All right, Clown—where's that package?"

"Clown?" gasped Henry. "Oh, my goodness!"

The other man came in at the other side. "Old High-Pockets is out cold," he announced. "Didja find it?"

"Package?" murmured Henry. "What package?"

"The package Borden gave yuh. You know damn well what package!"

"I—I haven't any package," denied Henry.

"Git out of that buggy!"

Henry climbed carefully out, and one man held a gun against him, while the other searched the buggy, swearing that if he did not find it he would shove Henry into the canyon. But the package was not there. Then the man searched along the grade for a short distance.

"Tell me where the package is, or I'll drill yuh," gritted the man.

"My dear fellow," said Henry, "I cannot answer, because

I have no idea where the package is. Someone has made a mistake."

"You fat-nosed liar! Nick Borden gave you that package and we saw him do it. You put that package into this buggy. Where is it?"

Henry had an inspiration. "True, true," he admitted. "But that did not prevent us from giving that package to another man after we left Scorpion Bend. I am afraid you took too much for granted, gentlemen."

"Who did you give it to?" demanded the bandit.

"Would that not be telling?" countered Henry calmly.

"What the hell good would that do us—now?" asked the other bandit. "They ain't got it. Let's high-tail it out of here."

"I'd like to kick this tub of lard into the canyon."

"What good would that do?"

"No good," added Henry quickly.

One of the men laughed shortly, and they walked away, disappearing in the darkness. Henry walked over to Judge, who was sitting up.

"What happened?" asked Judge.

"Are you hurt, Judge?" asked Henry anxiously.

"Naturally."

Judge got slowly to his feet and felt himself over carefully.

"No bones broken," he said thankfully. "Skinned knees and skinned hands. Otherwise I seem to be in fairly good shape. Now, if I have relieved your mind, Henry—what in hell happened?"

"Just another hold-up," replied Henry wearily. "You saw the masked men."

"Vaguely, sir—vaguely. It all happened so quickly. Our horse?"

"Our horse is dead."

"Hm-m-m-m. Dead, eh? I remember you whipping the horse—"

"A bright idea of running the gauntlet, Judge."

Judge cleared his throat raspingly and flexed his muscles.

"Hold-up!" he snorted. "Poor fools! Not over five dollars between us."

"They wanted that package—the one Nick Borden gave us, Judge."

"Borden's package? Why—what do you suppose was in it?"

"I have no idea," sighed Henry.

"They got it, of course."

"Of course, they did not, because I heaved it over the rim of the canyon, unseen. Then, Judge, I lied to them. I told them that we gave it to another man after we left Scorpion Bend."

"Hm-m-m-m. Over the rim of the canyon. Five hundred feet, if it is an inch. Why, the devil himself could never find it."

"The devil," said Henry quietly, "is hardly interested."

They lighted matches and examined the horse, which sprawled almost against the inner wall. They would be unable to move the obstruction from the road, but there would be little danger, as it is in an exposed spot, and there was little night travel over the road.

"As painful as it may seem," said Henry, "there are only two ways for us to get to Tonto City—and one of them is to walk."

"What is the other?" asked Judge quickly.

"Run," replied Henry dryly.

10

SLIM PICKINS SHOVED back from the bunk-house table, and scowled at Lightning Mendoza. Frijole Bill sucked on an unlighted cigarette and looked carefully at the pips on his cards, while Thunder Mendoza merely grinned. Most of the chips were in front of Lightning, who stacked them carefully.

"How you like heem, eh?" asked Lightning. "I draws myself ten-spots to bobs-tail flosh. Pretty damn smarts, eh?"

"Smart!" snorted Slim. "Payin' a dollar to draw a card to an inside straight. Yo're crazy."

"I made heem," beamed Lightning.

"You stayin' in that pot, Slim?" asked Frijole.

"Ask Lightnin' first," said Slim. "If he stays, I don't."

"I reckon I better wash the breakfast dishes," said Frijole.

Slim tossed his cards to the center of she table.

"Learnin' a damn *Mejicano* to play poker," he growled. "How many chips yuh got there, Lightnin'?"

Frijole reached over and made the count, took a look at the chips in front of Thunder and estimated quickly.

"We owe Lightnin' eleven dollars, Slim, and we owe Thunder a dollar."

Slim dug into his pocket and brought out a ten-dollar

bill, while Frijole furnished the two silver dollars. Lightning shoved the bill aside and shook his head slowly.

"Geeve me the real money," he said. "That stoff ees no good."

"No good?" snorted Slim. "Since when?"

"Paper money ees no good," declared Lightning. "Een Tonto Ceety, everybody ees say that those paper money ees all benefits money."

Slim stared at Lightning, while Frijole began to chuckle.

"Counterfeits, he means," laughed Frijole.

"Yuh mean that all the paper money is counterfeit?" asked Slim.

"That ees w'at they say een Tonto Ceety. All those paper money ees not wort' the eenk it am printed on."

"Lovely dove!" breathed Slim. Frijole scratched the back of his neck and squinted at Slim.

"Ain't that hell?" he asked quietly. "All of it. Well, I'll wash the dishes."

Thunder and Lightning left the house. Slim leaned against the door-frame and watched Frijole scrape out the pans.

"What," asked Slim, "happens if yuh try to pass counterfeit money?"

"All I know is what I've heard," replied Frijole. "It's either fifty or seventy-five years in the penitentiary."

"Yuh ain't sure which, eh?"

Frijole looked up at Slim. "Now what the hell difference would it make to either one of us?" he asked.

"Yeah, that's right, it wouldn't. Now what are we goin' to do with our wealth? I shore don't want to spend even fifty years in jail."

"I reckon we better bury it for a while. No use goin' to jail."

"Yeah. Mebbe we better go in and talk with Henry about it."

"Yuh mean—about our money?"

"No, I mean about the counterfeit money."

"Well, yeah, we could. I want to take him a jug of my last batch. Him and Judge must be about out."

They finished up the dishes, saddled their horses and went to Tonto City, carrying a jug of freshly made prune whiskey. They found Henry and Judge in the office, not at all in good humor, and both wearing slippers on their sore feet.

Judge groaned from sore feet and rheumatic twinges. It had been a long walk.

"Yore feet look comfortable," remarked Slim.

"They are not," declared Judge. "You try walking ten miles in boots—and at night."

"You boys came at a very opportune time," said Henry. "I want you to ride out about ten miles from here on the canyon grades, where you will find a dead horse. Dump him into the canyon and bring back the buggy."

"Did the horse have heart trouble?" asked Frijole.

"The horse," replied Henry, "had lead trouble. Two men tried to hold up Judge and I last night as we came back from Scorpion Bend."

"And yuh killed 'em both?" asked Slim quickly.

"Thank you, Slim."

"Livery horse?" asked Frijole.

Henry nodded. "Yes," he said, "and it will cost the county at least fifty dollars to replace him."

"Speakin' of money," said Slim, "what's this we hear about counterfeit money around here?"

"Even if you heard lies—they are true," replied Henry.

"Lots of it, huh?"

"I understand there is quite a lot."

"Is it against the law to pass it?" asked Frijole.

"Get caught at it," suggested Judge, "and you will be very unhappy."

"What did them hold-up men get off you and Judge, Henry?"

"Mostly experience, Slim."

"They must shore be beginners," said Frijole, "when they pick on you two."

"The primary grade," said Henry dryly. "Please do not forget to remove the harness before you dispose of the horse. You better take a horse from the livery stable."

They went over to the livery stable and told Tommy Roper what they wanted.

"Don't ask questions and don't argue, Tommy," advised Frijole. "All we want is a horse to drive back with that buggy."

"Wh-wha-wha-wha—"began Tommy, but Frijole interrupted.

"Ask Henry," he said. "All we are is jist his humble servants, and all we want is a plain horse, no harness and no buggy behind it. Jist a plain horse 'tached to a tie-rope."

They got one. Frijole dallied the rope around his saddlehorn, and they rode out of Tonto City.

About an hour later Nick Borden drove in from the Shoshone Chief. He was all smiles, as he came into the sheriff's office, but Henry and Judge looked at him glumly.

"Thanks to you two gentlemen," said Nick, "I got the payroll of the Shoshone Chief mine through safely. I'll take it now, if you don't mind."

Henry groaned softly and rubbed his nose, while Judge effected indignation.

"The—the payroll of the mine?" queried Judge.

"That package I gave you at Scorpion Bend yesterday evening."

"Oh," said Judge, "that package. You—er—gave it to Henry."

"Well, I—"

"He gave it to both of us," said Henry. "The payroll, eh? Nick, just how much money was in that package?"

"How much? Well, what difference does that make?"

"Well," said Henry quietly, "if it was only ten thousand dollars—you only lose that much. If it was—"

"My God!" gasped Nick Borden. "Where is it, Henry?"

"Please be calm," advised Henry. "After all, money isn't—"

"What did you do with it?"

"I—I threw it into Lobo Canyon, Nick."

Nick Borden stared at them for several moments.

"You—" Nick made queer noises in his throat. "You threw it into Lobo Canyon?"

Henry made a throwing gesture. "Like that," he said.

"You threw my money into—why, Henry! Why did you do that?"

"We were held up by two masked men, Nick. They said they saw you give us that package. But I—I threw it into the canyon—and they never saw me throw it. I—we did not know what was in the package."

"You threw my money into the bottom of that canyon."

"It was night," reminded Henry. "I could not see the bottom. By all the laws of gravity, it should be down there."

"They killed our horse," said Judge.

"They killed a livery horse," corrected Henry. "The county will have to pay for it."

"They shot your horse? Two masked men? What did they say?"

"They—one of them wanted to kick me into the canyon," said Henry. "The loss of that package seemed annoying. I told them that we gave it to another man outside of Scorpion Bend—and they believed me."

"They must be strangers," said Judge.

"Why?" asked Nick quickly.

"They believed Henry Conroy."

"Do you know where you threw it into the canyon?" asked Nick.

"The dead horse marks the approximate spot," replied Henry.

"Then why are we waiting?" asked Nick quickly. "Get your horses, while I buy up all the rope in the store. We'll get that money."

Judge groaned, as Nick Borden hurried out. Henry rubbed his nose and looked at Judge.

"Down into the canyon on a rope," said Henry. "My goodness!"

11

SLIM AND FRIJOLE were in no hurry to reach the scene
of the attempted hold-up. Neither of them had any liking
for the long ride, especially Frijole.

"Why don't he dig up Oscar and send him on this kind
of a job?" complained Frijole. "This ain't my work noway;
I'm the cook."

"Distiller," corrected Slim dryly. "Incinerator and
distiller."

"I notice you ain't never late for meals, Slimmie."

"Yeah, I know, but you can cook a hunk of cow harder
than any cook I ever seen. Yo're pretty good on aigs. Yeah,
I'd say that aigs is yore masterpiece. You ain't so awful bad
on spuds, and you do passable on a white bean, but yore
biscuits squeak. Atchally squeak."

"What'r yuh a-gettin' at, Slimmie?" asked Frijole mildly.

"Oh, I'm jist tryin' to point out to you that yore kinda
cookin' hadn't ort to exempt yuh from doin' other chores."

"Well, I never made no squeaky biscuits."

"Yuh do so. And they are also rusty from sody. Mind
yuh, I ain't makin' no complaints—I'm jist a-pointin' out
yore failures."

"I suppose," said Frijole, "that you figure yo're a top-hand
puncher, with no faults worth mentionin', Slim."

"Yeah, I've got faults, too," agreed Slim. "I like to take a bath every couple weeks. I shave on Sundays. I like clean shirts once in awhile. Oh, I've got faults—and I admit 'em."

"My Gawd!" breathed Frijole.

"There's the dead horse," said Slim. "Knowed we was gettin' close, because of the buzzards."

They dismounted in the shade of the rocky wall, but neither of them saw the man who was working his way down through the broken rocks to a-point above them. They removed the harness from the dead horse, and put it aside, after which they pulled and tugged at the horse, trying to get it off the grade and over the rim of the canyon. Both men were sweating and swearing long before they managed to get the heavy animal off the road, where it sent showers of gravel and rock from the wall of the canyon.

Slim was on his knees at the edge, watching the fall, when his eyes caught sight of an object only a few feet below the rim, lodged in a manzanita bush. He pointed it out to Frijole.

"It's a package, all tied up," insisted Slim.

"Aw, it's somethin' that's been throwed away," said Frijole.

"No, it ain't either, Frijole. I tell yuh it's a package that ain't been opened. We'll tie our two ropes together and I'll let yuh down there."

"You won't let me down no place, cowboy. I decline. If you want that old package so bad, I'll let you down on the rope."

Slim meditated, but finally got the two lariats, knotted them together, untied one of the horses and led the animal out near the edge of the grade, where he tied one end of the rope to the saddle-horn.

Then he tied the other end around his slim waist and sat down on the edge of the canyon.

"I'll let m'self down," he told Frijole, "secure the package, and then you help haul me back. That saddle-horn is jist an emergency."

"Uh-huh," nodded Frijole. "And if yuh slip, mebbe you'll take the horse with yuh—I dunno. But go ahead."

"I'm a pretty good accerbat," said Slim soberly. "You watch."

Easing himself carefully over the edge, he swung down swiftly to the manzanita, where his flailing feet found a foothold. That small, hard-twist rope was hard to grip. Slim looked below the manzanita, and took a deep breath. It looked a mile deep, and straight down.

After a short wait he secured the package, tied it to his belt and looked up at Frijole.

"Start haulin'," he ordered.

Frijole said. "I was jist a-thinkin' what you said about my cookin'."

"Go ahead and haul me back," urged Slim. "This damn bush ain't rooted any too strong."

"About the cookin'," persisted Frijole. "You talked about squeakin' biscuits, yuh know—and too much sody. And yuh said—"

Slim turned a perspiring face up to Frijole.

"Frijole," he said soberly, "yo're such a hell of a good cook that yuh get runty if anybody jokes about yore cookin'. Personally, I like everythin' yuh cook. Best grub I ever et."

"Uh-huh. I cook beef pretty good, eh?"

"Good? Man, it can't be beat. You shore can make food stand up on its hind legs and talk."

"Uh-huh. Well, yuh look like yuh meant it; so yuh can start comin' up."

Slim kicked all the loose rocks into the canyon, but managed to fall over the rim, where he rolled away and began unfastening the rope.

"That package ain't never been opened," remarked Frijole.

"I—I told yuh it hadn't," panted Slim. "I got good eyes."

Slim got to his shaky legs and untied the package from his belt.

"Might be a pair of shoes," said Frijole. "Kinda shaped thataway."

Slim started to cut the string, when a voice said sharply:

"I'll take that box, if yuh don't mind!"

Both men jumped and looked around, but there was no one in sight.

"Look up!" snapped the voice.

The man was on the rocks about fifteen feet above them, masked, and covering them with a rifle. Slim and Frijole gawped at him.

"Where in hell did you come from?" asked Slim blankly.

"Never mind that—toss me that package. Quick, too!"

Frijole took a chance and dived for cover under the overhang of the rock. The rifle blasted, but the bullet merely hummed into the canyon.

"Don't shoot!" yelped Slim. "I'll throw it. Here!"

Slim tossed the package straight into the air, much higher than the man on the rock, who jerked forward, intent on the package, and Slim went to cover beside Frijole. The man swore witheringly, as the package fell into the middle of the road.

"Come and get it!" yelled Slim, a cocked Colt in his hand.

"Don't invite," complained Frijole.

"He don't dare come," chuckled Slim, " 'cause he knows I'll bust him."

"I don't believe he can get down here, unless he jumps," said Frijole.

"Mm-m-m-mebbe," said Slim.

A couple of minutes passed, and Slim became anxious. He slid along the rocky wall, almost to the turn. He heard the crunch of gravel, and a man stepped into view.

Wham! Slim did not hesitate, but shot quickly. The man went down. Slim yelled, "I've got him, Frijole! C'mon!"

Slim went running past the turn. There was another man, running down the grade, a hundred feet away.

Wham! Slim's old .45 blasted against the cliffs. Evidently the bullet struck short of the running man, but a handful of gravel hit him square in the rear. He jerked to a stop, whirled, flung up his hands and sat down heavily, when his heel caught on a rock. Slim had ran past his first victim. Frijole yelled:

"Slim! My Gawd, you've shot the editor!"

"Huh?" yelled Slim. "An editor, didja say?"

"James Wadsworth Longfellow Pelly! You slew him, I reckon."

"C'mere, you!" Slim called to the other man, who came limping. He was a very frightened man.

"Who are you?" asked Slim bluntly.

"Who am—why, I—I am Donald Heaslip, the cashier of the bank at Scorpion Bend."

"Which one of yuh shot at Frijole a few minutes ago?"

"Shot at—no, no! We never shot at anybody."

"This jasper ain't dead, but he's bleed-in'," called Frijole.

"I'll be a liar!" breathed Slim. "I'll jist be that."

James Wadsworth Longfellow Pelly had been scored just above the left ear, knocked unconscious for a few moments, but was not badly hurt. The skin was broken and there was considerable gore. He dabbled his fingers in the blood and stared at Frijole and Slim. Slim said to Heaslip:

"Where did you two fellers come from?"

"Scorpion Bend. Pelly wanted to come down to Tonto City, so I got the day off and came with him. Back there, beyond the turn is our horse and buggy. From over there on the grade we saw you over here. Then there was a shot fired. Pelly wanted to see what was going on; so we left the rig back there and walked up here."

"Who hit me?" asked Pelly weakly.

"Oh, Lord!" groaned Frijole. "Here comes Henry, Judge, Oscar and Nick Borden."

The four men rode up. Nick Borden saw the package in the middle of the road, and went after it quickly.

"My goodness!" exclaimed Henry. "It must have jumped out of the canyon. Hello! What happened to Mr. Pelly? Frijole, can't you talk?"

"If I knowed what to say," nodded Frijole.

"The man must have been shot," remarked Borden.

"By golly, I'll bet that's what happened!" exclaimed Slim. "Can yuh imagine that?"

Nick Borden quickly untied the package, looked at the contents and grinned happily.

"Man, I'm lucky!" he exclaimed. "Eighteen thousand dollars!"

"Will somebody tell what happened?" bellowed Judge. "Who shot the editor?"

"We heard the first shot," offered Heaslip.

"It dang near hit me," said Frijole.

"So somebody shot at you, too, eh?" said Judge.

"I hope to tell yuh!" exclaimed Frijole. "He was up on the rocks, had a mask on his face and—"

"Did the same man shoot at the editor?" asked Henry.

"I'll betcha he did!" snorted Slim. "The son-of-a-gun!"

"Who shot me?" asked Pelly.

"Not a very good shot—" replied Judge, and added, "unfortunately."

"I didn't see any masked man," said Pelly. "I'll bet—"

"What'll you bet?" asked Slim quietly.

"Nothing. I must get to a doctor; I've been shot."

"Brilliant deduction," said Judge.

"I'll take you back," offered Heaslip. "You do need a doctor."

They went hurrying down the grade toward their horse and buggy.

"Now," said Henry to Slim, "I would like the truth, Slim."

"I'll bet somebody'll get hell in that newspaper," chuckled Slim, and proceeded to tell Henry the truth of the whole affair.

"It's plain enough now," said Borden. "The men who held you up last night were not satisfied with your story so they waited in the rocks to see what happened next. I'm sure glad that Slim and Frijole out-smarted them. It saved my payroll. I'll see that Slim and Frijole get a hundred dollars apiece."

"In silver," said Frijole dryly. "We're scared of rag-money."

"So is everybody else," smiled Borden.

12

MARY McLEAN WAS fast becoming a favorite in the King's Castle honkatonk. Casino Evans seemed to watch over her closely. Even Joe Mills, the piano player, was called to account for being a trifle confidential with her. She occupied a small room at the hotel, where she spent much of her leisure time. Henry and Judge rarely saw her, except at the show. She had shown no preference for any of the cowboys or miners, who came regularly to applaud her violin solos.

Her first appearance was at nine o'clock, and at eight-thirty, Henry Conroy knocked quietly on her door. She opened the door a few inches, saw who it was and opened the door quickly.

"Come in, Mr. Conroy," she said smiling.

"Thank you, my dear—thank you. My, what a comfortable little room!"

"The hotel has been very kind," she said. "Won't you sit down?"

Henry sat down in a rocker, placed his hat on the floor. Mary sat down and they looked curiously at each other.

"I know your act starts at nine," he said quietly, "so I will not take too much of your time, my dear. I have received a report from a detective agency in San Francisco—regarding you—and your father."

Her eyes narrowed slightly and she made a nervous gesture with her hand.

"A report?" she said blankly.

"Yes," he nodded. "I wondered if you went under a different name in that city."

"Why—" she hesitated—"no."

"You told me where you worked," he said. "The report shows that no one by the name of Mary McLean ever worked there. In fact, a check of all the department stores shows the same report—no Mary McLean."

"I see," she said quietly. "No Mary McLean. Odd, isn't it?"

"Odd, yes. It is also odd that James McLean, who possibly owned and operated an engraving business in San Francisco, had no daughter."

Mary's lips were a tight, hard line for several moments.

"That seems to make me a liar, Mr. Conroy," she then said.

"Or badly mistaken as to parentage, my dear," he said dryly. "You play the violin divinely, but as an actress—not fit for the role. My dear, you lose a father too easily. You identify a ring, but you paid little attention to the hand on which the ring was found. That was the hand of a laborer—not an engraver."

"And," said Mary, "I heard a man say that you are dumb."

"My dear, we are all dumb at times. But you did note the hand?"

"Of course. Please, I am not *that* dumb, Mr. Conroy."

"I see," mused Henry. "Your idea, perhaps, was to—well, just what was your idea?"

Mary walked to the door, opened it quietly and looked down the hall. Then she came back and sat down.

"I feel that you are to be trusted, Mr. Conroy," she said quietly. "I am Mary McLean. It was only a coincidence that my name was the same as that of James McLean, whose name was not James McLean."

"Possibly—er—Ormsby?" said Henry.

Mary looked keenly at the red-nosed sheriff.

"How much *do* you know?" she asked.

"As you proceed, my dear, I may show flashes of intelligence."

Mary smiled. "In fact, his name was Dan Ormsby. Erstwhile employee of the Bureau of Engraving, later a most successful counterfeiter, who saw the error of his ways, and, lastly, became an operative for the Treasury Department."

"His last bit of employment, I suppose," said Henry.

"Who knows?" replied Mary.

"And you are a detective, my dear?"

"An operative. James McLean, or Ormsby, was an engraver in San Francisco. He handled a certain variety of supplies. And certain orders purchased by a man from this valley, caused Ormsby to suspect counterfeiting. He reported to the Treasury Department, and was assigned to come here, after contacting this man, and try and buy into the work. His name was a sure-fire opening with any counterfeiting gang, because Ormsby really knew his job.

"The money I believe was marked and in large bills. Ormsby came here—and never has been heard of since. The counterfeiters probably knew his name was Ormsby. I came here to find my father, James McLean. The job at the King's Castle was an opportunity. But, Mr. Conroy, I have a feeling that I am watched, that everything I say is handed over to those men."

Henry nodded slowly. "No doubt of it, my dear. Those men are smart. Do you know anything about the counterfeiting of the Shoshone Chief stock certificates?"

"That was the beginning, Mr. Conroy. We knew about that. But I do not believe they attempted counterfeiting money, until Ormsby came here."

"You believe Ormsby is making the plates?"

"The department does; I am not an expert."

Henry got to his feet and looked at his watch.

"You have barely time to change and reach the stage," he said. "Thank you very much, Miss McLean; we understand each other now."

He walked to the door and opened it quietly, but there was no one in the hallway.

"Did you have private detectives on that investigation, or was it the San Francisco city detectives?" she asked.

"Oh!" Henry smiled quietly and shook his head. "There was no investigation, my dear; I made that all up. Good evening."

HENRY WALKED BACK to his room, where Judge was writing a letter. He looked at Henry curiously, as he said, "I suppose, sir, you made an ass of yourself."

Henry chuckled and sat down.

"You and your intuition," said Judge. "Well, what came of it?"

"The lady," replied Henry, "confessed."

"Eh? She confessed? To what, if I may ask, sir?"

Henry explained his talk with Mary McLean, and

Judge grunted his amazement. Finally he said, "Now we are getting somewhere, Henry!"

"Just where?" queried Henry. "I have merely confirmed a suspicion."

"But you *have* confirmed it, sir. We know now that Mary McLean is not a poor, unfortunate girl, we know that James McLean was Ormsby, and we are mighty sure that the counterfeiting is done in this valley. It is all valuable knowledge, Henry—mighty valuable."

"The Treasury Department has probably known it for months—and little good it has done them, Judge. A private detective, named Ed Ward, has been murdered, presumably, by the same gang. How this pseudo James McLean came to his death, we do not know. Perhaps Dan Ormsby is dead.

"He has been missing for months, at any rate, and he was acting for the Treasury Department. Judge, we just know enough to get ourselves killed."

Judge shuddered and laid down his pen.

"I believe," he said quietly, "we both need a drink."

"That," replied Henry, "is a sensible reaction. Get your hat, Judge."

They went over to the King's Castle, where they had a drink, and listened to Mary McLean's music. They talked with the three owners of the Doubloon Mine, Jeff Ort, Pete Halley and Dave Miller, and to Casino Evans, who was very much in evidence.

"The little lady with the fiddle sure draws 'em in," remarked Dave Miller.

"She's the finest attraction I ever had," declared Casino Evans. "The men like the sort of music she plays."

Henry and Judge went back to their room about midnight, and were undressing, when a revolver shot thudded somewhere in the building. Someone ran down the hallway, past their door, and, judging from the sound, turned left and went down an outside flight of stairs to the back yard.

Henry and Judge, half-dressed, stepped into the hallway. There were no lights in the hall. The elderly clerk had just come up from the lobby, trying to find the location of the shot. He called to Henry, asking if they had heard the shot, and then went down toward Mary McLean's room. His call brought Henry and Judge, and just outside of Mary's door was the body of a man.

Henry turned him over, and with lighted matches they looked down into the pasty face of Joe Mills, the piano player at the King's Castle. Joe Mills had played his last piano. The clerk swore that no one had come through the office, as far as he knew. Henry sent Judge to get Doctor Knowles, while he went over to the saloon.

They finished dressing before leaving the hotel. Henry sauntered into the King's Castle and up to the bar, where he bought a drink. Things were normal, it seemed. The last act was on at the stage. Henry knew that Mary had finished possibly thirty minutes ago. Joe Mills worked one act after she had finished.

Henry went back to the hotel, asked the still dazed clerk to go with him, and they went to Mary's door. It was locked, and she did not answer their knock on the door. But the clerk had a pass-key, and they went into the room.

Mary was not there, but the lighted lamp disclosed a

small sheet of paper, folded once, lying on the carpet near the door. On it was penciled:

> Keep your door locked tonight and leave Tonto tomorrow.
> You are in danger so don't wait to ask questions.
>
> A Friend.

Henry slowly folded the note and put it in his pocket. Judge and the doctor were coming up the hallway; so Henry took the lamp, closed and locked the door, and went out to them.

Doctor Knowles' examination was brief. "I'll get some of the boys to carry him down to my place," he said.

Henry and Judge went over to the King's Castle. They found Casino Evans at the bar, having a drink with one of his gamblers. He invited Henry and Judge to join them.

"You will have to find another piano player before your show tomorrow night," said Henry quietly. Casino looked at him curiously.

"Another piano player?" he queried. "Why—what is wrong with Joe Mills?"

"Joe Mills was shot and killed a little while ago in a hallway at the hotel."

Casino's amazement seemed genuine.

"Do you mean that?" he asked. "You're joking."

"His body is down at Doctor Knowles' home by this time, Casino."

"Joe Mills, shot and killed? Why, damn it, that doesn't seem possible!"

"In the midst of life, we are in death," said Judge solemnly.

"That's a hell of a thing to say," growled the gambler.

"I always thought so, too, but they are still using it," said Judge.

"I'm going down and see about this," declared Casino. "I still can't believe it. Joe was with me a long time. Want to go along, Tony?"

"Not me," replied the gambler. "You take the look, Casino."

Henry watched Casino leave the saloon, and lingered over his drink. He recalled that Joe Mills laughed, when it was suggested that Casino was law-abiding. Just why did Joe Mills laugh, he wondered.

13

THE MURDER OF Joe Mills caused considerable speculation next morning, but nothing compared to the furor caused, when it was reported that Mary McLean, the violinist, was missing. She had never come back to the hotel, after her last performance. Only Henry and the hotel clerk knew about the note, and the hotel clerk did not know what it contained.

Later, Henry showed the note to John Campbell, the prosecuting attorney, and told him who Mary McLean really was.

"It is my impression," said Henry, "that Joe Mills knew she was in danger. He went to her room, shoved the note under her door, and was murdered. Judge and I heard the killer run past our door and go down the outside stairway. He did not dare to wait and try to get into her room, if he knew that Mills had written her a warning. It is evident that the killer followed Joe, who must have come up the back stairs, because the clerk says he did not come through the office."

"Could Joe Mills have been connected with the counterfeiters?" asked Campbell.

"I do not believe it, John."

"Just why?"

"Joe Mills was more or less of a dope addict. He smoked

marijuana in his cigarettes. I believe he admitted it. No sane criminal organization would have used him. No, I do not believe he was one of them, John; but I do believe he knew who they are. That is what killed him."

Campbell nodded soberly. "And what about the girl, Henry."

"I wish I knew," sighed Henry. "She was in a dangerous position. It is possible that she learned something last night; something dangerous to the gang. Joe Mills wanted her to make a getaway, but they got her ahead of Joe's warning."

Judge met Henry on the way to the office, and Judge was boiling with indignation. The Scorpion Bend *Clarion*, a special edition, was the cause.

"An editorial on the front page in half-inch letters!" roared Judge. "It says Conroy, Van Treece and Johnson must go!"

"Go where?" asked Henry mildly.

"Out!" Judge waved the folded paper. "He should have been strangled at birth. Damme, I would like to have him between my hands right now. He dilates on the man who was shot in the buggy. He howls about the attempt to rob the Shoshone Chief payroll. He says he was attacked and rendered unconscious by a bullet intended for his brain— and he says that two of your men were on the scene—and did nothing. He says that too long have we been a blot on the fair name of this state. Henry, I have a notion to go up there and horse-whip him within an inch of his life."

"Does he get personal?" asked Henry.

"Personal? He calls us a pair of alcoholic parasites."

"Hm-m-m-m!" mused Henry.

"Are you going to stand for such things?" demanded Judge hotly.

"It is really too bad," sighed Henry. "Really too bad, Judge."

"What is too bad?"

"Slim Pickins' marksmanship," smiled Henry. "Shall we go in and get out of the sun. Forget James Wadsworth Longfellow Pelly. No doubt his head still aches—poor fellow. He says the bullet was intended for his brain?"

"He certainly does."

"Well, he is optimistic, at least. Brain, indeed. He should have said it was intended for his head. To those who know him, it would be much more convincing. If there is any of Frijole Bill's last batch left in that rear cell, I could use a little. Alcoholic parasites. Not bad. With practice he will finally succeed in saying something scathing."

"You, sir," declared Judge, "have the skin of a rhinoceros."

"But with a heart of gold, Judge. Fetch the jug, before we have words."

"Words! My God, that is all we ever have!"

Judge shuffled back to secure the jug, while Henry hastily glanced at the special edition, with its heavily printed editorial, the heading of which blared—THE SHAME OF ARIZONA MUST GO!

Casino Evans came in, and Henry shoved the paper aside. Casino scowled at Henry and said, "Well, how do you like that editorial, Conroy?"

"It is gaudy, to say the least," replied Henry.

"Gaudy!" Casino snapped his long fingers nervously. "I have never made a practice of criticizing you and your office, Conroy," he said, "but I'm agreeing with the editor of the *Clarion*. To that, I can add the murder of Joe Mills and the disappearance of Mary McLean. And what have you done? Not a damn thing—and you know it!"

"Better than you, my dear sir," replied Henry calmly.

"Better than—oh, so you admit your inefficiency, do you?"

"Why hide it?" queried Henry. Casino stared at him for several moments. Then he said, "I'll be damned!"

"Very likely," said Henry quietly. Judge came in and placed the jug on the desk.

"I don't understand you," said Casino.

"I am not exactly complex," replied Henry. "Possibly you are nonplussed at meeting an honest man. I admit that I am inefficient—and you become perplexed. Judge, fetch an extra cup for Mr. Evans."

"Not for me," said Casino quickly. "I have heard stories of that liquor, and I don't care for any."

"Some men," said Judge, "are natural fools. Henry and I drink this to get ourselves in that frame of mind. This, my dear Mr. Evans, makes one think."

"Think? Think what?"

"Think what damn fools men are to drink such stuff. Well, here's to you."

"To the little violinist—wherever she is," said Henry quietly.

"That's your job!" snapped Casino.

Oscar Johnson came into the doorway, unseen by Casino Evans, and stood there, looking at Henry.

"Yes—my job," said Henry slowly.

"Then get into it!" snapped Casino. "Alcoholic parasites! That editor told the truth. You should all be kicked out of office. Why, damn you—"

There was a ripping sound, as Casino's collar yielded to Oscar's grip, a strangled cry was jerked from Casino's vocal cords, as he was lifted from the floor, with Oscar's other hand taking up the slack in the seat of Casino's pants. A moment later Casino Evans was far out in the street on his hands and knees, bruised, humiliated and half-choked.

"I'll—get—you—for—this!" wheezed Casino.

"Yah?" queried Oscar. "Yust vait!"

Oscar started out of the doorway, but Casino Evans did not wait. He broke all speed records for crossing the main street of Tonto City, and dived through the doorway of the King's Castle, followed by the laughter of those on the street, who had seen the incident.

Oscar came back into the office, cool and collected. He took the third cup and filled it from the jug.

"Am Ay doing all right?" he asked.

"Not too bad," replied Henry. "Fill the other two, Oscar."

CASINO EVANS WENT straight to his room over the saloon, where he bathed his sore knees and hands, while Larry Steel, gambler, and Mazie tried to salve his wounded feelings.

Mazie and some of the girls had seen the incident from a window of their room, and Mazie was trying to be sympathetic, when she wanted to laugh.

"So you saw it from your window, eh?" growled the suffering Casino.

"We just happened to be looking out," said Mazie. "That Swede is a regular Hercules."

"Who was Hercules?" asked Steel, looking up from opening a bottle.

"Oh, he was a strong man of long ago."

"You mean Sandow, don't you?"

"I mean Hercules. Sandow was the guy who got his hair cut and lost his muscle. Hercules was the fellow who whipped a lot of snakes when he was a baby."

"Oh shut up!" snapped Casino. "I got half the skin scraped off my body, and I have to listen to a snake story."

"What do you suppose happened to Mary?" asked Mazie.

"How do I know?" growled Casino.

"Ran out on you?" queried Steel, reaching for a glass.

"With me owing her twenty dollars?" countered Casino.

"I'd like to know who shot poor Joe," said Mazie soberly. "He was just a poor dope who never hurt anybody. Do you suppose Mary shot him and pulled out? Joe was always whispering to her."

"Hell!" rasped Casino. "Her fist wasn't big enough to hold a forty-five. Guess again."

"Well," sighed Mazie, "she's gone and Joe's dead. What was he doing up there at her room?"

"I wish I knew," said Casino painfully.

Mazie squinted thoughtfully. "Mary went to her room right after her last act. Joe had to play for me and Dolores, and then he pulled out. He must have headed straight for her room. But she wasn't in her room, and she didn't change her dress. She wouldn't pull out in that dress; it was that spangled thing that Dolores loaned her. Something happened to her—and I wonder what it was."

"Leave that to law, sister," laughed Larry Steel.

"The law!" snorted Casino.

"Personally," said Steel, squinting through his glass of liquor at the light, "I wouldn't want to make any bad guesses about the law. They look dumb enough, but their past record isn't so bad. Conroy cleaned up a couple of tough cases, Casino."

"Bull luck," growled Casino.

"Mebbe his luck will hold good. I saw a man make twelve passes with the dice—and he wasn't halfway smart, to look at him."

"I hope he gets the buzzard who killed Joe Mills," said Mazie. "Joe went to Mary's room to either get something or to warn her."

"It's none of our business," said Casino. "Joe stuck his long nose into something—and look what he got. The safest thing to do is to mind our own business, and keep out of things that don't concern us."

"Let the law handle it," smiled Larry Steel.

"That's the idea."

Nick Borden came into the office to see Henry, and it was easy to see that the owner of the Shoshone Chief was disturbed. Henry was alone in the office.

"I've got a Federal man out at the mine," he told Henry. "He works in the office. That payroll we got from the Scorpion Bend bank had almost twenty-five hundred dollars worth of counterfeit tens and twenties."

"My goodness!" exclaimed Henry. "That much?"

"That much," said Borden grimly. "And the bills are good enough to fool anybody, except an expert. This man is going to check over the currency at the bank."

"Nick," said Henry quietly, "I want you to tell me the circumstances, regarding that payroll. Who knew you had it, and all that?"

"John Marshall, the banker and cashier, and Donald

Heaslip, the assistant cashier and bookkeeper. They both knew that there was a real package and a dummy package. The real package was taken over to the stage-office, where I received it the same as an express package. This one I gave to you and Judge. The other I got at the bank. The clerk at the stage office knew nothing about its contents, as it was not even insured."

"I see. The payroll was made up at the bank?"

"That's right. I gave them the list of bills I wanted. The dummy was made up of old newspapers."

"When does the Federal man make his investigation of the bank's money?"

"He is on his way up there right now. He came here with me, and went on to Scorpion Bend."

Henry nodded thoughtfully. "There has been a leak, Nick," he said. "Your scheme of the express package misfired. Thank you very much."

"You have an idea, Henry?" asked Nick Borden quickly.

"Let us say, an idiot's inspiration," smiled Henry. "I never have an idea."

Judge groaned over the idea of riding to Scorpion Bend. He would have to do the driving, and he hated the cramped quarters of a buggy.

"The next time," he said darkly, "they will shoot us instead of holding us up."

"Why?" asked Henry.

"The reason," replied Judge, "will not soften the impact of a forty-five. Even if they merely shoot our horse, it is a long walk back."

"If they shoot us," said Henry, "we will know they do not read the *Clarion*. No one ever shoots an alcoholic parasite."

They were starting out of the office, when the postmaster came in.

"I have a letter here for that missin' girl," he told Henry. "It was dropped into the office some time today. I thought it might be somethin' that would help you out—in some way."

He placed the letter on the desk. The envelope was soiled, the name and address printed with a soft pencil, with badly made letters. Henry looked it over thoughtfully. It had been mailed in Tonto City, and it might be a love missive from some cowboy or miner. But it seemed a bit bulky for a love letter. Henry looked up at the postmaster.

"I want you to witness the contents," he said. "The law cannot overlook anything that might give us a clue."

The flap raised easily, and Henry drew out the contents. Judge gasped. The postmaster swore softly. The contents were six one thousand-dollar bills. There was no note enclosed.

"Six thousand dollars!" husked Judge. "My God!"

Henry examined the address again. Who on earth, as illiterate as that, would send Mary McLean six thousand dollars? At least, who in Tonto City? Then Mary McLean's words flashed through his mind, "The money was marked and in large bills," when she spoke about Dan Ormsby.

HENRY EXAMINED THE money closely, but was unable to detect the marking. Naturaly, the work had been done by an expert. But who had sent the money back to Mary McLean—and why? Henry put the money back in the envelope, carefully sealed it with sealing-wax, and gave it back to the postmaster.

"You put that in your safe," he said.

"Suppose she calls for it, Mr. Conroy?"

"Give it to her—it belongs to her, I suppose. And thank you very much."

Judge walked over to the doorway, as the postmaster went out. He looked up the street, swore quietly and turned back to Henry.

"Now is the winter of our discontent," he quoted sadly. "Here comes James Wadsworth Longfellow Pelly."

"Unaccustombed as I am to murder—" began Henry.

"Enter, scrivener," invited Judge. Pelly squinted at the tall deputy.

"I came here," he announced, "to confirm the rumor that one, Mary McLean, is missing."

"And one piano player murdered," added Henry. "My dear Pelly, Tonto City is fast becoming a storehouse of valuable news for you and the *Clarion*. Sit down, man."

"Thank you."

Pelly sat down and looked at Henry.

"And what have you done about it?" he asked.

"My dear Pelly!" exclaimed Henry reprovingly.

"Nothing, I suppose."

"You may bandy words with this—er—scavenger," said Judge angrily, "but I will have nothing of him."

Judge stalked angrily from the room and went up the street.

"Then," said Pelly, "you admit that the girl has been kidnaped?"

"My dear fellow, all I know is that the young lady is missing. Whether she has been kidnaped or left Tonto of her own volition, I have no way of knowing. I am very certain that one Joe Mills, a piano player, was shot and killed near her door in the hotel."

"Why?" queried Pelly.

"For no known reason, except, perhaps, to give you the basis for another denunciation of my office."

"The *Clarion,* sir, is the voice of the people."

"And you, sir," said Henry, "have the pen of a sadist and the imagination of a damned idiot."

Pelly got quickly to his feet.

"I didn't come here to be insulted," he said.

"One never goes to a place to be insulted, does one?" asked Henry calmly. "It is a chance that must be taken, my dear sir. If I have thoroughly insulted you, I am pleased. If not, please bear with me awhile, and I may think of something really insulting. I may not be able to tell you anything about the missing girl nor the deceased piano player, but, sir, I can tell you many, many things about you."

Pelly jerked out of his chair and went to the doorway, where he turned around and glared at Henry.

"You go to hell!" he snapped angrily.

"Very well," said Henry smiling, "I'll meet you at the corner of El Diablo Avenue and Brimstone Street."

James Wadsworth Longfellow Pelly went up to the Tonto Hotel, where he secured a room, determined to stay in Tonto a day or two. Anyway, there was more news in Tonto than in Scorpion Bend, and he wanted to write a lead editorial, while he was still in the mood, and in this one he would not mince words. Wild Horse Valley would know exactly what he thought of Henry Conroy.

14

IT WAS EARLY in the afternoon, when Henry and Judge drove into Scorpion Bend next day. Judge was exasperated because Henry refused to say why they came to Scorpion Bend.

"I do not know why," he told Judge several times. "It is merely that I have an urge to come here. Perhaps it is a vain effort to be doing something."

"Something must be done," agreed Judge wearily.

"That is it exactly. Ergo, we go to Scorpion Bend."

"For no reason, Henry."

"Perhaps just for a ride, Judge."

"Why say perhaps?"

"Because you never can tell what might happen."

They stabled their horse, and while Judge talked with some men near the stable, Henry met John Marshall, the banker, near the post office. The conversation naturally turned to counterfeit money. Marshall said:

"Sheriff, something queer has happened. You remember that Nick Borden's payroll contained quite a sum of bad money?"

"Yes, I heard that, Mr. Marshall," agreed Henry.

"Well, yesterday a Federal expert, named Tom Dunn, came up from the valley, and just finished an investigation of the currency in my bank. Sheriff, not a piece of the currency in my bank was counterfeit."

"My goodness!" exclaimed Henry. "Isn't it rather coincidental—wait a moment! Mr. Marshall, what do you know about your assistant?"

"Don Heaslip? Oh, Don is all right. A very fine young man, and capable."

"Granted. Where did he come from, and how did he secure the position?"

"Don came from San Francisco, Sheriff. He was recommended by a banker friend of mine."

"By letter?"

"Why—er—yes, of course. But the letter—"

"The letter—of course," interrupted Henry. "But have you ever taken the application up with your friend in San Francisco?"

"The application was—no, I haven't. As a matter of fact, my friend was on his way to New York, where he was to sail for Europe, when he wrote the letter. Why, you don't—Sheriff, do you suspect Don Heaslip?"

"Mr. Marshall, there has been a leak in your bank—and I do not suspect you."

"No, of course not, but—well, I never suspected him for a moment."

"Mr. Marshall," said Henry quietly, "can you act?"

"Act? You mean—"

"Can you tell an untruth, or something you believe untrue, and make it sound like the truth."

"Well," Marshall smiled wryly, "I have been banking many years."

"Good man! I want you to tell Don Heaslip, in all confidence, that I have evidence that will convict the counterfeiters and hang the murderers to the highest tree in Wild Horse Valley. Tell him that I let enough slip to enable you to know that it is someone connected with a mine. That is a good shot in the dark because there are a lot of mines. Tell him that by this time tomorrow my office will have the ringleaders behind bars, and that every man connected with the operations of this gang are already in the shadow of the gallows."

John Marshall stared at Henry. "Is there any basis of truth in that?" he asked anxiously.

"Who knows?" replied Henry. "It may be true."

"Well!" John Marshall's chin jutted obstinately. "I will surely do my part, Sheriff. And if Don Heaslip—"

"You must pay no attention to him, Mr. Marshall. If he is guilty, he will make his move."

Henry met Judge, talking with Tom Dunn, who had introduced himself. Dunn had ridden a horse from Tonto City, and was still sore from the effort.

"If you do not mind," said Henry, "you will ride back with Judge, and I will ride the horse."

Knowing Henry's apathy for horseback riding, Judge looked at him in amazement.

"I wish to conduct a sort of experiment," said Henry. "But I do not want you to drive away, until about dark."

Dunn smiled broadly. "You have taken a weight off my mind, Sheriff," he said.

"And added extra weight to the poor horse," said Judge dryly. "If you gentlemen will join me, I shall purchase a drink."

It was nearly dark, when Judge, Henry and Dunn went

to the stable, but only Judge and Dunn rode away in the buggy, after arranging with the stableman to turn Dunn's horse over to Henry, who sat down near the wide door-way of the stable, where he could watch the street. It was nearly seven o'clock, when Henry left the stable and met John Marshall near the post-office.

"I told Don exactly what you told me to say," confided Marshall, "but he made no comments. I believe you made a mistake in your man."

"That is possible," sighed Henry. "Where does Heaslip live?"

"At the Scorpion Bend Hotel. He keeps a saddle horse in a private stable near the rear of the hotel."

"A private stable? So he has a horse. Show me that stable."

In a few minutes they reached the stable and went inside. Don Heaslip's horse and saddle were gone.

"What time did he leave the bank?" asked Henry.

"At four o'clock," replied Marshall.

They went to the hotel, and the clerk said he saw Don Heaslip, wearing riding clothes, leave the hotel about half past four.

"I remember a tongue-twister in vogue when I was a young man," said Henry, "and it applies to this case. It was this—the sly fox creeps, while the sleek hound sleeps. Try saying it fast."

"Why?" asked Marshall.

"Oh, just to make me forget what a damn fool I've been. Good night."

Henry hurried to the stable, saddled the horse and left town swiftly.

"Mr. Heaslip," he told the horse, "was smart enough to leave town by a back road; and that fact has upset me, no end."

JAMES WADSWORTH LONGFELLOW Pelly actually bought a drink. He had been unable to get any information about the missing Mary McLean; so he conceived the idea that by treating the bartender and getting confidential, he might get a valuable tip. Then the bartender treated Mr. Pelly, and the episode was over. The bartender was a busy man.

But those two large drinks of raw, Tonto City whiskey gave Mr. Pelly a decided lift. He remembered that he had been insulted by Henry Harrison Conroy, and right now his mind was full of barbed repartee. Would he slay Henry Harrison Conroy in verbal combat! There was a light in the window of the sheriff's office; so the mentally-reinforced Pelly strode in, all primed for debate.

But the office was empty. He stopped in the middle of the room. From behind him at the doorway someone gently cleared their throat. Pelly turned to see Oscar Johnson in the doorway. That giant Swede looked even larger in the lamplight.

"Do you want something?" asked Oscar gently.

"Oh, my!" whispered Pelly. The very person he did not want between him and the doorway. There would be no use exchanging quips with Oscar. A clatter of footsteps were coming down the sidewalk, and a moment later four men were peering past Oscar. They were Slim Pickins, Frijole Bill, Thunder and Lightning.

"What does he eat—peanuts?" asked Slim soberly.

"Judge says," remarked Frijole, "that he eats nitric acid and writes with his fingernail."

"I will thank you to get out of the doorway and let me depart," said Pelly. "You can't hold me here against my will."

"He's smart," said Frijole. "He's made out a will."

"I demand that you stand aside and let me leave this office," said Pelly.

"Sure," agreed Slim. "We'll divide up on each side—and let him make it."

"Where-at is Henry?" asked Frijole.

"He vent to Scorpion Bend," replied Oscar.

"Shucks!" snorted Slim. "We want to draw some money."

"And I got him a gallon of prune juice," sighed Frijole.

"Yudas!" exclaimed Oscar. "A gallon! I'll get de cups."

"Wait!" exclaimed Frijole. "We've got to squirsh this bug, before we have a drink."

"Geeve heem a drink," suggested Lightning. "Those prunes juice mus' be good for keel the bogs."

"I won't have it," declared Pelly. "You haven't any right to force me to stay here. I am a citizen, and I have my rights."

"We ain't goin' to hurt yuh," assured Slim. "We like yuh. If we didn't like yuh, do yuh think we'd ask yuh to drink with us?"

"I don't want a drink."

"After thinkin' it over," said Frijole quietly, "I'll betcha yo're as dry as a sidewinder's belly in Death Valley."

Oscar came in with the tin cups and lined them up on Henry's desk, where he filled them to the brim from Frijole's jug. Pelly counted them, and there were six. He said:

"I—I can't drink that much."

"Don't fool yourself—you only get one," said Slim.

"I meant—one."

"One at a time," agreed Slim. "Well, here's to yuh, gents."

Pelly slopped some on his necktie, but most of it went down his throat. It wasn't bad—after the first swallow. Pelly brightened visibly, but saddened a moment later, when the cups were filled again.

"I'm a little afraid," he said. "My stomach hasn't been right for …"

"Must have been somethin' yuh et," interrupted Slim. "But this'll fix it."

"What do you boys know about the missing girl?" asked Pelly.

"Jist about everything" replied Frijole. "Here's over the lips and past the gums; look out insides; here she comes!"

Pelly's hand shook a little, as he put down his cup.

"I—I had two drinks before I came over here," confessed Pelly.

"Yuh did?" exclaimed Slim. "Why, you damned drunkard! Pelly, yuh don't mean it!"

"I did so," grinned Pelly. "Two whiskies. Whee-e-e-e!"

"Sh-h-h-h!" cautioned Frijole. "What do yuh think this is—a saloon?"

"I am sincerely shorry," said Pelly. "I beg your pardon."

"That's all right," assured Slim. "Maybe yuh didn't have no bringin'-up. It shore comes out on a feller."

"I stand c'rected," said Pelly.

"Ay vill be damned!" exclaimed Oscar quietly. "His stummick is very kvick. Va'al, are ve going to drink or yust talk about it?"

None of them saw Donald Heaslip, when he came to Tonto City, because Donald Heaslip did not want to be seen. Judge and Tom Dunn did not come to Tonto City. Judging from the elapsed time, Donald Heaslip must have gone some place, before coming to Tonto City. At any rate, he slipped quietly into the rear of the King's Castle Saloon, where he was lost in the crowd, which was celebrating a payday at most of the mines.

The six men left the sheriff's office and decided to go over to the King's Castle, but were nearly run over by a team and wagon, which pulled in at the saloon hitch-rack. The driver swore at them.

"Ay t'ink that vars Pete Halley," said Oscar. "For dose vords Ay vill push in his nose, you bat you. Come on, yentlemen."

Whoever the driver was, he preceded them into the saloon. As a matter of fact, they did not enter the saloon. They were near the doorway, when a man staggered out of an alley and almost into them. He was Donald Heaslip, the assistant cashier of the Cattlemen's Bank at Scorpion Bend. Blood was running from his nose and mouth, and one eye was fast swelling shut.

"My gug-goodness!" exclaimed Pelly. "What happened to you, Don'ld?"

Slim grasped Heaslip by the arm, turning him around.

"Damn you, let loose of me!" rasped the young man. "You can't—"

From the entrance to the dark and narrow alley, only a few feet away, came the flash and report of a gun. Heaslip went to his knees, clawing at Pelly, and nearly knocking him off his unsteady legs. Heaslip fell full in the lights from the saloon window. There was so much noise in the saloon that few paid any attention to the shot.

A rider went away from the hitch-rack in the dark, traveling fast, but in the excitement no one noticed that. Slim went to his knees beside Heaslip.

"Who shot yuh, Kid?" he asked sharply. "Who shot yuh?"

"… said I was yellow," babbled Heaslip. "I'll… get… even. Doubloon… Mine… that… girl…"

"Doubloon Mine?" queried Slim. "What about that girl?"

"Get out… there… quick."

Several other men had joined the group, staring at the man on the sidewalk. Slim jumped to his feet.

"Doubloon Mine!" he exclaimed. "That wagon out there! C'mon, boys!"

The tragedy had shocked some of the liquor from their brains and legs, and they raced for the hitch-rack. Pete Halley had untied the team and was starting to climb aboard, when the six men reached him. Oscar shoved Pete aside, bumping him against the top-rail of the hitch-rack.

"Damn you, get away from the wagon!" yelled Halley. "You can't—"

Oscar's right fist thudded square into Pete Halley's face, and Pete went under the hitch-rack this time, losing all interest in his team and wagon. Slim got the lines, while the others piled in over the sideboards, and swung the team into the street. While men crowded out of the saloon doorway, trying to discover the cause of so much excitement, that team went out of Tonto City, like a fire department heading for a blaze.

Henry Harrison Conroy never rode a horse as fast in his life as he did that night. Just why such excessive speed, he had no idea.

He was certain that Donald Heaslip had stolen a march on him. Henry had sort of a vague idea that if Heaslip was guilty of wrong doing, he would try and get in touch with whoever he was working for. It looked as though Henry's suspicions had been correct, but his quarry had flushed too far ahead of the gun.

Just where Heaslip might be going, Henry had no idea. He rode off the grades and down into the valley, traveling at a more moderate pace. He was near where the road forked to the Doubloon mine, when he heard the beat of galloping hoofs. Henry reined quickly off the road, and saw a rider, traveling at full speed, swing onto the Doubloon road.

Henry rubbed his nose thoughtfully, flexed his cramped muscles, and wondered why anyone would be in such a hurry to reach the mine. In fact, Pete Halley, Jeff Ort and Dave Miller always traveled by wagon. Henry could not remember ever seeing either of them on horseback.

"Hm-m-m-m," mused Henry aloud. "Doubloon mine. My gracious! Just suppose—and me all alone, unarmed. What a fool a sheriff is to not carry a gun! Well, it is less than two miles to the mine. Nothing ventured, nothing had."

Henry rode slowly over the old road, bordered by heavy desert growth. At one time the Doubloon had been a promising prospect, and many thousands of dollars had been spent for machinery and development. Most of the machinery had been taken away, but the gaunt, old shaft-houses still reared their blackened timbers above the skyline. A five-hundred-foot shaft had been sunk, and there were a number of tunnels and huge stopes, where the original company honeycombed the hill, seeking the gold vein. Many of the big ore dumps were nearly covered again with desert growth.

When Henry reached a point a few hundred yards from the buildings he drew off the road into a little clearing behind a heavy thicket of mesquite, and almost rode into a horse and buggy, which had been left there. Examination disclosed that it was the horse and buggy driven by Judge and Tom Dunn.

Henry was really puzzled. What on earth would Judge and Dunn be doing at the Doubloon mine, he wondered? Had they discovered something and were making an investigation? He tied his horse nearer the buildings and went ahead on foot to see what he could discover.

TIED IN THE deep shadows of the old blacksmith shop was a saddled horse, still wet from a long run. The windows of the mine building were dark, but there was a tiny thread of light from a crack in the door. Henry worked his way around to a covered window, but could only hear a faint hum of conversation. He was wondering what to do next, when he heard the sounds of a galloping horse.

Henry dropped flat against the house, hoping that in the darkness he would not be discovered. The horse came within a few feet of him, and the rider dismounted quickly. The door was flung open, and there was a babble of voices. The light from the window identified the newcomer as Pete Halley.

Jeff Ort and Dave Miller came out to him, and then Casino Evans came out behind them, as though reluctant to join them. Casino saw Pete.

"What the hell!" he exclaimed. "Where is the wagon—and that girl?"

"They jumped me at the hitch-rack," panted Pete. "I—I tried to stop 'em, but one of 'em hit me. They got the wagon, damn 'em! But that ain't all. Heaslip wasn't dead, Casino—he talked! I stole a horse—and got here."

Casino Evans swore bitterly. "We've got to do something—quick!" he declared. "Pete, you damn fool, you stopped to get a drink—and look what happened! They've got the girl, but she can't prove anything. We've got to get rid of Van Treece, the stranger and Ormsby—now. Where is Van Treece and the stranger?"

"Up in the shaft house," replied Ort. "Ormsby ain't been brought from the stope yet."

"All right, we've got to work fast. Get Ormsby and take him up to the shaft house, and when you get him there, dump all three of them into the old shaft. Then cut the cable on that old cage, and let it drop. If we can get everything cleaned up, maybe they can't prove a damn thing. Get going, boys. I'll head back to Tonto City and clean out my safe. They haven't anything on me, but I want that money out of the safe; so we can make a split, if anything goes wrong."

Before anyone could voice an objection, Casino ran to his horse, got quickly into the saddle, and went racing away in the darkness. Miller said:

"There he goes—and there goes our money—while we have to do the dirty work. He'll empty the safe, and leave us to swing on the end of a rope. To hell with it—I'm not murderin' anybody."

"You'll do yore share, you chicken-hearted cry-baby,"

declared Ort. "I'm tired of yore squawlin', Miller. We're all in the same boat, and we float or sink together."

"I've never killed anybody," declared Miller, "and I won't be any party to throwin' three men into that old shaft. Go ahead, if yuh want to, but I'm pullin' out right now—money or no money."

"Yo're quittin'?" asked Ort, his voice tense.

"Right now—and so will you, if you've got any brains. Casino has thrown us all down. To hell with this job."

A revolver shot blasted in the dark, and a man cried sharply. Henry was around the corner from it, but realized that Miller had been shot.

"Deader'n a door-knob, Jeff," said Pete Halley. "Damn it, we've got one more. But you done it; so you'll have to pack him up to the shaft."

"Leave him lay there," growled Ort. "We'll dump the live ones first."

"All right, c'mon; we'll pack Ormsby up there."

The two men went out past the blacksmith shop, and Henry heard them climbing over a rough trail. He went out and found the body of Dave Miller. They had forgotten to take Miller's gun; so Henry took it for himself. He knew the trail up to the shaft house. It was a hard climb, and Henry was all out of breath long before he reached the tall, old structure, an inky-black silhouette against the starlit sky.

At one of the entrances he paused to catch his breath. There was not a sound, except the sleepy calling of a mocking-bird. Henry knew that at nearly the center of this building was the old shaft, which had been sunk over five hundred feet. Casino Evans' idea was to throw Judge, Dunn and Ormsby into the old shaft, and then cut the cable and let that huge, steel cage crash down on top of them.

Henry called quietly, his voice echoing back from the old wooden walls, but there was no response. He called again, and from somewhere in the building came a dull thumping sound, as though someone was beating on the floor with their heels. It was an eerie old place in the dark, but Henry went quietly across the rough plank floor, searching for the sounds.

He stopped and called softly. "Judge! Make a noise so I can find you."

Again the thumping sound indicated the position, and in a few moments Henry almost fell over a trussed figure. Cautiously he lighted a match. Judge and Dunn were stretched out on the floor, bound and gagged, Henry quickly cut away the gags, and slashed the ropes loose.

But he was none too soon. Ort and Halley were coming up to the opposite entrance. A weight was dumped on the floor, and Ort said:

"Light that lantern, Pete; we'll have to take a chance."

Henry crouched behind an old pillar, holding the gun in both hands. Pete Halley lighted the lantern, and Ort began dragging the body of a man across the rough floor. Neither of them ever gave a thought that anyone else might be there. They dumped Ormsby beside the other two, and Halley went over to remove a couple of planks from the mouth of the shaft. It was then that Ort discovered that his two prisoners were no longer gagged, no longer bound. He sprang back, drawing his gun.

Halley was stooping over, as Ort yelled:

"Look out, Pete!"

Pete Halley was out of balance. He tried to draw his gun. For a moment he sagged sideways, and then tried to leap across a corner of the shaft, but fell short. He screamed as he struck waist-high against the edge, and then bounced back into the shaft.

Ort whirled around, trying to locate somebody, but the lantern on the floor gave little illumination. Henry said:

"Drop your gun and put up your hands, Ort!"

Henry was not over a dozen feet away, but partly protected by the wooden pillar. Ort was game. He shot three times, the bullets smashing into the old twelve-by-twelve. Henry shoved his .45 past the side of the timber, shooting by instinct, and pulled the trigger. Ort went down, shot through the right leg. Henry yelled to him to surrender, but Ort still had three shots in his gun.

Cursing Henry, he started to try and crawl outside, but this time Henry stepped out, held the gun in both hands, and shot again. Ort lurched forward and sprawled, arms outspread.

"My God, Henry!" gasped Judge. "You got him, man!"

"My goodness, I believe I have!" exclaimed Henry. "That accounts for Heaslip, Miller, Ort and Halley. If you gentlemen will excuse me, I shall try and make it a full-house. Get your buggy and come to town."

Without any further explanation, Henry picked up the lantern and went stumbling down the steep trail.

"You may think he is crazy, Mr. Dunn," Judge said, "but I assure you that you are not the only one who feels that way. But who is this third party?"

Dunn lighted a match and looked into the bearded face of a man who looked as though he had suffered greatly.

He removed the gag from the bearded lips and said, "You are Ormsby?"

"What there is left of me—yes. What happened?"

"I wish I could tell you, sir," replied Judge. "Ormsby? Ormsby? Why, yes, I have heard of you, sir."

"He's all right, Judge," said Dunn. "He is one of us."

"You mean—a Federal man, Dunn?"

"Tried to be," answered Ormsby. "I made a hell of a botch of it."

"Haven't we all—except Henry Conroy."

"Conroy?" queried Ormsby. "They told me he didn't have any brains."

"And look where they are," said Judge.

15

IT SEEMED AS though everybody in Tonto City was crowded in the yard of Doctor Knowles, and a great many of them were in the house, where Mary McLean, stretched out on a sofa, was explaining what she knew about her kidnaping. Crowded around close were the men who had found her—Oscar Johnson, Slim Pick-ins, Frijole Bill, James Wadsworth Longfellow Pelly, and the inimitable Thunder and Lightning.

Mary had explained that two men had grabbed her in the dark, just as she was about to enter the hotel. They took her away to an old shack, where she was kept without food or water, until tonight, when a man had carried her out, put her into a wagon and covered her with old sacks. She could hear the sounds of men talking and laughing, when the wagon stopped at Tonto City, and there were sounds of a row, and then it seemed as though everyone in town had climbed into the wagon and walked over her.

"I am try for seet on her," grinned Lightning. "I theenk she ees old sack, but w'en I'm seet down she go *squik-squik*."

"A fine story," said Pelly, "but it doesn't tell us anything. Where is Conroy and Van Treece? As usual, they are very likely asleep somewhere."

"Listen, you parrot-voiced pelican," said Slim. "One

more word against Henry and Judge and I'll hit you so hard that you'll talk bass for the rest of yore life—if yuh live."

John Campbell, the prosecuting attorney, turned to Pelly.

"You say that Peter Halley was the driver of that wagon, and that Heaslip told you that the girl was at the Doubloon Mine?"

"I think that is what he said, Mr. Campbell."

"That team and wagon are from the Doubloon Mine," said Slim.

"And Halley tried to prevent you from taking the team?"

"He vars very mad," said Oscar, grinning widely, "but Ay cooled him off."

"What became of Halley?" asked Campbell.

"I don't know what became of Halley," said Slim, "but I do know that my horse is missin' from the hitch-rack. This town is gettin' so that nothin' is sacred."

"If we had some decent men in that sheriff's office—" began Pelly, but Oscar put a big paw over the editor's mouth.

"Yust von more vord from you—and Ay vill yerk," promised Oscar.

"This is no place for a quarrel," said Doctor Knowles. "Wait until you get outside."

"Suits me," said Oscar. "Ay can yerk as hord outside as Ay can inside."

"Aw shucks, let's go uptown," said Slim. "No use botherin' around here any longer. Dog-gone it, I wish Henry and Judge would show up."

The five men filed out of the room. Pelly went with them, because Oscar was behind him, and they all headed for the

King's Castle Saloon. Most of the crowd around Doctor Knowles' house had gone back to the main part of town.

Business was booming at the King's Castle. Casino Evans came in from the rear. He had changed from his riding clothes at the stable, but was not exactly immaculate. Everyone was talking about Mary McLean. Nick Borden asked Casino if Mary would come back there to work.

"If she wants the job, I can sure use her," said Casino. "Does she have any idea who kidnaped her?"

"I guess not. She says she never saw anybody, because they kept her blindfolded."

"It's a queer thing," said Casino, "and doesn't make sense."

"What was this I hear about this youngster from the Scorpion Bend bank being shot, and telling that the girl was at the Doubloon Mine?"

"I don't know, Nick. Maybe he was out of his head."

"But the wagon was from the Doubloon Mine, and several men said they saw Pete Halley here just before Heaslip was shot."

"It does sound queer," admitted Casino. "Probably the sheriff will investigate—as he usually does."

HENRY HARRISON CONROY slid the last fifteen feet down the hill, and stopped just about where Dave Miller's body had been. But there was no sign of the body. Henry lighted matches, but beyond splashes of blood on the ground, there was no indication that a man had died there. Henry discovered that he had taken Ort's gun, which gave him two.

"Two-Gun Conroy, that's me," he panted, "A woolly wolf of the wilderness. If Broadway could only see me now!"

He ran down the road to where he had left his horse, tucked both guns inside the waist-band of his trousers, and mounted. A half-mile down the road he told the world that a holster was the proper place to carry a gun. Both of those heavy .45s had slipped down, and right now the muzzles were sticking in the tops of his boots, while the butts and frame were playing havoc with his shins and ankle-bones. With his left hand holding to reins and saddle-horn, and the other hanging onto his sombrero, Henry Harrison Conroy raced for Tonto City.

CASINO EVANS MADE his way through the crowd to the stairway, where he went quietly up to his room. Locking the door securely he proceeded to open his private safe. The sight was rather gratifying to him, as he tumbled packages of currency into a handbag. Packing them carefully and locking the bag, he took a length of small rope from his desk, and tied it to the handle of the bag.

Then he carefully opened a window and leaned out. Satisfied with the inspection, he quickly lowered the bag to the ground, dropped the rope and closed the window. He could hear the music from the honkatonk as he searched his desk. Satisfied that he had everything of value, he went out, closed and locked the door, and went to the stairs.

In his little stable was the fastest horse in Wild Horse Valley. It would not take him long to reach Scorpion Bend, where he could get a train and be many miles away from Tonto City before any investigation could connect him with any wrongdoing.

Casino did not know how much Joe Mills had told Mary McLean, but he did know that when he told Joe who Mary was, and that they would have to put her where she could not harm any of them, Joe had gone to warn her. That was why Joe Mills was killed—he talked too much.

Casino had no ideas of splitting that money with Ort, Halley and Miller. On the evidence of what Heaslip had said, and the fact that Mary had been found in their wagon, the law would deal with the three from the Doubloon mine. There was no doubt in Casino's mind that one of the three would confess and implicate him; but he would be very far away by that time.

He came slowly and nonchalantly down the stairs, while the crowd milled below him. He stopped to look over the room. Over by the bar were Oscar, Slim, Frijole and Pelly, talking with John Campbell. There was an open space near the door, and he saw Thunder and Lightning Mendoza come in. Casino jerked back, stifling a curse. Lightning was carrying the valise he had lowered from his window, the rope dragging.

He heard Slim say, "What the hell are you doin'—goin' travelin'?"

Lightning's reply was not audible. Casino did not know what to do. All of his money, except what he had in his pocket, was in that valise. A dozen different plans flashed through his mind, but none of them were practical. He came down to the bottom. Men shoved past him, jostling him, as they went to the roulette layout, but Casino Evans paid no attention to them.

Suddenly there was a commotion of sound. The men near the doorway separated quickly. A man, hatless, disheveled, his face plastered with blood and dirt, staggered into the room. It was Dave Miller, unarmed, uncertain on his feet. Slim Pickins grabbed him by the sleeve.

"What's wrong with yuh, Miller?" he asked. The buzz of conversation had died. A stack of poker-chips rattled loudly, as they were upset onto the floor.

"I've got to find a man," panted Miller. "They shot me, because I wouldn't murder other men. I'm goin' to find him. He's the one I want."

"You ain't even got a gun," said Slim.

"I'll get him," said Miller. "He's a yellow killer. I don't need a gun."

Casino Evans started to back up the stairs. A man bumped him from behind, and he turned to look into the face of Henry Harrison Conroy. Casino gasped. But his gambling nerve stood him in good stead. He said, "Get down there—a man has been shot, Conroy."

"I saw him shot, Casino," replied Henry wearily. "You are the man he means. You are through, Casino."

Casino seemed to take a forward step, but it was only to whirl facing Henry. Two guns thudded so close together that there was only one report. Casino went down, plunging into the crowd, while Henry dropped to the stairs, sprawled flat and gently slid the rest of the distance to the bottom. Only Oscar Johnson had seen the two men on the stairs. Now he went through that crowd like a swimmer doing the Australian crawl.

The place was in an uproar. Oscar had Henry in his arms, yelling for everyone to get out of his way. Luckily Doctor Knowles was at hand, and persuaded him to place Henry on the floor. Casino Evans had been killed instantly. Oscar and Slim held the crowd back, while the doctor made his examination. Judge, Tom Dunn and Ormsby came in, but no one paid any attention to them. The doctor removed something from Henry's waistband and held it up. It was a Colt .45, and there was still a gob of lead sticking to part of the frame and the edge of the cylinder.

"He ain't dead, Doc?" asked Slim anxiously.

Henry gasped, choked, wheezed and tried to sit up. He opened his eyes and looked around.

"If I am dead," he whispered huskily, "the world had better revise its ideas of heavenly angels."

"The bullet," said the doctor, "smashed up on that extra gun."

John Campbell shoved in close and looked down at Henry.

"What is this all about, Henry?" he asked. Henry blinked and took a deep breath.

"Where is Dave Miller?" he asked.

"He's right here in a chair," replied Frijole. "I'm a-keepin' him."

"Miller is the last of them," said Henry painfully. "Heaslip, Ort, Halley and Casino—what about him?"

"He's dead," said the doctor quietly.

"All dead, except Miller," said Henry. "I am sure he will talk."

Miller would. They put wet towels on his head, a drink of whiskey into his stomach, and he talked. He said that Casino Evans was the leader. He conceived the idea of counterfeiting mining stock. Casino made it himself, but was not competent to make counterfeit money. He bought all his supplies from an obscure engraver in San Francisco—Dan Ormsby, who was operating under the name of McLean.

In some way Evans discovered that McLean had tipped

off the Treasury Department to the sales. He confided enough in McLean to cause McLean to want to buy in on the deal. Evans suspected that it was a ruse to find their plant; so when McLean came down there, bringing enough money to buy a share in the business, McLean was put under lock and key and forced to engrave plates, under threat of death.

"What about the detective who was shot in the buggy with Josephine Swensen?" asked Judge.

"Casino and Ort done that job. Casino knew this man, and he was afraid of him."

"Who," asked Henry, "was the man they dressed in McLean's, or Ormsby's, clothes, and left in the desert?"

"A desert rat," said Miller weakly. "He came to the mine, dyin' from tuberculosis. Me and Halley took care of him. Casino felt that someone would be lookin' for Ormsby; so when this feller died, they put Ormsby's clothes on him, put Ormsby's ring on his finger and left him in the desert. Casino said that the buzzards would do the rest."

"Heaslip tipped you off to that Shoshone Chief payroll?" asked Henry.

"He tipped off Ort and Halley. Casino didn't have anythin' to do with it. Ort went back next mornin', and he knew that the payroll was recovered."

"What about the money Ormsby brought to buy into the scheme?" asked Henry.

"Casino was scared of it. He swore it was marked, and that it would be poison for anybody to cash a thousand-dollar bill. So they had an idea that the money on the corpse would cinch the identification. Anyway, they emptied Ormsby's pockets and put it all on the corpse."

"My God, what a story!" exclaimed Pelly. "It is the biggest one I ever had a chance to publish. Mr. Conroy, I want to be the first to congratulate you."

"My goodness!" exclaimed Henry.

"Ormsby," said Judge, "was that money marked?"

The bearded man shook his head.

"No, it wasn't," he replied. "I know that Casino was smart; so I took a long chance. No, Judge, that money is not marked. I played a dumb part in this deal. I don't know what they'll do to me for making plates, but, if I do say it myself, I made them good enough for the Treasury Department to recognize my work. It was do or die—and I had no desire to die. The credit must all go to Henry Harrison Conroy. A few minutes later, and we would all have been in the bottom, of the Doubloon shaft."

Oscar had Lightning's valise. They put it on a table and opened it, disclosing thousands of dollars worth of currency. Lightning told where they found it.

"That's all the money we made," said Miller. "Casino kept it."

"And he was all set for a getaway," said Campbell. "A few hours more, and Mr. Casino Evans would have been gone. Henry, you did a grand bit of detective work. I congratulate you, sir."

"Thank you, John. I—I did very well with what I had to go on."

"What was that?" asked Judge.

Henry rubbed his nose thoughtfully. "I am afraid I am just a bit too modest to talk about it, Judge," he said. "Suffice to say, Wild Horse Valley is law-abiding once more—we all hope."

"I am going to buy a good drink for everybody in the room," offered Nick Borden.

Slim and Frijole were suffering from thirst, but slipped out quietly. While the rest of the crowd edged in close to the bar, Slim and Frijole leaned against opposite sides of a porch-post.

"Good money," murmured Slim. "Not even marked. Anybody could spend it. And all my life I've hankered to set in the shade of a cocoanut tree, and have cocoanuts fall into my lap."

"I'm jist a cook," sighed Frijole. "I know how to fry, roast and bake, but when it comes to havin' brains—I'll die a cook. Six thousand dollars! Slim, we're jist a couple of them there phil—phil—phil—what do yuh call fellers who give away money in big gobs?"

"Yuh don't mean to say that there's another feller who is as a big damn fool as we've been, do yuh?"

"Is there? Why, one time down in Abilene, I knowed the biggest damn fool on earth. His name—"

"I know it," interrupted Slim. "His name was Frijole Cullison. He picked up another damn fool named Slim Pickins. Let's go home."

TRACKS IN THE SAND

Henry felt that there was something rotten in the State of Denmark—and likewise in the State of Arizona

1

"DOC" DARNELL, ERSTWHILE Arizona mine promoter, Oklahoma oil promoter, and so on down the line, including confidence schemes, shell games and marked cards, spread his two hundred and twenty pounds of well-dressed avoirdupois on a bench in Golden Gate Park and wondered what was to be his next move to keep his bankroll from further shrinkage. And what Doc would do for a dollar would amaze anyone—excepting honest work.

Doc had a bland, open countenance. In fact, he was benign, with his gray hair, honest-looking eyes, and an habitual smile under his close-clipped gray mustache. But Doc Darnell belied his looks. The police had a name for him, and that name was Dangerous.

A squirrel came across the grass, leaped to the top of the bench and looked Doc over carefully. But Doc was not interested in the little animal. In one pudgy hand he held a newspaper, which he proceeded to unfold. On the front page was a large picture of a man in dinner clothes, and above the picture was the headline:

MILLIONAIRE TURNS GOAT-HERD AND
WRECKS SWANKY NIGHT-CLUB

The story, loaded with humorous details, said that Frank

Travis had loaded a borrowed truck with goats, taken them to a famous roadhouse, where, at the height of the midnight festivities, he had driven them into the place. Both goats and patrons, the paper said, became hysterical. A famous band leader was later removed from the depths of a kettle-drum, where a four-legged battering-ram had put him. Women had fainted, and the place was n scene of wild disorder. Travis, the millionaire, according to the police, had probably left town.

Doc Darnell knew Frank Travis. In fact, he had, at one time, selected Frank Travis as a victim, but the police recognized him too soon. He knew that Frank Travis had inherited several millions from his father. He was an orphan, nearly thirty years of age, a wild spender, who even refused to retain a law firm, because of the fact that they might advise him.

Doc Darnell also knew that quite recently this same Frank Travis had acquired ownership of the Shoshone Chief gold mine in Wild Horse Valley, Arizona, at which

mine one of Doc's personal friends was general manager. It had been reported that Travis had paid nearly a half million for the Shoshone Chief. Doc closed his eyes and estimated what he could do with that much money. Travis' father had made his millions in mines; so it was quite natural that the son would look favorably upon mining investments.

Doc sighed and opened his eyes. Dreaming never put any gold into his pockets—but it was nice to dream, anyway. The squirrel cocked his head inquiringly, as Doc took a handkerchief from his pocket and removed a speck of dust from his left eye.

A MAN CAME sauntering past the bench and sat down on the next bench, where he proceeded to fill his pipe. He was not exactly down-at-the-heel in appearance, but did not look at all prosperous. He needed a shave, and his shoes had not been shined for days. He also looked as though a good meal under his belt might not be amiss.

But Doc Darnell was not so much interested in his outward appearance, as he was in the man's face. Slowly he unfolded the paper again and looked at the face of Frank Travis. He didn't need to do that, because he was very familiar with the face of Frank Travis. He folded the paper again, tucked it into a crack in the bench, and got slowly to his feet.

The squirrel had deserted Doc to go over to the newcomer, and the man seemed amused over the antics of the little fellow. He looked up as Doc approached.

"Friendly little devil," he remarked.

"Ah, yes," replied Doc. "They are always begging for nuts."

"Very likely recognized me at first glance," said the younger man soberly.

"Very good!" chuckled Doc. "Lovely day, my friend."

"I really hadn't noticed," he replied, poking a finger at the squirrel.

Doc took a long, black cigar from his pocket and carefully lighted it. A closer view of this man's face had caused Doc's blood-pressure to climb several points. The resemblance to Frank Travis was remarkable.

"Haven't we met before?" he asked. The man looked sharply at him, but shook his head.

"Sorry," he said. "I'm a stranger here."

"Remarkable resemblance to a friend of mine," said Doc.

A mounted policeman came along. Doc became engrossed in his nails, and he noticed that this stranger did not look up, until after the horse and rider had gone on. Could it be, he wondered, that this man was also just a bit police-shy. Finally Doc said:

"Are you working here in San Francisco?"

"Jobs," replied the man, "are pretty scarce."

"That's right," agreed Doc. "No work—no eat."

The man looked closely at Doc. "You haven't missed many meals," he said.

"A smart man eats," smiled Doc. "I do not work—but I eat."

"A smart man, eh?" mused the stranger aloud. "Maybe I'm not smart."

"Maybe," suggested Doc, "you haven't thought along the right channels."

"Such as?" suggested the man quietly.

Doc puffed thoughtfully for several moments. Then he said, "As I diagnose your case, my friend, you are a stranger here, out of work, nearly out of money. Am I right?"

"You said nearly," reminded the stranger.

Doc laughed quietly. "Did you ever hear of Doc Darnell?" he asked.

"Sorry, but it doesn't click in my brain. Who is he?"

"I am Doc Darnell."

"Medico, tooth carpenter or horse doctor?"

"No, no, my friend—none of them," laughed Doc. He moved closer on the bench, although the nearest ears were on a baby and her nursemaid, two hundred feet away.

"Would you," queried Doc, "like to make a fortune—very quickly?"

"And if I did," replied the stranger, "how much of it would I enjoy outside of prison walls?"

"Very, very well put!" exclaimed Doc. "You have brains, my friend."

"Possibly an instinct to remain free, Doctor."

"We all have this instinct," smiled Doc. "You and I are not the kind to go blindly into a thing. But when Doc Darnell steps into a situation, my friend, there is nothing to fear from the law. Can you act a part?"

The man laughed. "So you are promoting a play, Doctor?"

"I am not, sir. But as the immortal Bard put it so aptly—"

"I know! but usually the characters are miscast, Doctor."

"True, true. Wait a moment."

Doc went back to the bench and secured the paper, which he took back and opened it to the front page.

"You have a mirror," he said. "Look at that face."

The man studied the picture, rubbed his stubbled chin and handed the paper back to Doc.

"It does look a little like me," he admitted. "But newspaper pictures are never very accurate."

"I know Frank Travis," said Doc, "and you look like him. In fact, the resemblance is remarkable. You, my friend, could double for Frank Travis."

"Who is this Frank Travis, Doctor?"

In a few words Doc Darnell outlined Frank Travis. The man smiled.

"The interesting part," he said, "is the fact that Travis has a million dollars, and in that respect all resemblance between us has faded. It is nice to know that I look like a moneyed man, Doctor. But you spoke about making a fortune—quickly."

"Ah, yes—a fortune. How quickly?" Doc shrugged his shoulders. "It takes a little time to work out a plan. It must be fool-proof, this plan, my friend; but the reward—"Doc licked his lips in anticipation—"will be worth all of it. Would you—" Doc hesitated thoughtfully, "be willing to be Frank Travis? And if there was no Frank Travis—later, of course—would you mind being Frank Travis—always?"

"Let me get this straight," said the stranger, no longer smiling. "You ask me to masquerade as another man. Then you add a hint that this other man might cease to exist. Doctor, I don't go in for murder."

"Tut, tut, man!" said the Doctor hastily. "Nothing like it. You merely play the part. My friend, it means a million dollars to us. Ease and comfort, with every luxury—for life."

"That sounds all right. In fact, it sounds crazy. What is the deal?"

"Not so fast, my friend. You are interested, it seems."

"You spoke of a million dollars," reminded the stranger.

"Or more," added Doc. "What is your name?"

"You quoted the Bard of Avon," smiled the stranger. "I will reply, What's in a name? Make it Smith, if you must have a name."

"Ah, yes—Smith. Frank Smith, perchance?"

"If you want it that way, Doctor. What next?"

"Just this, Smith. Is there anyone liable to pop up and recognize you, or any relative—"

"Rest your mind on that," smiled the man. "There is no one."

"Good! Where are you living?"

"In a dump down on the Embarcadero. But I can go with you at—"

"No, no! We must not be seen together. Here is a little money, Smith."

Doc Darnell took a ten-dollar bill from a thin billfold and gave it to him.

"I'll gamble that much on your integrity, Smith," he said. "Meet me here a week from today, at this time, and everything will be settled."

"Thanks, Doc; I'll be here. That deal looks too good for me to miss."

"Good! Don't make any friends, Smith. Keep away from people. I'll see you a week from today."

"If I'm out of jail—I'll be here, Doc. So long."

Doc took the newspaper over to a rubbish box dumped it inside and went away, deep in thought. It was almost too good to be true. For once in his life he had given up a ten-dollar bill—gladly.

IT WAS ABOUT three weeks after that meeting in Golden Gate Park, when Henry Harrison Conroy, sheriff of Wild Horse Valley, and "Judge" Van Treece, the deputy, stood at a bar in Scorpion Bend and had one more drink, before starting the long trip to Tonto City. A queer pair of peace officers, these two. Henry was short and with an ample girth, a very red nose, and a moon-like countenance, while Judge was six feet, four inches in height, very thin, and with a long, lean face, long nose and huge, bushy eyebrows. It was the face of an undertaker or tragedian. Judge was past sixty.

Together with Oscar Johnson, a giant Swede, they made up what the Scorpion Bend *Clarion* was pleased to call "The Shame of Arizona." For most of his fifty-odd years Henry Harrison Conroy had been well known in legitimate shows and vaudeville. Featuring his red nose and a droll ability at juggling, he made millions laugh. But when vaudeville waned, Henry was nearly broke and entirely discouraged. It was then that an uncle he had never known died and left him the JHC Ranch in Wild Horse Valley.

With no knowledge of the West, Henry came to claim his inheritance. His rather extreme raiment, including spats and a gold-headed cane, amazed and amused Arizona. His courtly manners and droll humor appealed to them. He had only been there long enough to establish a residence, when a county election was held. One cowboy intimated that he was going to write Henry's name on the ballot for sheriff. The idea spread quickly, and Henry swept the country.

He realized that it had started as a joke. Well, if Wild Horse Valley liked a joke, he would go along with the idea, and appoint Judge Van Treece as his deputy. Drink had made Judge a dignified derelict, but had ruined a promising career as a criminal lawyer. His manner of getting drunk appealed to Henry, who also had a thirst. To add to the joke, Henry made Oscar Johnson, the giant Swede, the jailer.

Wild Horse Valley was no place for weakling officers. The discovery of huge gold deposits down there changed Tonto City from a sleepy cow-town to a wild mining camp, with all its attending vices. But in some way, Henry and his crew operated efficiently. No one knew why, but they did. It was very evident that they did not in any way resemble the popular conception of Arizona peace officers. Judge invariably wore a long, rusty Prince Albert coat, stringy black ties and a flattop, black sombrero. Except when riding he encased his feet in elastic-top shoes, the kind known as Congress gaiters.

On his infrequent trips to Scorpion Bend Henry usually wore a tailored suit, which fitted like the skin on a sausage, a derby hat—and those spats. Just now they stood at the bar, facing each other. It was nearly midnight.

"My wish for a very good health to you, sir," bowed Henry soberly.

"Thank you, sir," murmured Judge. "And to you, sir—a health."

They touched glasses again, bowed soberly and drank. The bartender turned away to hide a chuckle. That sort of thing might go on for hours. The men around the roulette wheel turned to smile.

A PAIR OF Mexicans came into the saloon. One of them halted near the doorway, while the other came slowly up to the bar, knocked his hat off in an attempted military salute, and said:

"*Señor*, eetees meedsnight; the boggy waits weethout."

"Without what, my good servant?" queried Henry soberly.

"I be damn eef you know," replied Lightning Mendoza. "That ees w'at you tell me to say, eef I am not meestaken—I hope."

"Perfectly correct, my good man," nodded Henry. "If you are ready, Judge, we will proceed home."

Judge hiccoughed slightly, adjusted his hat, and nodded.

"We will away, sir," he said solemnly. "Precede me, Henry."

Soberly and in single-file they left the saloon. Thunder Mendoza, the other Mexican, held back and fell in behind Lightning. A babel of conversation and laughter broke out after their exit. The four men went to the saloon hitch-rack, where a buckboard and team awaited them.

"I theenk I drive," suggested Lightning.

"Your thoughts, my good man, are far astray," replied Henry. "Those narrow grades around Lobo Canyon need a strong and steady man at the lines. I shall do the driving tonight."

"I was afraid of that, sir," sighed Judge. "Strong and steady! My, my!"

"I have never dropped you into that canyon yet, Judge," reminded Henry, as they settled into the buckboard seat, with the two Mexicans sitting in the back, their feet over the rear.

"Frijole Beel ees say that I am bes' driver you ever saw, I expect," suggested Lightning.

"Have done!" ordered Henry, and then swung the team around in the middle of the street, nearly upsetting the buckboard.

WITHIN A FEW yards that team was running at top speed, and they went out of town in a shower of gravel, with Judge hanging onto his hat with both hands. Henry let them run.

There was only the stars and a faint crescent moon to guide them, but Henry felt that the horses would keep on the road, and that the run would be all out of them, before they reached Lobo Canyon. The buckboard rocked and swayed dangerously, but they were outrunning the clouds of dust, churned up by the eight hoofs and the four wheels.

Henry took off his derby hat and put it between his feet. Judge said:

"Henry, are you showing off—or haven't you the lines in your possession?"

"I have the lines, sir, and I am in complete control."

"Then demonstrate, Henry! Thunder fell out, and is running behind, clinging to Lightning's feet."

Henry checked the team long enough for the exhausted Thunder to regain the buckboard.

"I'm bomps out," panted Thunder. "I'm grab something and those are my leetle brodder's foot."

"Damned reckless driving, if you care for my opinion," said Judge.

"I never have cared for it," replied Henry, "so I do not see why I should make any exception at this time. All set Thunder?"

"I theenk sometheeng ees on fires!" exclaimed Lightning.

"Possibly Thunder's feet?" suggested Judge gravely.

"No, no, up the road!" blurted Lightning. "Sometheeng burn, I theenk."

Judge and Henry turned in the seat. About a quarter of a mile up the road, and off to the left, flames were piling above the mesquite.

"That old prospector's shack up there against the mesa," exclaimed Judge. "It is on some of the old road, Henry!"

"Hang on!" shouted Henry, and away they went. Henry knew where the old road intersected with a more recent highway, and was swinging his galloping steeds to the left, the buckboard careening on two wheels, when he caught a flash of two riders, almost into them.

Guns blasted from the hands of the two riders, the team whirled wider, skidding the buckboard against a mesquite thicket, where it proceeded to upset. Henry landed in a sitting position in the sand, dazed from the impact with the earth. The team went on for fifty yards, where they tied up in more mesquite, and proceeded to kick everything in reach.

Henry staggered out to the road and looked around. The dim figure of Judge came limping down the road, his voice reeking with complaint as he stated painfully.

"You *will* fasten those lines together, Henry! How many times have I told you to not buckle them?"

"This," gasped Henry, "is no time for arithmetic, Judge. Are you all right?"

"Being dragged with one foot caught in the loop of a pair of damned lines is not my idea of a healthful exercise, sir. What happened? Did I or did I not see and hear shots fired at us?"

"You certainly did, Judge. Hah! Smell that smoke! Kerosene! Where are Thunder and Lightning?"

"Yoo-hoo!" called a voice weakly. "How am I, you hope and trus'?"

"Are you all right, Lightning?" asked Henry anxiously.

"Sure—all right. But I'm can' gets down. One foots ees high as your head and you can' get heem loose."

"Hung up in the mesquite," groaned Judge. "Where is Thunder?"

"I am seeting on heem," said Lightning blandly.

"Is he hurt?"

"I'm don' theenk so; he don' keek about notheeng."

They tore their way through and managed to rescue the two Mexicans. Thunder was unable to talk for awhile, but he soon recovered. They untangled the team and examined the buckboard, which was little the worse for wear. With everything on an even keel again, they tied the team and limped up to the burning shack, which was more than half consumed. It was an old, tinder-dry, one-room dwelling, which had not been occupied for years, as far as they knew. There was still a decided odor of kerosene in the smoke, indicating that the shack had been deliberately fired.

Henry and Judge were puzzled. Why would two men fire the old shack, and then shoot at them? Was there something in the shack that they wished to destroy? And did they fire the shots to distract the occupants of the buckboard from any chance of recognition? It was rather puzzling.

Henry walked around the fire, looking at it from every angle, but was unable, on account of the heat, to get very close.

"You have no idea of the identity of the two riders, Judge?" asked Henry.

"Have you?" countered Judge.

"Have you, my leetle brodder?" asked Lightning, anxious to say something.

"Have I wheech?" queried Thunder.

"Me, too," said Lightning. "I never see anybody."

"We were facing the light," said Henry. "Judge, I believe they recognized us."

"Undoubtedly," said Judge dryly, but added, "Unless they are the sort of persons who go around, taking pot-shots at total strangers. Gad, my rheumatism is killing me! This job is almost a guarantee against old age. I can hardly bend my left knee."

"No wonder!" exclaimed Henry. "You have a mesquite snag run up your left pant-leg."

Judge sat down, while Lightning pulled the snag out. It

made the left leg of Judge decidedly more supple, but did not help his disposition, because the pant-leg was ruined. They limped back to the buckboard. Judge groaned, as he climbed into the seat.

"More rheumatism?" asked Henry.

"No," replied Judge, "I was merely visualizing our ride around Lobo grades, with you at the lines."

"Cowardice ill becomes a deputy sheriff, sir," said Henry soberly.

"At our ages, Henry, we should use our accumulated wisdom."

"Senility has not reached me as yet, Judge," replied Henry. "And as for my driving ability—I am still alive."

"Due to the grace of God, and the fact that you landed on the seat of your pants in the sand—yes—but no thanks to your ability as a driver. I ask you in all sincerity—drive carefully for the rest of the way."

"Well," sighed Henry, "I suppose I *have* had my fling. Be of good cheer, my friend, as we plod our weary way homeward. Are you ready, boys?"

"Let heem go," said Lightning. "I'm mak' bet weeth Thonder. The firs' one fall off lose *uno peso.*"

"No shove," warned Thunder.

"Good men with stout hearts," laughed Henry as he swung the team around, narrowly missing another upset, and they headed for Tonto City again.

But as they turned to the left on the main road, they saw, in the dim light, a man staggering toward them. Henry drew up quickly, as the man almost bumped into their team. Henry handed the lines to Judge and got out. The man stopped and by the light of a match Henry discovered that he was Johnny Riley, manager of the livery stable in Scorpion Bend. He was hatless, his face streaked with half-dried blood, due to a cut on the left side of his head.

"What in the world happened to you, Johnny?" asked Henry.

"I dunno," replied Johnny dazedly. "Where's my horse and buggy?"

"We haven't seen any horse and buggy," replied Henry. "You recognize me, do you not, Johnny?"

"Why, shore—yo're the sheriff. I know you. But I'll be danged if I know what became of my horse and buggy."

"Where were you going, Johnny?"

"Going? Oh, yeah. Gee, I must have forgot. Why—why, I was takin' a man to Tonto City. That's right. Two men stopped us. That's funny—where's the man?"

"Who was this man, Johnny?" asked Henry quietly.

"I don't know. He—he said somethin' about ownin' a mine. Yeah, that was it."

"Did he," asked Judge, "say his name was Frank Travis?"

"No, he didn't tell me his name."

"Frank Travis?" queried Henry. "Judge that is the new owner of the Shoshone Chief. What made you think—"

"It was in the *Clarion*," interrupted Judge. "I read it today. Just a short article, saying that Frank Travis would arrive tonight. I paid little attention, because—"

"Get in, Johnny," said Henry. "There is room between Judge and myself. You need a doctor. I guess we may as well stay all night in Scorpion Bend, as it will soon be morning, anyway. Are you feeling better, Johnny?"

"No," replied Johnny earnestly, "I don't. I wish I knew where that horse and buggy went."

"Did you," asked Judge, "get a good look at this man, Johnny?"

"Nope. It wasn't very light in the stable. He said he just came in on the train. Had a valise, I know that much. The boss will sure give me hell, if anythin' happens to that horse and buggy."

"Do not fret about the horse and buggy," advised Henry.

"Well, my Lord!" exclaimed Johnny. "What became of the man I had?"

"That," replied Henry, "is of more importance than a horse and buggy."

JAMES WADSWORTH LONGFELLOW Pelly, editor and owner of the Scorpion Bend *Clarion,* was not an impressive figure, as he sat at his littered desk, tapping his teeth with a pencil, as he tried to figure out an editorial for his next issue. He was scrawny, near-sighted, and usually ink-stained, and very proud of his ability to spread vitriol via his editorials. There was no love lost between himself and the sheriff's office of Tonto City, and J.W.L. Pelly never overlooked an opportunity to comment caustically on the operations of that office.

There had been no visible crime in Wild Horse Valley for months, and Mr. Pelly was hard-put for anything to write about. Deep in thought, he heard the outer door close softly, but did not look up. He knew that someone was standing at the little counter. Pelly wrote a few words at random on a piece of old paper. Finally he looked around.

Henry Harrison Conroy was behind the counter, idly surveying the establishment and paying no attention to the editor. Pelly's lips drew into a thin line. He had never been able to exchange quips with Henry.

Finally Henry said quietly, "Nice place you have here, Mr. Pelly. It would be interesting to see what one might find below the surface. A good cleaning might disclose—"

"Was there something you *wanted*, Mr. Conroy?" asked Pelly.

"Ah, yes," sighed Henry. "In this so-called newspaper you publish there was an item to the effect that one Frank Travis, new owner of the Shoshone Chief mine, was due to arrive here yesterday evening."

"Yes, I printed that item."

"Thank you, sir; you are very frank. Would it be presuming to ask where you received such information?"

"It would," nodded Pelly.

"I see. That, of course, is merely your reply to a citizen. As sheriff of Wild Horse Valley, I demand a full and complete explanation as to where you received such information."

"Oh!" said Pelly. "Well," he sighed deeply, searched his desk-top and came up with a letter, which he gingerly handed to Henry.

IT BORE AN ornate heading, Frank Travis Properties, San Francisco, California. Apparently written as publicity, it stated that Frank Travis, owner of the Shoshone Chief mine, would arrive at Scorpion Bend on this date, on his way to Tonto City, where he expected to plan improvements in machinery for a complete exploitation of the newly acquired mine. It was not signed.

Henry nodded and gave the note back to Pelly, who was curious to know what Henry wanted with such unimportant information.

"Did Mr. Travis arrive?" asked Pelly.

"I have no information, sir," replied Henry. "A man

arrived. He started for Tonto City in a livery vehicle, driven by Johnny Riley. Past midnight last night I found Johnny Riley wandering on the road, suffering from a beating at the hands of someone. His companion disappeared. Johnny remembers very little. Men are now searching for the horse and buggy and the missing man."

Pelly drew a deep breath. "Frank Travis is a millionaire," he said.

"That fact," said Henry soberly, "will probably protect him from all harm. Well, good day, sir."

"Wait a minute!" blurred Pelly. "What is your office doing about it?"

"Nothing for publication," replied Henry. "Please leave my name out of it, Mr. Pelly; I am a very modest man, and I do not care to have my name in the paper. In addition to that, sir, I may say that it is none of your infernal business. Good day, sir."

Henry joined Judge and the two Mexicans on the main street, and they rode out to the burned shack, which was now only a heap of ashes. Two men rode in and reported that the horse and buggy had been found, but no trace of the missing man. Henry nodded soberly and stared at the ashes.

"Yuh don't think he'd be—in that, do yuh?" asked one of the men.

"I'm wondering, boys," replied Henry. "Take your ropes, tie them to each end of that old fence rail, and one of you ride on each side of that pile of ashes. I believe the pole is heavy enough to scatter the ashes."

The two cowboys quickly obeyed the suggestion, and after a couple of attempts dragged out the charred remains of what had once been a man. At least, it had once been a human being, but now burned beyond any possibility of identification.

A wagon was secured, and the body taken back to Scorpion Bend, where it was turned over to a doctor. There was no doubt in Henry's mind that the remains was that of the man Johnny Riley had started with to Tonto City. James Wadsworth Longfellow Pelly rubbed his hands in anticipation of a mystery, which the sheriff could not handle, and which would give him plenty of opportunity to again flay the Shame of Arizona.

"What a story!" he gloated. "A millionaire murdered and burned. Or don't you believe this is the body of Frank Travis, Mr. Sheriff?"

"Millionaires burn practically as readily as a poor man, I believe," replied Henry. "If you can identify that incinerated remains as the body of Mr. Travis, you have a story. However, you have a flair for being a bit premature, Mr. Pelly—and if I may say so, sir, a decided leaning toward journalistic inaccuracies; so what you may write about this will not in any way surprise your few readers."

"Some day," said Pelly icily, "I shall drive you out of office."

"I hope it will be a nice day," said Henry blandly. "I should hate to attend your funeral in the rain, Mr. Pelly."

"I can use just such a statement," said Pelly.

"Verbatim, I hope," smiled Henry. "It will please nearly everyone in Wild Horse Valley. Good day, Mr. Pelly."

2

NUMBER 79 WAS an hour late into Scorpion Bend that night. Doc Darnell and his protege from Golden Gate Park were on that train. This man, to be known as Frank Travis, was well-dressed, and his baggage was of the very latest.

"Just one more leg to this journey," said Doc Darnell, as they walked down the main street to the stage depot. "This stage trip from here to Tonto City is nothing to brag about."

"I can stand it," replied Travis. "Do any of these people know you?"

"Some," admitted Doc. "Down here they know me as a mining engineer, as I told you. They accept you at face value in Arizona, my boy. Don't worry about a thing. You are bringing me here to expert the Shoshone Chief."

"More truth than poetry in that," said Travis dryly. "Expert is right!"

They came to the lighted stage depot and turned off the street. There was a woman standing at the counter, and she turned toward them, as Travis came in ahead of Doc. Her bags were on the floor beside her. Travis halted and looked sharply at her. She was modestly dressed in a gray traveling suit, with a perky little hat on her head, and Travis thought she was quite the prettiest girl he had ever seen.

But she was staring past him at the doorway, as though transfixed. He looked back, but there was no sign of Doc Darnell.

Then the girl blinked and looked away for a moment, but again looked toward the doorway. Her gloved hands were clenched at her sides.

"I beg your pardon," said Travis quietly, "but can you tell me when the stage leaves for Tonto City?"

"I—" The girl looked at Travis for the first time. "Oh! I beg your pardon, I—I didn't realize—"

"The stage," stated a masculine voice from a rear room, "left an hour ago. Yore train was too late for him to wait."

"Time and the Tonto stage waits for no man," smiled Travis, as he placed his two bags on the floor.

"Who was that man with you?" asked the girl.

"With me?" queried Travis. "Oh, you mean the man who was behind me? Why, I believe his name is—er—Jones. That's it—Cyrus Jones."

"Cyrus Jones?"

"Yes. You were saying that you wanted to go to Tonto City?"

"More than anything," she replied earnestly. "That train was an hour late, and it is absolutely necessary for me to be in Tonto City tomorrow morning. It means so very much, don't you see?"

"No," replied Travis, "I don't see, because I haven't the slightest idea why you have to be there. However, I want to be there, too. Now, it might be possible to secure a vehicle in which to make the trip."

The clerk at the depot had been listening, and now he

said, "Yuh can hire a rig at the livery stable. It's across the street."

"Thank you very much," said Travis.

"I would pay my part of the expenses," said the girl.

"Naturally," said Travis dryly. "Shall we try it?"

Johnny Riley was willing to rent them the livery rig. Johnny, whose head was swathed in bandages, said, "I started to take a man to Tonto City last night, and danged near got killed. I reckon they killed the man I was with."

"Don't they want folks to go to Tonto City?" asked Travis anxiously.

"I dunno," replied Johnny. "I'll have that horse hitched in a jiffy."

The girl and Travis stood in the livery stable doorway and waited. There was no sign of Doc Darnell, and Travis wondered what had become of him. Finally the girl said, "My name is Nola Terry."

"Thank you," said Travis. "My name is Frank Travis. I'm from San Francisco, California, and I am very glad to meet you, Miss Terry."

Johnny drove the horse and buggy out to the doorway, and Travis said, "Aren't you going to drive the horse for us?"

"Can't do it, Mister," replied Johnny. "I've got the place alone tonight. That's a right gentle horse, and you won't have any trouble."

"I can drive," said Nola.

"You can? By jove, that's fine. I never have. That will pay your part of the expenses."

He handed Johnny a piece of currency and told him to keep the change.

"But, Mister," said Johnny, "you gave me—"

"I know," interrupted Travis. "That's all right, my boy."

"Gee, that's swell. Mind givin' me yore name, Mister? I've got to have it for the book, yuh see."

"My name is Frank Travis."

"Frank—hu-u-uh?"

"Travis, T-r-a-v-i-s."

"Holy Henhawks! Why—why, they said that was the name of the man who got killed last night!"

"Who said that?" asked Travis quickly.

"Well, you was supposed to come in on the train—and they thought—"

"They did, eh? Then what happened?"

"Well, the man came here to the stable and I was takin' him to Tonto City, but two men stuck us up and hit me over the head. This mornin' the sheriff dug the burned body of a man out of a shack. Somebody set fire to the shack last night. And they thought it was the body of Frank Travis."

Travis was silent for several moments. Then he said, "Could you describe that man to me, son?"

"I didn't get a good look at him, but I think his hair was kinda gray on the sides, and he had sort of a long nose."

"I see-e-e," said Travis quietly. "Thank you very much."

HE CLIMBED IN beside Nola, and they drove out of Scorpion Bend.

For a mile or more Travis was too preoccupied to talk, but finally he said: "The moonlight is beautiful, Miss Terry. In fact, I have never seen it so blue as it is out here. Do you live out here?"

"I have never been here before in my life," she replied. "I am from Chicago. I taught grade school in a little town outside Phoenix, where the salary was very small, but I stayed to the end of the term. I had applications in every-where, and when I was about ready to give up, I got a letter from Tonto City. But in order to get the position, I must be there in the morning. So you can see that my need was urgent, Mr. Travis."

"Yes, I can see how urgent it must be," he agreed.

"I shall never forget your kindness in helping me to be there," she said.

"That is nothing."

"It means a living for me, Mr. Travis. Is this your first trip down here?"

"Yes." Travis laughed shortly. "I expected to see hard-faced women and Indian squaws—and I saw you."

Nola laughed. "But all women in Arizona are not hard-faced, Mr. Travis. I have seen many beautiful women in Arizona."

"And I," said Travis, "have only seen one. By the way, you asked about the man who was behind me at the stage depot. Do you know him?"

"For a moment I thought I did. But he moved away so quickly. I knew a man once who looked like him; a man without an ounce of manhood, and with the predatory instincts of a coyote."

Nola clucked to the horse, and they went up the long winding road to the top of the mesa. Nothing was said until they reached the top, where she drew up the horse for a breathing spell.

"You are a fine driver," he said. "Where did you learn?"

"I was raised on a farm. I drove a team when I was ten."

"That was wonderful. We were speaking about the man you disliked. What was that man's name?"

"James Wilton. He married my mother. My father had sold a big farm, and we moved to Chicago, where he made some fine investments. When he passed away, he left everything to mother. We were well off. But James Wilton came along. He was very rich, he said. He married my mother, and through trickery beat her out of every cent, and then disappeared. That was twelve years ago. Mother died. She couldn't stand poverty. I was twelve years old. Since that time I have made my own way in the world, Mr. Travis—and it hasn't been easy."

"That was tough," said Travis quietly. "His name was James Wilton, and he looked like the man who was behind me. Could he have recognized you, Miss Terry? I mean, if he was James Wilton."

"Possibly. But I suppose it was a trick of the light, or my imagination."

"Possibly."

"You said his name was Cyrus Jones, Mr. Travis."

"After all," replied Travis, "names mean little."

"No, that is true. Well, we better go on if we expect to be there by morning. Wasn't it queer that they should report your death in Scorpion Bend this morning?"

Frank Travis was silent for several moments, and then he said, "Do you mind if I smoke, Miss Terry? I think better at that time."

"I do not mind it in the least."

"Thank you. Yes, it is queer—me being dead. I can't quite understand it."

"Could there be two Frank Travises?" she asked innocently.

"Two? Why, I—yes, I suppose it is possible. Rather

a coincidence that two men of the same name should come to Scorpion Bend within twenty-four hours of each other—both heading for Tonto City. They mistook someone else for me because the newspaper said I would be in last night."

"And killed the wrong man?" asked Nola fearfully.

"I never thought of that," said Frank Travis. "I wonder."

3

IN ORDER TO catch up on their sleep, Henry and Judge slept at the JHC ranch.

Not long after daybreak they were awakened by an unearthly squawk, and sat up in bed to behold Bill Shakespeare, the rooster, sitting on the foot of their bed. Bill was tall and scrawny, and almost entirely out of feathers. As Henry and Judge sat up in bed, Bill gave another convulsive squawk and fell backward, hitting the bare floor with a dull thud.

"Bill," said Henry quietly, "seems indisposed."

Bill apparently got up, because he stalked out in the middle of the room and fell down again. Then he got up and proceeded to walk squarely into the wall near the doorway and fell down again.

"That, sir," said Judge, "should be an object lesson. Bill Shakespeare has been eating Frijole Bill's prune whiskey mash again. An innocent rooster is the victim of acute alcoholism. What a pity!"

"What abject bliss!" exclaimed Henry. "Not a care in the world. Probably dreaming, that he is an eagle—or perhaps an ostrich."

"Rooster dreaming!" snorted Judge. "Bah!"

Henry chuckled. "One more tilt with a wildcat, and Shakespeare will be entirely nude."

"Do you believe Frijole's lies about Bill Shakespeare and the wildcat?" asked Judge.

"Absolutely."

"You are a bigger fool than I thought. Frijole is the biggest liar unhung."

Frijole appeared in the doorway, half-dressed. Frijole Bill Cullison was past sixty, little and scrawny, with a mustache entirely too large for his small face. Soaking wet, and with all his clothes on, he might weigh a hundred pounds. Frijole Bill was the cook at the JHC, but spent most of his time distilling prunes, to which he added anything handy, even to horse-liniment.

"And how is the latest batch of whiskey?" asked Henry.

"That bunch," declared Frijole, "is the *e pluribus perotinitis* of all I've ever made. It atchellay snapped at me when I bottled it. It's as soft as a baby's caress and as devilish as an Apache full of gin. Henry, you've never tasted anythin' like it."

Slim Pickins came and peered over Frijole's shoulder. Slim was six feet four inches tall, with a long, lean face, an acrobatic Adam's-apple, and a prodigious thirst. Slim had just ridden in from Tonto City.

"H'lo," he said wearily.

"This," said Judge severely, "is a fine time to be getting home."

"Better stay f'r breakfast," suggested Slim blandly. Judge snorted, and started to rebuke Slim more plainly, but Slim interrupted.

"I thought somebody said that Frank Travis was killed. He ain't. Hell, he came to town last night in a horse and buggy."

"In the buggy, I presume—not in the horse, Slim," said Henry. "You say—wait a minute! Did you say it was Frank Travis?"

"Tha's right. And he brought the mos' beautiful lady I ever seen with him. 'S a fact. She's the new school teacher, I unnerstand."

Henry and Judge looked at each other for several moments.

"Identification all shot to smithereens," said Judge.

"Well, I'll start breakfast," sighed Frijole. "If yuh want a snifter of that last batch, Henry—go easy until yore pipes get heated."

"Thank you—not before breakfast, Frijole," said Henry.

"I stepped in some of that mash," declared Slim, "and she done et the heel off m' boot. What kinda whiskey will that make?"

"Blended stuff," replied Frijole soberly.

"Blended with what?" asked Judge.

"Potato alcohol and turpenteen," replied Frijole, "and with jest a slight tech of red paint to give color. She's shore smooth, gents."

"I'll take a jug back with us," said Henry. "It should be well aged by two o'clock this afternoon."

"She'll be a patriarch by noon," declared Frijole, and hurried to the kitchen.

Life was like that on the JHC; no one took it seriously. Slim Pickins, with the assistance of Thunder and Lightning Mendoza, handled the cattle, kept the water-holes open, and repaired the fences. Henry was not critical. Judge Van Treece's lectures on efficiency fell on deaf ears. He advocated the discharge of the two Mexicans, but Henry vetoed such an idea. Henry loved to laugh, and what was funnier than those two mishandling the King's English?

What if Frijole Bill neglected his work to manufacture prune whiskey, while Slim Pickins slept in the shade, while there was branding to be done? It was all right with Henry. Somehow the cooking would be done, the cattle branded.

THEY ATE BREAKFAST, and Slim took them back to Tonto City. Henry always sighed as he looked over Tonto City. When he had come there it was a sleepy cow town, with no worries for anyone. But gold had changed all that. Ore wagons, drawn by six span of mules, churned up the dust of the street, the hitch-racks were crowded, the sidewalks crowded with people. Music blared from the King's Castle, the biggest saloon and gambling place in the country, now owned by Bart Silvaine, a huge, gross-faced, overdressed gambler. Henry did not like Bart Silvaine, because the gambler was too suave, too overbearingly affable at times.

They arrived at the office and sent Slim back to the ranch, after taking a gallon jug of Frijole's latest concoction into the rear of the office, where Judge covered it with a tarpaulin. He came back to find Henry talking with a stranger.

"Judge," said Henry, "I want you to meet Frank Travis, new owner of the Shoshone Chief mine."

They shook hands, and Travis said, "I believe my demise was rumored in Scorpion Bend yesterday."

"Slightly premature, I imagine," said Henry gravely. "I am glad to know it was an error, and what may we do for you, Mr. Travis?"

"It is rather personal," said Travis soberly. "I came here

last night with a Miss Terry, who is seeking the position as school teacher in your school. A very lovely young lady and of great talent, I presume. The cold, hard fact of the situation is that she needs the job. It now develops that the situation is sought by a number of applicants, who have been asked to apply this morning, regardless of how far they may have been obliged to travel; so that the trustees may make their selection."

"Is there anything wrong with the method involved?" asked Judge.

"Only," said Travis, "that Miss Terry was led to suppose that she would get the position if she arrived in time. She didn't know it was a contest."

"I see," nodded Henry solemnly. "And what am I supposed to do, Mr. Travis? I can not very well arrest the other contestants, nor threaten the trustees."

"You have influence," said Travis. "Or I don't know just what to say—but she needs the position very badly."

"You—uh—haven't heard any comments on the lady by a trustee, have you?"

"One man," replied Travis, "whom I am told is a trustee, remarked that she was, in his words, too damn purty to teach school."

Henry smiled. "I shall see what I can do, Mr. Travis. After all, Tonto City has no laws against beauty. God knows, it is drab and sordid enough."

"If she gets the position, I will make it worth your while, Sheriff."

Henry looked at him searchingly. "You will do what?"

"I'm sorry," said Travis quickly.

"Young man," said Henry quietly, "this *is Arizona*—and even with your millions you can't buy things like that."

"Thank you—I had that coming. I'll appreciate what you may do."

"That is all we want—appreciation—it is mighty scarce."

Frank Travis left the office. Judge rubbed his long nose and looked at Henry.

"You read that in a book, Henry," he said.

Henry chuckled. "I had that line in a play years ago, Judge. "If I do say it myself, I delivered it well after all these years. You can alter it to fit any state. The Conroys, sir, have never lost their honor."

"It must have been tied on," said Judge.

"Tightly, sir—tightly. Well, I suppose I must add my influence to the pleas of a beautiful young lady. Where is my—ah, there it is!"

"Overalls, boots—and a cane," said Judge. "But why the cane? You are not crippled—physically."

"I ignore the slur on my mentality, Judge—and I may need something a bit more potent than my influence."

AFTER HENRY HAD gone, Oscar Johnson came in. The office seemed very small, after Oscar came in.

"Hello, Yudge," he said. "You know law pretty good, eh?"

"I have a very comprehensive knowledge of law, Oscar."

"Va'al, Yudge, is de penalty yust de same if you kill a vite man or a Svede?"

Judge looked narrowly at Oscar, but the big Swede was in earnest.

"The only difference," replied Judge, "is that for killing a white man they will hang you on Friday. For killing a Swede, they hang you on Thursday."

"A day ahead or a veek later, Yudge?" queried Oscar.

"With my permission," replied Judge, "you may go to hell!"

"Are you yoking, Yudge?"

"I am not. You have my permission and blessings. I hope you are not thinking of killing anyone."

"Yust von," said Oscar. "Chris Sonderson."

"Oh, the new cook at the Tonto Hotel."

"Ya-ah! Das fuud wrastler. He vants Yosephine."

Josephine Swensen, maid of all work at the Tonto Hotel, was Oscar's light-o'-love. Josephine was six feet tall, as angular as a rail fence, hard of jaw and harder of fist. Josephine's I.Q. was equal to Oscar's, but, if anything, she had a more potent right-hand punch.

"After the trials and tribulations you have suffered at the hands of Josephine," said Judge, "you should thank and congratulate Chris."

"Ay don't like the cut of his yib," declared Oscar. "Yudge, Ay heard somet'ink about a man being borned to death in Scorpion Bend."

"You did, eh? And what did you hear, if I may ask?"

"Ay heard he vars dead."

Judge snatched his old hat off the desk and yanked it on his head.

"It is such as you that drive sane men to drink," he declared. "Stay right here and debate your own problems—I must have alcohol. If Henry Harrison Conroy insists on having a bunch of imbeciles—" Judge's voice faded in the distance, as he hurried toward the King's Castle.

Judge found Bart Silvaine at the bar, talking with a man he had never seen before.

"Judge, I want you to meet my old friend, Doc Darnell," said Silvaine. "Doc is a mining expert, coming here to plan an expansion of the Shoshone Chief mine."

"I am certainly honored, sir," boomed Doc. "Superior or Supreme?"

"Retired, sir," replied Judge, not to be outdone, as he sized up Doc Darnell. "Just now I am assisting the law enforcement of this county. It has been nice meeting you, Mr. Darnell."

"Thank you, Judge," said Doc soberly. "But in a lovely community like this, you surely do not mean that there is anything for the law to do."

Judge drew himself up to full height and looked keenly at Darnell from under beetling brows.

"Either you are a damn fool, sir, or you mistake me for one," he said coldly and walked on.

Doc Darnell looked after him, a quizzical expression in his eyes. Finally he turned to Bart Silvaine and said: "Just a little crazy, eh?"

"Right now," replied Bart Silvaine quietly, "is the proper time to get that idea out of your mind, Doc. Wait until you see the sheriff. They look like the damnedest pair of goofs on earth—but go easy. They've cleaned up some tough cases in this country, and they've got their signatures on Boot Hill."

Doc Darnell laughed quietly. "Bart, you are still barking at shadows. Inside of one week I could sell either of them the Mississippi River."

"That's true," agreed the gambler, "but after you've made

a getaway, you'll find that the check they gave you is no good."

"Hm-m-m-m. That smart, eh?"

They walked to the doorway, and saw Henry and Judge meet across the street. Henry was still swinging that gold-headed cane. Judge looked him over critically. Henry seemed in good spirits.

"Well, sir," he said, "the young lady secured the position."

"She did, eh?" queried Judge. "Coercion, I suppose."

"Not at all, Judge. It was ridiculously simple. I am very pleased over everything."

"Just what," asked Judge, "did you threaten to do to the trustees?"

"I never even spoke to them, sir. In fact, I spoke to no one."

"Then how in the devil did you get her the job?"

"I didn't, sir; she already had it. Suppose we drop back to the office, lift the tarpaulin and find out just what Frijole has done for the past week to earn his salary."

"You spoke my mind, Henry. I went over to the King's Castle to get a drink, but a man at the bar irritated me so badly that I came away. Did you ever know a man named Doc Darnell—a friend of Bart Silvaine?"

"The name is not familiar, Judge. But if he is a friend of Bart Silvaine, I'm sure our paths have never crossed."

They entered the empty office and went to the rear, where Henry produced two tin cups, which Judge filled from the jug.

"This man," said Judge, "is a mining expert, brought here to plan some work on the Shoshone Chief. He is said to be a mining expert, but Henry"—Judge lowered his voice—"if he isn't a crook, may I never claim to know anything about human character."

"Snap judgment, perhaps," suggested Henry.

"Intuition," corrected Judge. "He has a honeyed voice, a diamond stickpin, and a pair of hands that never felt the rasp of a pick-handle. Well, here is confusion to crime, my friend."

Henry and Judge drank half the cupful, stopped and stared at each other, both unable to breathe or speak for the moment.

Judge Adam's-apple jerked convulsively and he closed his eyes. Then they both finished the drink. Henry leaned against the bars of a cell and heaved a deep sigh, his eyes closed.

"Steel shavings, ground glass and nitric," whispered Judge.

"The first swallow," wheezed Henry, "was terrific. After that I heard two distinct splashes, as my tonsils fell."

"And Bill Shakespeare ate the mash!" marveled Judge. "Well, I'd hate to think that a rooster had a better constitution than I. Shall we fill them up again, Henry."

"Pray do," replied Henry soberly. "It will be a noble experiment."

DOC DARNELL PACED up and down the living-room of Jim Wade's cottage at the Shoshone Chief mine, while Jim Wade, a big, hard-faced man, sat in an old rocker, his feet on a table, as he smoked his pipe.

"Set down, Doc," he said irritably. "Stop wearin' out the floor."

Doc came back to the table and started to say something, but stopped when he heard the sound of wheels on the rocky ground outside. Someone knocked on the door, and Wade told them gruffly to come in. It was Frank Travis.

"You sure took your time," growled Doc Darnell.

Travis flung his hat on the table and sat down.

"What the hell happened to you in Scorpion Bend?" he asked. "You sure disappeared quick."

"Never mind that part of it," replied Doc. "Meet Jim Wade, manager of *your* mine."

Neither of them offered to shake hands.

"What was your idea in chasing around with that girl, Frank?"

"She's a good driver, Doc," grinned Travis. "We both wanted to get to Tonto City; so I hired the horse and buggy, and she did the driving."

"I told you to keep away from folks as much as possible. Damn it, can't you understand that we are playing a damn dangerous game. One mistake, and we're stuck. When you're playing the part of a millionaire—act like one."

Travis lighted a cigarette and flung the match into the fireplace.

"I've been thinking this thing over, Doc," he said. "There's a lot of bad angles in the deal. Suppose Frank Travis shows up. Suppose someone from his organization comes. Oh, I know the deal. I've practiced signing Frank Travis' signature until I can do it in the dark. I sell you the mine for a big price. You are backed by eastern capital. You pay me twenty-five thousand—and I drift. But what happens to you when Frank Travis shows up?"

"You won't be here," replied Doc, "so why worry? We'll handle it ourselves."

Travis turned to Wade. "I suppose you'll tell him you were fooled by my likeness to him, eh?"

Wade laughed shortly. "He's never been here. I was hired by his father."

"Well, that's settled," said Doc. "When the transfer is made, I fire Wade. He takes his cut and pulls out. Later, after we're sure that everything is safe, Wade can come back. I'm the nominal owner of the mine, and I've got brains enough to outsmart anything that comes up."

"When do we pull this job?" asked Travis.

"After pay day," said Doc. "We'll let Travis' outfit square up everything, and we start a clean slate."

"And I get twenty-five thousand, eh?" mused Travis. "The mine is worth half a million. Pretty small percentage to the leading role, Doc."

Doc and Wade exchanged quick glances.

"Twenty-five thousand is more than you could make in a lifetime," said Doc.

"I admit it," said Travis, "but that doesn't change the fact that I'm the key in this situation. Without me—you may as well go back home."

"How much do yuh want?" asked Wade bluntly.

"Enough to make it worth my while," replied Travis quietly. "Settle it between you—and let me know the figure."

"All right, all right," said Doc hastily. "You won't lose. Move up here from the hotel tomorrow, where we know you'll be safe—and handy. We can't take any chances on you making a fool remark to somebody that might queer the whole deal. And keep away from that girl."

"What's that girl to you?" asked Travis curiously. "Suppose she does recognize you?"

Doc Darnell stared at the floor for several moments. Finally he said, "I recognized that girl—after twelve years. I haven't changed much, and she'd recognize me very easily."

"Why not get rid of—" began Wade, but Doc silenced him.

"What did you mean by that, Wade?" asked Travis.

Wade spat toward the fireplace, but did not answer.

"I can stay away from her," said Doc. "She doesn't know I'm here. In fact, I'm not sure she got a good look at me in Scorpion Bend. And you keep away from her, too, Frank. We're playing for the biggest stake of our lives, and I'm not letting anything interfere with things. At my age, I can't afford to make a failure out of this deal—and I won't."

Travis got up and walked the length of the room, finally stopping in front of Doc Darnell.

"Speaking about that girl," he said quietly. "Nothing is to happen to her. The day this deal is to be settled she is to be working in Tonto City and perfectly safe—or it won't be settled, Doc. And if she is molested after the deal is settled—"

"She won't be," said Doc quickly. "I'm not fighting women. You have my word."

"After what I know about you, Doc," said Travis evenly, "I should go a lot on your word. Don't get red in the face. We're all crooks; so we may as well speak our minds."

"The kid's right," said Jim Wade. "We're in this together. If he wants to protect that girl—I don't blame him."

"She'll be protected," promised Doc quickly. "No use getting riled over her."

"And I'm not moving out here," added Travis. "I'll come up every day, but I'll live at the hotel—if that's what they call it. And if I want to see that girl—that's my business, Doc."

"All right, all right! Go ahead. Far be it from me to guide you."

"The kid has his rights," said Jim Wade. "I'd do the same."

"That's right—we all would," said Doc.

4

THE INQUEST AT Scorpion Bend, for lack of witnesses, was merely a formality. The local doctor testified that the man's skull had been smashed by a blunt instrument before being nearly incinerated, so the jury brought in a verdict of murder, committed by a party or parties unknown. As there was no means of identification, the body was buried by the county.

James Wadsworth Longfellow Pelly's story of the inquest was filled with barbed criticisms of Henry Harrison Conroy and his staff. It said, in part:

"Had the sheriff and deputy been even partly sober when they met the killers at the forks of the road, as they testified, they might have identified the men. But this is only a phase of the unpopular regime of the Shame of Arizona."

Judge exploded in righteous wrath.

"We were not drunk!" he declared huskily. "You know we were not, Henry."

"I do not suppose we had to exceed twelve drinks apiece, Judge," replied Henry solemnly. "The man exaggerates."

"Ay got drunk vonce," said Oscar Johnson soberly.

"You did, Oscar?" queried Henry. "What happened?"

"That was two years ago," said Judge, "and he never sobered up."

"My goodness!" exclaimed Henry. Nola Terry was standing in the doorway of the office.

"I presume you are Mr. Conroy," she was saying.

Henry disengaged his feet from the desk and managed to get to his feet.

"Yes, indeed," he replied. "You are Miss Terry, I believe."

"Yes. I wanted to thank you for helping me get the position as teacher in the Tonto school."

"My dear," smiled Henry, "I did nothing."

"You are modest. Mr. Travis told me."

"My regards to Mr. Travis. Won't you sit down, Miss Terry?"

"Thank you, I will, because I wish to speak to you on a little matter. I haven't the slightest idea what it is all about, and I—I would like a little advice."

Nola took a letter from her purse, extracted the one sheet of paper and seven twenty-dollar bills, which she placed on the desk.

Henry picked up the letter and read it aloud:

Dear Miss Terry: If you are wise you will leave Tonto City at once. You are in great danger, which I can't explain. I am enclosing a hundred and forty dollars for your expenses. Say nothing to anybody, but go quickly.

A Friend.

"My goodness!" exclaimed Henry. "A friend! And hard cash, too. Miss Terry, this is rather remarkable."

"I thought so," she replied quietly.

"A joke, perhaps," suggested Judge.

"At a hundred and forty dollars, Judge?" asked Henry.

"That is good old coin of the realm. Hm-m-m-m-m. A friend. Miss Terry, have you made any friends since arriving here?"

"I haven't been here long enough to know anyone," she replied. "That is the queer part of it."

"Are you afraid?" asked Henry.

"I—I really do not feel any too secure, Mr. Conroy."

"No, of course not. Well, well! Someone does not want you here; someone who is willing to pay you money to get out. Just who could that be?"

"I wish I knew. I am boarding and rooming at the Gibson home, but I have been there such a short time that I haven't really become acquainted with the Gibson family. This letter is a mystery, Mr. Conroy."

"Ah, yes, indeed—a mystery," agreed Henry. "But that is what we are here for, my dear; to unravel mysteries. I'm sure we will get at the bottom of it in a short time."

"Do you wish to keep the letter, Mr. Conroy?" she asked.

"Ah, yes. You keep the money. Spend it, if you wish."

"But it isn't my money."

"Well, suppose you keep it until the rightful owner comes and asks for it, Miss Terry."

"Thank you, Mr. Conroy. I will run along now."

"Good day, my dear," smiled Henry. "Do not worry—all will be well."

After she had gone, Judge snorted aloud.

"Of all the unmitigated asses I have ever known—you carry the flag, Henry," he declared. "We are here to unravel mysteries, are we? Sherlock Holmes Conroy! Sir, you would promise the moon to a pretty woman."

"She vars owful purty," remarked Oscar.

"Hm-m-m-m!" snorted Judge. "Beauty in distress. Ah, yes, all will be well, my dear! Honeyed words—and nothing behind them, except a vacuum."

"Hast finished?" queried Henry soberly.

"Hast," replied Judge grimly.

"Oscar, get the jug," ordered Henry. "Bring three tin cups, too."

The huge figure of Doc Darnell loomed up in the doorway.

"Make it four, Oscar," said Henry. "Good day, sir."

"And to you, Sheriff," boomed Doc genially. "I am Darnell, gentlemen. I am, at present, making an expert survey of the Shoshone Chief for Mr. Travis, the owner. Oh, how do you do, Mr. Treece. Pardon me for not recognizing you at once. And—er—what have we here?"

Oscar came in with the jug and the cups. Henry smiled, as he lined up the four cups on the desk-top.

"In England," he replied, "it is tea; in Tonto City it is prune liquor. You indulge, I hope, sir?"

"I have never tasted prune liquor," said Doc, "but I am agreeable."

Henry poured the liquor to the top of the cups. Doc sniffed at the aromatic liquor, a rather unusual odor.

"To you, Mr. Darnell," Henry said. "Bottoms up, gentlemen."

DOC DARNELL EMPTIED his cup, his right arm dropped limply to his side, while he braced his left solidly against the desk. His breathing was little more than convulsive shudders, which finally passed, leaving him fairly normal, but with a florid complexion and a husky throat.

"That," he declared in a wheezy voice, "tops anything

I have ever sent down my throat. Of what is it made, if I may ask?"

"It is based on the plebian prune," replied Henry, "blended with potato alcohol and turpentine, with a minimum of horse-liniment. What else is in it, only Frijole Bill knows. Have another, sir?"

"My God!" exclaimed Doc Darnell, aghast at the thought. "Does one take more than one drink during the same decade?"

"The first one," smiled Henry, "is the initiation. After that, you will not mind. In fact, after the second one, you will scoff at any other liquor."

"After two of those," replied Doc, "I could scoff at mayhem. Well, if it is the custom—"

Doc drank another, but this time, except for a gasp or two, he was all right. He shrugged, placed the cup on the desk and smiled widely.

"Egad, it hath a glow!" he exclaimed quietly.

"Sit down, sir," invited Henry. "It is the safe thing to do."

Doc sat down and expanded. "I like it here," he declared. "In fact, if nothing happens, I shall be here indefinitely."

"After two drinks of that," said Judge dryly, "the future of all of us is in grave doubt."

"No, no, I did not mean the liquor," laughed Doc. "As a matter of fact, I represent Eastern capital. If my report justifies the investment, they will purchase the Shoshone Chief mine, with me in charge. Mr. Travis and I are negotiating at present. By Jove, that stuff sure has some authority!"

"We shall be pleased to add you to our citizenship," said

Henry. "Tonto City needs big men; men of your caliber, Mr. Darnell. We must expand."

"This town," said Doc expansively, "needs someone to give it a shove."

"True," agreed Judge quickly, "and then someone to pick up the pieces."

"You jest, my friend," chuckled Doc.

"I never jest," declared Judge soberly. "Remember, I have lived in this town a long time. It will not stand a hearty shove."

"How about another yigger of yuice?" suggested Oscar, motioning toward the empty cups.

"A noble thought," said Henry. "Fill them up, Oscar."

Doc got to his feet, but not without difficulty.

"If you will excuse me," he said huskily, "I will be going. I just remembered an important letter I must write. Next time—perhaps. Good afternoon, gentlemen; it has been good to see you again."

Doc hit his right shoulder against the side of the door, but managed to right himself and went up the street.

"Good to see us again," chuckled Henry. "Our friend Doc Darnell is as pie-eyed as possible. He felt himself slipping. Well, here's to his kneecaps—may they bear him well."

"That man," declared Judge, "is as crooked as a snake-track in a mesquite patch, Henry."

"Snap judgment, my friend. Perhaps an honest soul, with an exaggerated ego. You are too prone to smell out the criminal odor, Judge. He must be honest, or he would not be representing Eastern capital."

THE RANCH BUCKBOARD drew up in front of the office.

Slim Pickins was driving, with Frijole on the seat beside him, while Thunder and Lightning rode in the back, with their feet hanging over the tailgate. All four were dusty and dirty, as they climbed out and entered the office.

Slim tossed a small canvas sack on the table.

"Never gimme a job like that again," he said. "My Gawd, Henry, you ain't got no idea how many ashes there was to sift. And that's all we found."

Frijole grabbed the jug and a cup, spilling the liquor in his haste.

"Pour one for each," ordered Henry. "You look dry."

"What are they talking about, Henry?" asked Judge.

"I had them sift the ashes in that burned shack," replied Henry, and then dumped out some metal objects from the canvas sack. There were two large buckles, evidently from a suitcase, because the metal corners were also there, but Henry was more interested in three metal initials, which he spread out on the desk; initials about an inch high. As he laid them out in a line they were F H T. Judge looked them over critically.

"Who would be F.H.T.?" he queried. Henry swept them off the desk-top and put them in a drawer of his desk.

"That was shore a thirsty job," declared Slim.

"This *is* liquor!" said Frijole, wiping away the tears. "It shore takes the ashes out of yore gullet. How do yuh like it, Oscar?"

"Ay," exclaimed Oscar, "vant to sing!"

"No singing," said Judge. "Fill them up again; so the boys can go home and clean up."

"Jist a couple more," said Frijole. "I've shore got a thirst."

"Don' speel heem!" warned Lightning. "Those theeng burn hole een the overall."

Their drinks finished, the four men climbed into the buckboard and headed for the JHC. Oscar sprawled on the office cot, at peace with the world. Judge tilted his chair-back against the wall, hooked his heels over the lone rung, and looked quizzically at Henry, who sat there, eyes half-closed.

"Those initials are F.H.T.," mused Henry. "The *Clarion*, and may it strangle in its own vitriol, said that Frank Travis was to arrive that night. Queer, Judge—very queer."

"Something," quoted Judge hollowly, "is rotten in the state of Denmark."

"And likewise in the State of Arizona," added Henry.

5

THE SCHOOLHOUSE AT Tonto City was not a thing of any great beauty. It was a box-like, pine board structure, sans paint, and without a bit of grass or foliage around it. The shingles had curled from the heat, giving the roof sort of a moulty appearance. The front steps were in the sun, and on these front steps sat Frank Travis.

School had been dismissed at least thirty minutes, and Frank was waiting for Nola Terry to come out. She finally emerged, carefully locking the door, but paying no attention to Frank, who was uncomfortably warm.

She turned from the door, brushed a damp lock of hair away from her eyes and looked at him.

"I told you that you must not come up here to meet me," she said severely. "People are already talking about us."

"Isn't that good?" he asked innocently.

"Of course, it isn't good. The trustees won't like it."

"Jealous?" he queried. "They are all married, I understand."

"Of course, they are not jealous. But even the children notice it. One of the little boys came up to me before school was dismissed and said:

" 'Teacher—he's settin' on the steps'."

"I know," replied Frank quietly. "I bribed him to do it."

"You bribed him? Why, for goodness sake!"

"Mostly for my sake," said Frank Travis meekly. "Shall we walk back to town?"

"I suppose so. But I do hope that none of the trustees see us."

"They wouldn't fire you for walking with me, would they, Nola?"

"They might. Maybe they would object to the teacher walking home with a man. They will not hire a married woman, and when you take this job you must agree to not get married, as long as you teach the school."

"Well, that's all right," grinned Frank. "After we get married, you won't need to teach school."

"After we—don't be ridiculous, Frank Travis."

"I'm serious, Nola. I told you the night we came here from Scorpion Bend that you were the most wonderful girl I ever met."

"I know," she smiled. "You expected to see hard-faced women and Indian squaws."

"And I saw you," he added quietly. "Let's be sensible, Nola."

"Let's," she agreed quickly.

"If that was meant to discourage me—I never heard it," said Frank. "I'm a very persistent person."

"I am beginning to find that out. I don't want to marry you. Why, I don't know anything about you—nor you about me."

"Think of the things we'll find out about each other, after we are married. Like opening an old chest, after a treasure hunt."

"There might be skeletons," she suggested quietly.

"I love 'em," he said soberly. "They rattle so pretty."

"You don't discourage very easily," she said.

"Discourage? My dear!"

"Frank, let's really be sensible. I am here to teach school. What you are doing here, I do not know. All I know is your name."

"Names don't mean much down here, Nola. In many cases, I believe a brand mark is more honest than a name— and even a rustler can change that. If my name wasn't Frank Travis, what difference would that make?"

"Isn't your name Frank Travis?" she asked quickly.

"Why did you ask me that, Nola?"

"I don't know."

They had reached the wooden sidewalk and were walking down the main street, approaching the Tonto Hotel.

"You must leave me at the general store," said Nola. "I have some shopping to do."

"All right, Nola. I'm sorry if my meeting you has been annoying. I'll be more careful in the future; but I must see you. I mean it. If you—"

They had reached the entrance to the hotel, when Doc Darnell came out. He had likely imbibed more than the prune whiskey he got at the sheriff's office, and was not in a very joyful mood. His lurch from the doorway nearly caused him to collide with Nola, who drew aside quickly, staring at him.

"Pull yourself up, Doc!" exclaimed Frank quietly.

"Who, me?" queried Doc. "Why, I—I—hm-m-m-m!"

He saw Nola, and his lips tightened, as he swallowed painfully. If wishes were horses, Doc Darnell would have been riding far from that spot.

"James Wilton!" exclaimed Nola. Frank Travis watched Doc Darnell.

"Wilton?" queried Doc. "You called me Wilton, young lady?"

Doc was sparring, gathering his unlimited nerve.

"You are James Wilton," she said accusingly. "I'd remember *you*."

"I am sorry," said Doc. His nerves were working again. "Evidently you mistake me for another. But no harm done. My name is Darnell, and I have never known a James Wilton. My loss, I suppose."

He turned his head and looked at Frank, who was smiling slightly. It nettled Doc. He wondered if this young fool had told her something. It might ruin their whole deal. He said to Frank:

"Go up to your room, and I will meet you within the hour. Important." Then, bowing to Nola, "No harm done, my dear lady. You are excused for mistaking me; it has been done before."

Then he stepped off the sidewalk and walked across the street. Nola and Frank looked at each other, and her eyes were very frosty as she said, "I will leave you here. If that man is your employer—"

Then she turned and walked down the street. Frank smiled grimly, as he watched her trim figure disappear into the general store. He waited in the little lobby, until Doc came from King's Castle, and went up to his room, where Doc joined him.

The big man had imbibed more liquor, but was more worried than inebriated.

"Do you realize that that girl can kill our whole game?" he asked.

"I'm afraid that you have led a very dishonest life, Doc," remarked Frank.

"Dishonest? I've taken what I could. I've played every damn game on earth—straight or crooked. But that has nothing to do with this situation. Don't you realize that I could still be dragged back to face the charges of—well, it only amounted to about eighty thousand dollars. That is small change compared to this deal. But it would kill everything."

"They can't touch me," said Frank quietly. "I haven't done anything—yet."

"Go ahead and whitewash yourself!" snorted Doc. "What's that girl doing here, anyway?"

"She's the school teacher, Doc."

"She is, eh? Oh, yes, I knew that. Something has got to be done about *her*."

"Hands off, Doc," said Frank warningly.

"Oh, you're backing her, eh? So that's it. A lot of good that will do you. If she exposes me, you'll go down with me. She'd probably like to know that you are masquerading as another man."

"You'd tell?" asked Frank. "You'd expose our deal to the public?"

"You're damn right. It would take me about a minute to prove that you are not Frank Travis. I can tear down just as easily as I can build up."

"Just the old dog in the manger, eh, Doc?" remarked Frank. "You would. But where does this gambler fit in on the deal?"

"Silvaine? He's with Jim Wade and me. For your own information, Silvaine has ice-water for blood, and he's the best pistol shot I ever knew."

"I see. He's the gunman of the crowd."

"Don't overlook Jim Wade in that respect. It's damn plain to me that we've got to rush this deal. That girl bothers me. Wade says that the money for the payroll is due at the bank. You'll sign a check for that amount. The minute the payroll is disbursed, we buy the mine. You give us another check for the balance in the bank, and we give you your share."

"You get together with Wade and Silvaine and decide what I get," said Frank. "I'm entitled to more than twenty-five thousand."

"We'll settle that," growled Doc. "I didn't think you'd hold us up. But you've got the chance—and I don't blame you. I might do it myself, if I was in your place."

Frank laughed. "If we traded places, you'd ask for at least half."

After Doc left the hotel, Frank wandered down to the street, where he met Henry Harrison Conroy. Henry's moonlike face was rather grim, as he said, "Mr. Travis, I would like to talk with you—at my office."

Frank said, "Why, certainly," but he was wondering what the pudgy, red-faced sheriff had in mind.

They went into the office. Judge and Oscar were out somewhere. They sat down and Henry said, "Mr. Travis, something has happened that seems to be—er—rather a coincidence. The newspaper at Scorpion Bend carried the news that you were to arrive there the evening before you did arrive. On that train was a stranger. He hired a livery rig and driver to bring him here. A short distance out of Scorpion Bend, two men stuck them up, and the driver was beaten over the head. The stranger disappeared. Do you follow me, sir?"

"Very closely," nodded Frank.

"That same evening, and a little later, a shack was burned, and in that shack was burned the stranger, whose initials were F.H.T. We recovered the metal initials from the ashes. Have you a middle name, Mr. Travis?"

Frank was staring at the floor his features tensed. Henry noticed that his hands were clenched tightly.

"That sounds like murder, Sheriff," he said quietly.

"It was murder, sir. The man's skull was crushed. I asked you if you had a middle name."

Frank shook his head. "No, I have no middle name. But those initials could have been H.F.T., or any of several combinations of letters."

"As I say," replied Henry, "it is quite a coincidence—but still remains—murder, sir."

"I quite agree with you."

"Thank you, sir; it isn't often that anyone agrees with me. By the way, a man who calls himself Doc Darnell was in to visit us. He tells me that he is trying to purchase the Shoshone Chief from you."

"Yes, I believe that is his intentions. They will buy on his recommendation, I understand."

"I see. He goes over the whole situation; in fact, he makes a comprehensive survey of the physical assets, examines veins, machinery, and the general layout, looks deeper under the surface than the average human, and—"

"Oh, certainly," interrupted Frank. "It is a tedious job."

"Then," said Henry quietly, "why in hell don't he do it? Since coming to Tonto City he has been once at the mine, and for possibly an hour. He doesn't even know the location of the shaft-house."

"Well, I don't know," confessed Frank, looking with a certain degree of admiration upon the roly-poly sheriff.

"If he is a mining engineer, I am an Indian chief," declared Henry.

Frank smiled inwardly. Henry was painting a word picture of Doc Darnell.

"And one more thing, Mr. Travis," said Henry. "Your admiration for Miss Terry, the school teacher, is evident. I do not blame you—she is a very beautiful woman. Did Miss Terry tell you about a letter she received?"

"Letter?" asked Frank curiously. "No, she did not, Sheriff."

"A letter, together with a hundred and forty dollars in currency, which warned her of danger, and asked her to leave Tonto City at once."

"Why—why, that is ridiculous," spluttered Frank. "Warning her, you say?"

Henry nodded quickly. "The money was to pay her expenses, and the letter was merely signed, a friend."

Frank got to his feet and walked to the doorway, where he turned.

"I don't understand it," he said. "If she is in danger—I'll see you later."

Frank went hurrying up the sidewalk. Henry walked to the doorway and glanced up the street. Judge came in from the rear room, walking carefully and wiping his lips with a bandanna handkerchief.

"You seem to have stirred the young gentleman," remarked Judge. "I am sure he has something to do with it."

Henry turned and looked at Judge.

"I told you, sir, to sit back there and listen—not to attack that jug of prune whiskey."

"I was very discreet, Henry," smiled Judge. "I should like to see the expression on Doc Darnell's face, when Mr. Travis tells him your advice on experting a mine. And he will, or I am badly mistaken. Would it be amiss, if we adjourned to the jug, my friend?"

"And if it were—who cares," smiled Henry. "After a bit of the essence of the festive prune, Judge, we are going to Scorpion Bend."

"Why?" asked Judge flatly.

Henry waved the question aside. "Have you ever looked at the moon from the top of Lobo Grades, Judge?" he asked.

"With envy, sir," declared Judge.

"Envy? And why with envy, if I may ask?"

"The moon, sir," replied Judge, "is safe. It doesn't have to ride over dangerous roads with a nit-wit at the lines. Shall I pour, sir?"

"Pray do," nodded Henry soberly.

JAMES WADSWORTH LONGFELLOW Pelly had finished mailing his latest edition of the *Clarion*, and felt well satisfied with his handiwork. He elevated his slipper-shod feet to the top of his littered desk, spread the paper across his knees, and smacked his lips over his leading editorial, with its banner line—MURDER IGNORED AGAIN.

Pelly thought it was well written. It pointed out the inefficiency of Henry Harrison Conroy and his staff of incompetents, and demanded action on the latest murder. It was full of vitriol, and demanded that the commissioners immediately replace the Shame of Arizona with efficient, intelligent men.

Yes, Mr. Pelly thought it was very, very good. Yet, strangely enough, Mr. Pelly had advocated it before—and Henry Harrison Conroy was still in office.

Mr. Pelly did not notice that the front door of the office had been left open. In fact, Mr. Pelly did not know that anyone was inside the door, until he heard a gentle cough, and Judge's voice saying:

"I distinctly heard him smack his lips, indicating that he really *eats* his own words, Henry."

James Wadsworth Longfellow Pelly let the paper slide to the floor, as he twisted in his chair to see Henry and Judge at the counter.

"Well!" he exclaimed. "I didn't see you come in."

"You must have expected us," said Henry. "After that editorial—"

"The *Clarion* hews to the line," said Pelly firmly.

"And smells to High Heaven," added Judge.

Henry shook his head sadly at Pelly. "You fail to be original," he said. "After one good editorial, your supply of vitriolic vocabulary is exhausted. Since then you repeat, my dear boy, until your writings are odious and odorous. You should study more and fret less."

Pelly's face flamed. "What do you want?" he asked angrily.

"If you still have that letter-head from the Frank Travis organization," replied Henry, "I would like to note their address."

Pelly had it, and slid it across the counter to Henry.

"Have you seen Oscar Johnson today?" asked Judge.

"No," replied Pelly, "and I hope I never see him again."

"That isn't mutual," said Judge. "He said he wanted to see you. You see, he wants you to explain what a drunken, misfit Swede means. I explained, as best I might, but he wants your version. Getting technical, I suppose."

"If he comes here," declared Pelly nervously, "I—I will not be responsible for what happens to him."

"Isn't that strange?" queried Judge. "He said the same thing about you."

Henry shoved the letter back to Pelly. "Thank you very much," he said.

But Pelly wasn't interested in the letter. "I'll have him arrested," he said. "I'll have him put under bonds to keep the peace."

"Just because he wants to ask you a question?" queried Henry.

"And such a simple question," added Judge. "Or is it possible that you, in all your wisdom, cannot answer it, Mr. Pelly?"

"He—he is all muscle and no brains," wailed Pelly.

"The pen, my dear boy, is supposed to be mightier than the sword," said Henry. "Look him in the eye and read him soothing parables. Explain to him that 'drunken, misfit Swede' is a term of endearment. He will understand, I am sure."

"Be gentle but firm," admonished Judge. "If he is stubborn, show him that you are his master. Good day, sir."

They walked out, sober-faced, and went up the street. It was still early in the forenoon. Henry went to the depot, where he sent the following wire to Frank Travis' San Francisco address:

PLEASE WIRE ME PRESENT ADDRESS OF
FRANK TRAVIS AND WHAT ARE HIS THREE
INITIALS.

"Do you suppose Oscar will go down to the *Clarion* office?" asked Judge.

"Not likely," smiled Henry. "And still, I wish he would. No, no, I do not mean that I wish the annihilation of Mr. Pelly, but—it rather rankles to have him print that the county should abolish the sheriff's office, because nothing ever comes from there, except ribald mirth and odors of distillation."

"At times," said Judge quietly, "one may smell that prune whiskey even out on the street."

"I know that Judge," agreed Henry, "but *ribald mirth!* That is a gross misstatement. We may laugh, sir—but not in a ribald way."

"Not at all," agreed Judge. "I suppose we must stay here, until you get an answer to that telegram."

"Exactly; so we may as well enjoy the flesh-pots of Scorpion Bend."

Instead of hiring a rig from the livery stable, they came to Scorpion Bend in a two-seated spring-wagon, with Slim driving, and Oscar Johnson occupying the extra seat. Neither of them were expert drivers, but both were better than Henry or Judge.

They were both at the Ocotillo Saloon, when Henry and Judge came back from the depot.

"Ay am feeling like a vipporvill," declared Oscar. "Das is goot liquor."

"You better ease off a little, Oscar," advised Judge. "If James Wadsworth Longfellow Pelly sees you, feeling like a whip-poorwill—"

"Oh, ya-a-ah! Das newspaper faller. Ay don't like de cut of his yib."

"Never mind the cut of his jib," said Henry. "Keep away from him—and stay sober—both of you."

"Me, I'm perfee'ly shober," declared Slim. "I could drive a jerk-line team, hauling six wagons, over a pack-trail."

"And no doubt you would," agreed Henry. "But I want you able to drive two horses and wagon over a road; so take it easy."

At six o'clock that afternoon Henry received an answer to his telegram. It was from James Worth, who added, office secretary. It read:

AS FAR AS WE KNOW FRANK TRAVIS IS IN
TONTO CITY.

"That," said Henry, "is a big help to our side. No information about his initials."

"As far as they know," said Judge. "What do you think, Henry?"

"If Frank Travis' middle initial is H," said Henry, "then Frank Travis was burned in that shack, and this deal to sell the Shoshone Chief is the biggest steal ever pulled off in Wild Horse Valley. The Frank Travis we know is an impostor, Judge."

"I told you that Doc Darnell is a crook," declared Judge.

"He is behind the deal. A forged signature—and a bunch of crooks make half a million."

"I believe," said Henry quietly, "that something is about to happen."

"And," said Judge, "I hope it will not be to us."

6

BECAUSE OF THE intense heat of the daytime, the stage to Scorpion Bend left Tonto City at eight o'clock in the evening. Dave Leeds, the regular driver, had been drinking with Tony Vega, who was a substitute driver, and worked between times as a swamper at the King's Castle Saloon, and was in no condition to handle the team. Tony was a careful drinker, and was able to take over the job.

Just before the stage was ready to leave Tonto City, a woman got in. Perhaps Tony Vega was the only one in town who saw her get aboard. At any rate, the stage left Tonto City in a cloud of dust, and headed for the long trip over the Lobo Grades.

About nine o'clock Frank Travis walked into the Tonto Hotel, and the old clerk handed him an envelope, with the remark that he found it on the counter. Travis' name was on the envelope.

He opened the envelope and scanned the few lines. It was from Nola Terry, and read:

It is necessary for me to leave here at once. Do not look for me.

It was simply signed "Nola." Frank Travis' jaw tightened, as he turned back to the doorway. He knew that the stage had been gone an hour, and that the stage depot was closed.

He walked swiftly down to the Gibson home, where Nola had lived, and found them upset, too. A little Mexican boy had delivered a note to Mrs. Gibson from Nola. It read:

> *Will you please explain to the trustees that I must go at once. Have them pay you my salary to date for my board and room. Sorry, but this is very urgent—and thank you for your kindness to me.*

"She was so happy here," said Mrs. Gibson. "Never a word about leaving. Such a lovely girl, Mr. Travis."

"Yes," said Frank quietly, and went back to the main street.

There was still one possibility left. If he could get to Scorpion Bend before she could catch a train. He found Tommy Roper, the stuttering cowboy, who managed the livery stable, and explained what he wanted.

"Wh-wh-why dud-dud-don't you rur-ride a huh-horse?" asked Tommy. "It's quh-quh-quicker."

"I can't ride," said Travis impatiently. "You hitch up a horse—and you do the driving. Don't argue—I want speed."

AFTER SUPPER THAT evening Henry and Judge found Slim Pickins, trying to raffle off a stray dog in the Gilt Edge Saloon. He had sold Oscar Johnson four tickets at twenty-five cents apiece, and the big Swede was arguing for an immediate drawing, when Henry and Judge appeared. Slim reluctantly released the dog, and spent the dollar for drinks.

"I believe," remarked Henry, "that I shall drive the team."

"I was afraid of that," sighed Judge.

"Ay vill drive," announced Oscar. "Ay could drive a team in de dark over Lobo Grades, vit von hand tied behind me."

"And not even hang onto the lines," added Slim. "I've seen yuh do it."

However, Slim and Oscar sat in the back seat, while Henry did the driving, with the apprehensive Judge beside him. Henry was not a good driver. On sharp turns Henry was not interested in the fate of the rear wheels. The Lobo Grades were dangerous. In most places the road was not wide enough for two vehicles to pass, and the southbound vehicle must take the outside edge all the way across the grades. One mistake would plunge the vehicle into the bottom of Lobo Canyon, which in certain places was close to four hundred feet deep. The average depth along the grades would be over two hundred feet.

There was no moon that night. Slim and Oscar went to sleep, while Judge fumed and fretted, but Henry paid little attention. In the daylight, or in moonlight, it was possible to see far enough ahead from curves to observe the approach of another vehicle, thus enabling a driver to select a wide spot for the passing. But tonight there was no possible chance of that.

Judge lighted a match and looked at his watch.

"Where do you suppose we will meet the stage?" he asked anxiously.

"Who knows?" replied Henry. "But Dave Leeds is a careful driver, and he will realize the importance of careful traveling. You may rest assured, sir, that I will bring you safely home."

"Stay closer to the wall, Henry," urged Judge. "Plenty of time to tempt fate, when we meet someone."

"Timid soul," sighed Henry, but swung the team in a little closer to the inside.

There was a slight upgrade, as they approached one of the hair-pin turns. Neither Henry nor Judge saw the approaching stage, until it was nearly into them. Henry's team swerved to the left, and the light wagon took the brunt of the crash, which was terrific. It flung the lighter vehicle against the rocky wall, sparks flew from shod hoofs, a horse screamed. Then there was only dust-filled air, a few pieces of rocks rolling from the wall of the grade.

Henry found himself on his hands and knees on a horse, tangled in the harness, and so badly dazed that he hardly knew what happened. The horse never moved, but the other one was still kicking. Henry managed to get loose and stagger into the road where Oscar's voice complained:

"Who in de ha'al has been monkeying?"

Slim wailed, "All right, all right! Get yore damn feet off my neck!"

Henry said weakly, "Judge! Judge, where are you?"

"I am here," said Judge peevishly. "I fell between the seat and the dash, and that damn seat has pinned my neck so tight I can't get loose."

"I reckon it's yore feet—not Oscar's," said Slim. "My God, what a crash! What'd yuh do, Henry, hit the wall?"

Slim helped Judge loose, and they all stood in the road.

"It was the stage," declared Judge. "I saw enough to recognize it. But where in the devil—who have we here?"

It was Tony Vega, knocked silly, but still able to stagger around. Henry grabbed him by the sleeve, and kept him from walking into the canyon.

"Where's the stage?" panted Tony. "My Gawd, what did we hit?"

"You hit us," accused Judge. "You never gave us a chance."

"It—it threw me off," said Tony. "Where's the stage?"

"I'm afraid," said Henry painfully, "that the stage is down at the bottom of the canyon."

"My God!" exclaimed Tony. "There's a woman on the stage!"

"A—a woman?" panted Judge. "Who in the name of—"

"I dunno," said Tony. "She got on at Tonto. Wore a veil—paid me cash. I dunno who she is, I tell yuh. My God, she's dead!"

"I am very much afraid you are right, Tony," said Henry. "Where is Dave Leeds?"

"Had too much whiskey," said Tony. "I had to drive. And look what happened! I didn't see yuh at all. It was too dark. What can we do?"

"One of our horses got killed," informed Slim. "The other one seems to be all right. I'll yank off the harness and ride for help."

"A good idea, Slim," agreed Henry. "Bring plenty of men—and ropes. We'll need—"

"We can't get down from here," interrupted Slim. "We'll have to go in the lower end of the canyon, Henry. I'll go for help, and you fellers start walkin'. It's only about five miles to the end of the grades. So-long, I'll go as fast as that horse can travel."

But when Slim turned to get on the horse, that horse was already traveling away in the darkness.

"What the hell!" yelled Slim. "There goes that—"

"Wega took him!" snorted Oscar. "Ay saw him do it."

"Why would Tony Vega do that?" asked Henry. "Why, he—well, he has gone."

"I'll saw his damn ears off," promised Slim angrily.

They stood around in the darkness, each one rubbing some part of his injured anatomy, and wondering what to do next. Finally Henry said:

"We may as well walk. No doubt Tony Vega will sound the alarm in Tonto City; so we may as well be down at the lower end of the canyon."

No one approved nor rejected Henry's suggestion; they just started walking toward Tonto City. In about thirty minutes they met Frank Travis and Tommy Roper. They had seen a wild rider go past them, but had no idea who he was, until Henry told them what had happened. Travis got out of the buggy.

"That lady," he said huskily, "was Nola Terry."

"No!" exclaimed Henry. "The school teacher, Travis?"

"She left a note for me and one for Mrs. Gibson. She was leaving Tonto City. I—I wanted to catch her in Scorpion Bend."

They quickly unhitched the horse, and turned the buggy by hand on the narrow foad.

"Do you want to go back to Tonto, Travis?" asked Henry.

"No, I—I believe I'd rather stay here. Someone else go."

"Judge, you go with Tommy," ordered Henry. "You know what is needed."

7

IT WAS WELL after daylight, when the men from Tonto met Henry and his party at the mouth of Lobo Canyon. They brought extra horses, plenty of rope, and Judge was thoughtful enough to bring some food for Henry, Travis, Oscar and Slim. Lobo Canyon was full of brush and broken boulders, and the stream bed was difficult to follow. In places they had to dismount and lead their horses.

They were all more or less bruised and torn by the time they reached the approximate spot where the stage went over the edge. Frank Travis had hardly spoken a word during the hard trip, but was one of the first to see the wreckage of the stage—a smashed wheel, hanging to a manzanita snag on the side of the wall.

Henry was the first to reach the smashed vehicle, which was upside down, wedged between some boulders in the sand. He asked the men to stay back, as he went slowly up to the stage. After a close inspection, he asked them to come on. The doors had been torn off the vehicle, the top smashed almost to the floor—but there was no one inside.

The men stood around, staring at the cliffs. Henry drew a deep breath and studied the situation.

"Where is the woman?" asked one of the men quietly.

"Prob'ly flung clear of the stage," said another. "We better spread out and make a search."

For at least thirty minutes those twenty men searched. From the grade, far above them to where the stage crashed, there was not a bush nor a ledge, where the body could have been thrown. Not even a crevice was overlooked. Finally the men gathered around the stage again. Henry looked them over, and noticed that Frank Travis was not among them.

"Where is Travis?" he asked.

"Me and him went up the canyon," a man said, "but we didn't find anythin'; so I came back. Mebbe he went further on."

"See if you can find him," ordered Henry. "The rest make another search. If there was a woman in that stage, she must be here."

But that search was as futile as the first. The man came back from up the canyon and reported that he could not find Frank Travis. He said he yelled Travis' name, but there was no response.

"We will leave his horse here," said Henry.

"And prob'ly have to come back and hunt for him," growled a cowboy.

"Granted," agreed Henry. "Well, gentlemen, we may as well go back and report that there was no woman on that stage. Tony Vega must have had too many drinks."

The return trip down the canyon was as difficult as the one coming in, and the men were tired out when they reached its mouth. Henry and Judge were the last ones out, and the others were stringing along far ahead, as they emerged from the shadows of the cliffs.

"You will proceed to Tonto City," said Henry. "Contact Oscar and Slim, and the three of you keep a close eye on things. I am not at all satisfied with what we found. Watch for Tony Vega to come to Tonto. Have Slim watch the King's Castle. Tell Oscar to watch around the hotel—and you can watch from where you like. Do not miss Tony Vega, if he comes to town—and follow him when he leaves. Have your horses handy. You understand?"

"Perfectly," replied Judge stiffly. "But—about you, Henry?"

"I shall stay here."

"You think that there is someone still in that canyon?"

"I know that one man is in there, Judge."

"Oh, yes—Travis. Be careful, Henry."

"Do not be a fuss-budget! Watch for Tony Vega—and follow him."

Judge, a very slow rider, was last to reach Tonto City. He found Oscar, Slim, Frijole Bill, Thunder and Lightning at the sheriff's office. He gave Slim and Oscar their orders. Frijole said:

"We'll all watch. Hell, we'll picket this town so close that a lizard couldn't come to visit a cockroach, without us see-in' him."

"And no drinking," ordered Judge. "Not a single drink."

"Aw, Judge!" protested Frijole. Judge shook his head. "I reckon I spoke up too quick," sighed Frijole. "Yuh see, I just drawed off a new batch, and brought in a gallon. She's back there behind the door, strainin' at her leash. Pore little thing."

Judge smacked his lips, but shook his head.

"No liquor," he declared.

"Ay am hortsick," declared Oscar. "Ay could use about t'ree inches in a vashtob."

"Today," declared Judge, "there is a drouth in Tonto City."

IT WAS A long day for Henry Harrison Conroy. All he could do was to sit in the shade of a boulder and watch the mouth of the canyon. The sun went down early at that spot, but it was not long until the shadows of evening moved in. Darkness comes swiftly after sundown in that country. Henry moved in closer to the trail. His horse was concealed in the heavy brush further back on the slope.

Coyotes yapped on the brushy ridges, and Henry saw a wild-cat come out on the trail, stretch like a satisfied house cat, and go trotting toward the mouth of the canyon. A coyote cut the trail fifty feet away from Henry, stopped short, when a vagrant breeze brought it the scent of man, and faded into the brush like a puff of smoke.

It was an hour or more after dark, when Henry heard the scrape of shod hoofs on stone, and the dark bulk of horse and rider appeared out of the canyon. About a hundred feet from where Henry sat the man drew up. For a long time he seemed to be listening. For possibly ten minutes he waited, and then two more riders came out of the canyon, traveling in close single-file.

They joined the first rider, and they talked in low tones for several moments. Finally the one rider rode swiftly away toward Tonto City, while the other two followed him at a slow trot. Henry waited several moments, before getting his own horse and coming in behind them.

About two miles north of Tonto City there was a fork in the road, where an old road led to the Shoshone Chief mine. About three miles north of Tonto City was an old trail, little used, which also led to the Shoshone Chief.

Henry rode just fast enough to keep fairly close to the two riders, and when he came to this old trail, he quickly dismounted and by the aid of a match he investigated the trail. There was not a fresh track.

He mounted quickly and rode swiftly. The trail was not well defined, and in places the desert had overgrown it, but Henry depended on his range-wise horse to keep to that trail. And Henry never rode five miles faster in his life—on a horse. He was almost among the mine buildings, before he drew rein.

Henry wasn't sure where he was going, nor what he was going to do when he got there, but he had a vague idea. Avoiding the bunk-houses, and going carefully, so as not to meet anyone, he arrived at the main office building. There were no lights in the place. Henry rode around to the rear and tied his horse to a fence.

"I feel," said Henry to himself, "that I am as crazy as Jackson's mule, which swam a river to get a drink; but something inside me seems to say that I'm right. Maybe it is the lack of food and drink."

HE WENT UP to the rear door of the office and turned the knob. To his surprise, the door was unlocked. Carefully he let himself into the room. He stood there long enough for his eyes to become accustomed to the darkness. To his left was a counter, reaching about two-thirds of the width of the room, which was about twenty feet by thirty feet in size. Midway of the room, and to the right, was a large desk and several chairs.

To Henry's left was a door, evidently to a closet, or store-room. He went over to this door, but found it locked. As he started to move over to the desk his foot struck something that jingled on the rug. It was a key-ring on a broken chain, with two keys. He tried one on the door, and it opened.

But before Henry had a chance to investigate further he heard noises at the rear of the building. Someone was coming in the back doorway. There was only one thing for Henry to do and that was to hide in the closet. As he closed the door, someone came in, and he was afraid to entirely close the door for fear they might hear him.

There was no conversation out there. The rear door closed, and he heard someone hurrying around the room, pulling down the blinds. Then a lamp was lighted. He heard a scuffling, dragging sound, and a solid thump. Then a man said:

"Damn such a job! Feelin' better, eh? You sure got a solid whack on the head, young feller. That's what yuh get for bein' nosey. And that ain't all you'll get. But yuh made it easy for us. Even that fat-nosed sheriff knows you got lost in Lobo Canyon. If they never find yuh, they'll figure you fell and killed your fool self."

Henry eased the door open a few inches. Jim Wade, manager of the mine, was standing by the desk, looking down at the bound figure of Frank Travis. Henry only got a flash of the scene, because the door creaked. Wade whirled around, started toward the door, which Henry jerked shut.

Wade jerked at the door, but it was locked—and Henry had the key. Wade rapped sharply on the panels, and said huskily:

"Open that door, you fool! You can't get away. If you don't open it before I count three, I'll fill that place full of lead!"

Wade was close to the door, in order for Henry to hear

plainly; so Henry shoved the muzzle of his .45 within an inch of the panel, and pulled the trigger. The report almost deafened him, but he heard the crash as something or somebody fell down.

Quickly fitting the key in the lock Henry came out, coughing, his eyes filled with tears. If it had been a ruse, Henry fell for it; but it was no ruse. Jim Wade was sprawled on the rug, face down, his gun a few feet from his right hand, which clutched the rug. Henry took a deep breath and wiped his eyes with the back of a pudgy hand.

"Well, it was a nice night for it," he said quietly, and walked over to open the front door.

EVIDENTLY NO ONE outside had heard the shot, muffled inside the closet. He came back and looked at Wade. Then he looked at Frank Travis, who stared at him with dazed eyes. After a few moments Henry grasped Wade's legs and proceeded to drag him behind the counter. He closed the front door, and went over to Travis, intending to untie him, but he heard the sound of horses outside, and dived back for the closet. The smoke was nearly gone now.

Someone unlocked the front door, and several men came in. They were Doc Darnell, Bart Silvaine and Tony Vega. The door clicked shut behind them, and Darnell said, "Where's Wade? Would that fool go out and leave—"

"It's all right—the door's locked," said Silvaine. "Take a look at his ropes, Tony. He's conscious, Doc. That helps a lot. You've got the papers?"

"I've got 'em. All we need is that young fool to sign 'em."

"His ropes are all right," said Tony. "Where's Wade, do yuh reckon?"

"He wouldn't run out on us, would he?" asked Doc.

"Jim Wade never ran out on anybody," said Silvaine. "If he did—where's that girl? He's the only one who knows where she is, Doc."

"I know it, Bart. It was a fool thing to do, but he insisted that one man was enough to know that. Nothing could happen to him. Hell, he brought Travis here. He was all right when Tony left them."

"Aw, he's around," said Tony. "Nothing happened to Jim Wade."

"Untie Travis, Tony," ordered Darnell. "I want these papers signed."

Tony quickly untied Travis and removed the cloth gag from his mouth. Travis was conscious, but had been hit pretty hard.

"Yank him up here to the desk," ordered Darnell.

"My God, what's this!" exclaimed Silvaine. He dropped to one knee on the rug and held up his fingers, wet with blood. Tony shoved Travis into a chair. Silvaine and Darnell stared at each other.

"Blood!" exclaimed Doc quietly. "Whose blood? What has happened?"

"Something—sure," whispered Silvaine. "I don't like it."

"Mebbe Wade had a nose-bleed," suggested Tony. "Yeah, mebbe he did."

"Maybe he—didn't," whispered Silvaine. "Doc, I don't like this."

Doc Darnell shuffled the papers and forced a pen into Travis' fingers.

"Write that signature on this blank paper," he ordered.

Travis took the pen, but it slipped from his fingers. Darnell swore bitterly and rescued the pen from the floor.

"Wait!" exclaimed Silvaine. He saw a rug near the end of the counter had been twisted aside, when Henry dragged Wade's body.

In three strides the big gambler reached the end of the counter, with Doc close behind him.

"Wade!" gasped Silvaine. "Look, Doc!"

As Doc Darnell leaned in closer, Henry stepped from the closet. He was between them and the front door now, his big gun gripped in his right hand.

"Keep your hands in sight!" he snapped.

Silvaine and Darnell jerked upright, their hands in sight. With a slight whistle of astonishment Tony Vega started to lift his hands, and at the same moment Frank Travis reached out and took Tony's gun from his holster.

"Why, you damned—" gritted the big gambler. His right hand swung down, and the lamplight flashed on a sleeve-gun, as it dropped into his hand.

Henry's heavy Colt rattled the rafters again, and Silvaine staggered into Doc Darnell from the impact of the heavy bullet.

BUT DOC DARNELL was equal to the emergency. He grasped Silvaine, whirled him around between him and Henry, using Silvaine as a shield, and with a superhuman effort he swung Silvaine off the floor and came straight at the surprised Henry, in a bull-like rush.

Henry could not shoot Darnell, and when he tried to sidestep Darnell's rush a small Navajo rug slipped under his feet, and he went down with a crash. Over him went Darnell and his burden, crashing to the floor with Darnell on top.

Darnell got to his feet with surprising speed for a man

of his bulk, and fairly tore a gun from his shoulder holster. Henry was helpless for the moment, his gun-hand twisted under him.

Again the room shuddered from the concussion of a heavy shot. Darnell jerked around and the gun fell from his hand. For a moment he looked like a tight-rope walker, trying to catch his balance, and then he went down.

"I owe you that one, Doc," said Frank Travis, and at that moment Tony Vega tore the gun from Travis' hand, and in one leap skidded to the door. Before Henry could sit up and turn, Vega fired once at him, but the bullet went high, smashing into the wall.

The next instant he flung the door open, leaped outside— and landed in the arms of Oscar Johnson, who was lunging up the steps. Tony Vega yelled a strangled curse, and the next moment he was flung back into the room, flat on his back, the wind all driven from his lungs.

Behind Oscar came Judge, Slim, Frijole and the two Mexicans.

"Anyt'ing else you vant done, Henry?" asked Oscar blandly.

"Yes," replied Henry huskily, "you may go into that closet and bring out the school teacher, Oscar."

"The school teacher?" gasped Judge. "Wasn't she on that stage?"

Frank Travis, in spite of his injuries, beat Oscar to the closet. Nola Terry was quickly released. She was unhurt, except for the pains of returning circulation and shock. Travis tried to question her but she did not seem to know what had happened. Miners, attracted by the shooting, crowded into the place, but Oscar and Slim held them back.

Darnell and Wade were dead and Silvaine was badly hurt. The big gambler refused to talk, but not Tony Vega. As soon as he regained his breath, he was only too eager to talk, to answer questions.

"Silvaine and Wade killed Frank Travis and burned him in that old shack," panted Tony. "I dunno how they done it; I wasn't there. Doc got scared of the school teacher and sent her a note to git out. She didn't go, and then Silvaine figured out a scheme. He got one of the honkatonk girls to write them notes. They had to have a woman on that stage, in case anybody should see us start; so he hired another of the girls to go to Scorpion Bend, and he gave her money to buy a ticket east.

"They grabbed the school teacher and brought her out here. Wade didn't let anybody know where she was held. They wasn't goin' to hurt her, if the deal went all right. I mean, until the girl got to Scorpion Bend and got away on the train. Silvaine had to have an alibi."

"And then they were going to dispose of the school teacher," said Henry.

"Somethin' had to be done with her," admitted Tony. "That wasn't any of my business."

"Tony," said Henry, "when you grabbed that horse on the grade, you came and told Wade what happened. Then you and Wade beat us into Lobo Canyon, stole the body of that girl and took it away. Later, you knocked Travis on the head and kept him there until after dark."

"How'd you know this?" asked Tony.

"I saw the tracks in the sand beside the wrecked stage,

my boy. I know somebody got there ahead of us—and that you'd have to come out."

"And Doc Darnell said you was dumb!" exclaimed Tony wearily.

Henry turned to Travis, who was rubbing Nola's wrists. The girl was crying a little. "Travis, when you shot Doc Darnell a while ago," he said, "you remarked that you owed him that much. What did you mean? You were both in a crooked, murdering deal."

"For what he did to this girl," replied Travis quietly, "and because he murdered one of my best friends. At least, he planned it."

"Who was that friend?"

"Tommy Fuller. Oh, you don't know him. He was a private detective, who did most of my investigating. Oh, I know it don't make sense, Henry. I had too much money. I wanted excitement. Doc Darnell mistook me for a double of myself. It was a chance for some fun. My office knew what the deal was about. Tommy tried to get me to drop it, but I wanted something to do. Tommy came a day ahead of me. He said that if I was going to play a damn fool, he wanted to be in there ahead of time."

"His initials were T.H. Fuller?" asked Henry.

"That's right," nodded Travis.

"You have no middle name?" queried Henry.

"I have," replied Travis, "but I never use it. The name is Hezikiah."

"F.H.T.," said Judge. "How are you feeling, Miss Terry?"

"Better, thank you," she whispered. "Frank, I—I heard them talk. They were going to have you sign the papers, and then they were—they were going to put us in that horrible canyon—for the buzzards. Now I can go back and teach school again—and everything will be all right."

"My dear," said Travis quietly, "you are going to marry the biggest fool that ever came to Arizona, and if you can't get along without schoolhouses, I'll buy you a whole flock of them to play with. We will have the biggest wedding ever held in Wild Horse Valley—and Henry Harrison Conroy will be our best man."

"My goodness!" exclaimed Henry. "The last line spoken—and no one pulled down the curtain. Will someone please go after Doctor Knowles?"

THUNDER AND LIGHTNING Mendoza were selected to notify Doctor Knowles, the coroner. They got on their horses and started down the road toward Tonto City, puzzled over what had happened.

"Funny theeng happen tonight; I don' onnerstand heem," said Thunder.

"The way I meesonderstand heem ees like these," explained Lightning. "These ver' pretty *señorita* wan' schoolhouses; so they domp her eento Lobo Cañon on her *cabeza*—I don' know why, eef you onnerstand w'at I am talking about, my leetle brodder.

"Henry ees keel copple men, biccause I do not know why. Everybody talk togedder and nobody ees say mucho. But everybody green and ees ver' happy, excepts Tony Vega, and then they wan' doctor. W'at you theenk?"

"I am leesten for hearing pretty damn good," stated Thunder, "but I'm can' mak' heads from the tail. One man say he ees come here for play damn fool. He mus' be right, biccause he say he weel buy whole flocks from schoolhouse for the *señorita*."

"That ees exact from w'at I theenk," agreed Lightning. "Een sometheeng he ees ver' loco, but een sometheeng he ees damn smart."

"Een w'at theeng ees he so damn smart?" asked Thunder.

"W'en he say that Henry ees the bes' man."

BLIND TRAILS AT TONTO

*In many ways Henry was always
resourceful; a good quality in any sheriff*

HENRY HARRISON CONROY, sheriff of Wild Horse Valley, held up a water-glass filled with an amber-colored liquor, and squinted thoughtfully through it at the light from an oil lamp.

"Nectar of the gods," he said quietly. "Ambrosia—fit for the palate of a king."

"Judge" Van Treece, the deputy sheriff, had swallowed his drink, and his Adam's-apple was doing a devil's dance. A few tears trickled down his seamed cheeks, and he opened his eyes. Then he said huskily:

"The king is dead, Henry."

"Frijole Bill" Cullison, the cook, tilted back in a chair against the wall of the main room in the JHC ranch house, looked curiously at Judge, while "Slim" Pickins, a lean-faced cowpuncher, sprawled in a chair, an empty tin-cup dangling from a long forefinger.

Henry Harrison Conroy drank slowly and thoughtfully, his eyes closed, and his nose, the biggest and reddest in Arizona, seemed to glow with an added power.

"Egad!" he breathed. "It doth take possession."

"What in the name of the Lord did you put in that last batch, Frijole?" asked Judge. "There is more than the juice of the prune."

"Yea-a-ah," admitted Frijole Bill, "there is. I blended her

with potato alcohol, added some rice, a couple pounds of raisins, and topped her all off with a few shots of horse-liniment. Yuh see, I wasn't just sure how she'd act on the human frame. I had t' shrink a couple new hoops on that danged keg, because she kept a-swellin'.'"

"And she purred like a cat," added Slim. "Times she kinda groaned, too. I got kinda s'picious of that stuff, so I wrapped the keg in a tarp, tied a rope around her, and tied it off to the bunk-post."

"You'd lie, and Slim would swear to it," declared Judge.

"Personally," said Henry, "I believe it. I can still hear it crackle."

"I tried her out this mornin'," said Frijole soberly, "and I found out one thing, Henry. If she blows back on yuh, don't be perlite. Jist open yore mouth wide. I didn't, and it blowed off a pivot-tooth I've had for twenty year. It atchally did, and I found that tooth buried half out of sight in a pine board.

"And then I seen old Bill Shakespeare, the rooster. He'd

got hisself full of the mesh. Well, sir, he—"

"Have done!" snorted Judge. "No lies please, Frijole. No one ever sees that Bill Shakespeare, except yourself—and you'd lie about—"

"I seen him, Judge," interrupted Slim.

"Tell us more, Slim," urged Henry. "I am in the mood for a good lie."

"I am not," declared Judge. "I believe that, instead of listening to lies about an inebriated rooster, we should be planning just what we intend to do in this campaign. According to the Scorpion Bend *Clarion*, and may James Wadsworth Longfellow Pelly stew in his own grease, we haven't a chance on earth to remain in office. He says that Honest Ed Henderson will poll twenty votes to our one."

"And you, sir," said Henry patiently, "want me to waste my energies at such odds. Twenty to one—my godness!"

"And unless we bestir ourselves—he may be right in his odds," said Judge.

"Some day, when I'm in the right mood," said Slim Pickins, "I'm goin' up to Scorpion Bend and kill me an editor."

"And hang for it, I presume," said Judge.

"If yuh cut off his ears," said Friiole, "I'll bet yuh can't hang him; that rope would slip right over his head. How about another little snifter, gents?"

THEY WERE A queer pair of peace officers, Henry Harrison Conroy and Judge Van Treece. Henry, short and fat, with a big, red nose, was a well-known figure in vaudeville for many years. In fact, Henry grew up back-stage, with little knowledge of anything outside the theater. But when vaudeville waned, and Henry, confronted with the necessity of making a living, was willed a ranch in Wild Horse Valley by an uncle he had never known, Henry knew nothing about the West; and the West had never seen anything like Henry, with his tailored clothes, derby hats, gold-headed cane and spats.

Wild Horse Valley, and especially Tonto City, chuckled with glee. In Tonto City was Judge Van Treece, tall, angular lawyer, who drank himself out of the profession. With the figure and face of a tragedian, courtly manners and a frayed frock coat, he appealed to Henry's sense of humor.

And when Wild Horse Valley, during an election, wrote Henry's name on their ballots in sufficient numbers to assure his election as sheriff, Henry, in turn, appointed Judge Van Treece as his deputy. And then, to add flavor to the office, he appointed Oscar Johnson, a giant Swede horse-wrangler, as jailer.

"If Wild Horse Valley's sense of humor elected me," said Henry, "I shall give them more to laugh at."

But in spite of outward appearances Henry and Judge had proved their ability to handle the affairs of their office. Perhaps they drank too much, perhaps their methods were not of the approved Western sheriff, but the results were the same. Frijole Bill and Slim Pickins handled the work at the JHC, together with Thunder and Lightning Mendoza, two brothers, who mishandled the King's English, and loved to lie in the shade.

But things were changing in Tonto City. Jim Nelson, reputed a big-town gambler, had purchased the King's Castle, the biggest saloon, gambling house and honkatonk in the country. It was Nelson who was backing Ed Henderson, owner of the Circle H spread, for sheriff. Nelson didn't like Henry and Judge. Henderson was a cattleman, hard-faced, cold-eyed, who wore a fierce mustache and rode bad horses. Henry had nothing against Henderson, who had been in the valley about nine years.

The editor of the *Clarion* had coined the name "Honest Ed" Henderson.

Just where the honesty came in, he had never divulged, but it gave him a chance to work the honesty angle for all it was worth in his editorials against the regime of Henry

Harrison Conroy, although he could not say that Henry had ever done anything dishonest.

Frijole Bill was the cook—when he wasn't distilling prunes into a very remarkable whiskey, which had become rather infamous for its potency. Frijole was past sixty, with a heavy mustache on a face entirely too small for such an ornament, and he would not weigh over a hundred pounds, filled with his own concoctions. Slim Pickins was about forty, lean as a half-starved hound, with a lean, serious face and a pair of inquiring eyebrows.

"Yuh know what I'd do?" asked Frijole. "If I was runnin' for sheriff, I'd hire me a band, and I'd hire the Slim Princess to sing to the voters. By golly, I'll betcha I'd get votes."

"Even if I wasn't runnin'," amended Slim, "I'd take her. Wouldn't even bother about a band."

"Keep your mind on taking care of the JHC cows," said Judge.

The "Slim Princess," as she was known, was Jim Nelson's wife, and the principle attraction at the King's Castle. She was also an accomplished faro dealer. But the cowboy and miner worshiped from afar, because she paid them no attention, and Jim Nelson had let it be known that she was taboo.

Frijole filled their glasses again.

"I cannot quite grasp that twenty-to-one prophecy, Judge," said Henry. "I look at you, and I consider me. The odds are not fair, my friend."

"Too large?" asked Judge, sniffing at his liquor.

"Too small," replied Henry soberly. "If Honest Ed is half as good as the *Clarion* paints him—we will be lucky to vote for ourselves. In fact, after reading that last editorial, I doubt that I shall vote for myself."

"I feel thataway m'self," said Frijole. "He's a dinger."

Judge drank half the glassful, shuddered visibly and put down the glass with a trembling hand.

"You might at least blend it, Frijole," he said. "My last swallow was pure horse-liniment."

"It don't blend so good," said Frijole. "Yuh see, I stirred in that liniment, but soon's I quit, she comes right to the top again."

"The thing to do," said Slim, "is to take off the top, rub yourself good, and then drink the rest."

Henry got up and placed his glass on the table, his eyes closed tightly.

"O, Death where is thy sting?" he whispered.

"Listen!" exclaimed Slim.

Someone was coming up onto the porch. Suddenly the lamp chimney exploded into a million pieces of thin glass, and from outside came the blasting report of a rifle. A framed picture at the end of the room came down with a crash, as two more shots were fired.

ALL FOUR MEN were on their feet, staring at the door, where protruding splinters showed where a bullet had smashed through. For a space of perhaps ten seconds no one moved nor spoke. Then they heard the sound of galloping hoofs, receding in the distance.

"They got Uncle Jason!" exclaimed Frijole, pointing at the picture frame on the floor, the glass shattered.

Henry walked to the door and flung it open. On the porch, sprawled on his face, was a man. A rivulet of crimson was spreading across the boards. Frijole brought the lamp and they examined him. He was a middle·aged man, not very tall nor very heavy, roughly dressed, and quite dead from two bullets.

None of them had ever seen the man before. About fifty feet from the porch stood a saddled horse, reins down. Slim went out and led the animal over to the light, where he examined it.

"This is Russ Haley's horse," he said. "Now what would a dead man be doin' with Russ' horse?"

"He wasn't dead when he got it," reminded Frijole.

"Yeah, that's right—he wasn't."

"Such inane conversation!" snorted Judge. "Of all the damnable—"

"Slim," said Henry calmly, "will you please get a horse and go to town after Doctor Bogart?"

"I shore will, Henry."

"You might find him at the King's Castle," called Judge, "trying to make a pair of deuces beat a full-house."

They went back into the house, but left the door open. Judge said:

"This makes fine grain for the *Clarion* mill, Henry. A stranger is killed on the steps of the sheriffs home. And only two weeks before election. Why couldn't this have waited until the issue was determined?"

"A very constructive idea, my dear Judge," said Henry. "But unfortunately human passions are not guided by political necessity. Unless, of course, you feel that our opponents have stooped to murdering on our front porch in an effort to embarrass us. What do you think, Frijole?"

"We don't know the man—and he's dead," replied Frijole soberly.

"That is a sensible answer," said Henry. "Poor Uncle Jason!"

THEY WENT TO the back of the room and looked at the picture. It was a huge, crayon portrait of Jason H. Conroy, founder of the JHC Ranch. It was there, when Henry took possession, and out of respect for the man who had so kindly willed him the ranch, he left it on the wall. But now the ornate frame was cracked, the glass broken, and Uncle Jason was half-out of his frame. A bullet had cut the wire.

"It won't seem like home no more without Uncle Jason," said Frijole sadly. "I helped him hang that picture. A feller promised to enlarge the photygraft for two dollars and sell him a frame for ten. The bill was fifteen dollars for the picture and twenty for the frame. Uncle Jason said he hung the damn thing up there, so that every time a peddler came along he could look at it—and shoot the peddler."

"One time, when Uncle Jason came home drunk and lit the lamp, he thought the frame was a winder, and some whiskered *pelicano* lookin' through at him. So he throwed three shots, before the lamp blew out, but he never came within two feet of the picture."

"Uncle Jason," said Henry soberly, "must have had a fine soul."

"Well, maybe he did," replied Frijole doubtfully, "but it never showed."

"I feel," said Judge, "that we should consider the dead man, and why he was shot on our porch. It must have been with malice aforethought."

"And a thirty-thirty," added Frijole. "Look at that hole in the door."

They took the lamp out there again, and searched the

man's pockets. There was not even a cent in money, nothing, except, deep in a pocket they found a crumpled piece of paper on which was crudely penciled:

TONTO CITY—SOUTH OF SCORPION BEND.
STAGE LINE.

There were no marks on the clothes, as far as they could see. Judge examined the wrinkled suit and the heavy shoes.

"Penitentiary clothes, Henry," he said. "I'd bet my soul on that."

"I have never worn them, sir; I wouldn't know," said Henry soberly.

JIMMY SEARS, THE stage driver, admitted that he gave the man a free ride from Scorpion Bend. Said Jimmy, a good-hearted old rawhider:

"He said he didn't have a cent, and he wanted to go to Tonto City. Shucks, it didn't cost me a cent to let him ride. He sat on the seat with me, but he didn't talk any. That is, he didn't say much."

"Did he ask about anybody in particular?" asked Henry.

"No, he didn't, Henry. He said he ain't never been here before."

Russ Haley, the cowboy, whose horse the old man had stolen, laughed heartily over what happened.

"He stopped me in front of the King's Castle Saloon," said Haley, "and asked me where the sheriff's office was. I told him where it was, and I said there wasn't anybody there, 'cause I just came past. Then I told him how to get out to the JHC—and I'm a son-of-a-gun if he didn't steal my bronc to go out there."

Another man came to Henry and said he had seen the man in the King's Castle, listening to the Slim Princess singing, later, he said, he saw the man standing against the wall, watching the crowd.

THE STAGE FROM Scorpion Bend came in about four o'clock; so the man was in Tonto City from that time until about nine o'clock that evening. But no one had seen him in conversation with anyone. Something had happened during those five hours to cause him to need a sheriff's assistance; a need so great that he stole a horse to go after that assistance.

In the sheriff's office Oscar Johnson, the giant Swede jailer, was telling Judge Van Treece, "Ay am yust as good defective as anybody, Yudge. Ay hord," Oscar lowered his voice confidentially, "von of de girls at de King's Castle say to anodder girl, 'Das ha'ar faller come to me and he ask me who is sinking dat song, and Ay say it is de Slim Princess.'"

"In the same dialect, I presume," said Judge soberly. "And just what does that prove, Oscar?"

"Va'al, Hanry vanted to know who talked vit the dead man, Yudge."

"Very good, my dear Oscar. But every man who sees or hears her for the first time would probably ask the same questions. And for your information, the word is detective—not defective—although, in my opinion they work about the same.

"T'ank yu," smiled Oscar. "Ay vill listen some more."

"You better keep away from the girls at the King's Castle," advised Judge. "The next thing we know, you will be using perfume."

"Su-ure," grinned Oscar. "Ay bought bottle dis morning. Yockey Club."

"Better not let Josephine smell it on you."

Josephine, the maid-off-all-work at the Tonto Hotel, was Oscar's light o' love. She was a big, raw-boned person, with a hard jaw, and a punch in either hand.

"Ay am t'rough vit vimmin'," declared Oscar. "Dey are frickle."

Shortly after Oscar left the office Henry came back, sat down at his desk and tried three times to put his feet on the top. Failing in this, he sagged back in the chair and looked soberly at Judge.

"You seem a bit depressed," remarked Judge.

"I am not, sir," declared Henry. "Right now I am in the hands of a scientific detective; so there is no reason for depression."

"You jest, my friend?" inquired Judge, mildly interested.

"Far from it, sirrah. Came this morn to Tonto City, a stranger, whose card indicated that he is W. Ferguson, private detective. I found him at Doc Bogart's place, conferring with John Harper, our eminent prosecutor, as J.W.L. Pelly indicates him in the *Clarion,* and the good doctor. It seems that Mr. Ferguson is interested in our latest casualty. In fact, he is so much interested in that corpse that I have been asked to request that everyone in Tonto City come to see the corpse, and to try and identify same, while Mr. Ferguson, from concealment, mind you, observes their reactions.

"Doctor Bogart will place the deceased on a bier in the center of his main room, and while the curious throng moves in single-file from west to east, Mr. Ferguson will observe from between the portieres in the small archway, leading south. Is that fairly clear in your mind, sir?"

"The arrangement seems simple," nodded Judge. "In fact, everything seems simple, including Mr. Ferguson. Has he told you what his interest may be, and just who the dead man was?"

"He," replied Henry quietly, "is rather reticent."

"Does he," asked Judge, "expect the killer to come and examine the handiwork?"

"He hath an idea," replied Henry soberly. "He told me he had. Well, I must pass the word to the folk of Tonto City. The remains will be on display at two of the clock."

Jim Nelson, owner of the King's Castle, listened to Henry.

"What do you want me to do—close my place for an hour?" he asked sourly. "And why the hell should I order all the girls to go down there and look at a dead man, Sheriff?"

"You see," explained Henry confidentially, "we suspect that this man jilted one of the girls in your honkatonk, and she shot him. Now, if that girl was obliged to look at him—"

"You're crazy!" snorted Nelson. "One of my girls? Would one of my girls steal a horse and—Conroy, I've been told that you have some of the craziest ideas on earth—but this is the worst."

"Thank you, sir. Now if you will ask that they all come there—"

"All right," growled Nelson. "We'll all come, if it will make you feel any better."

"I would greatly appreciate it, Mr. Nelson. If I can solve

this case quickly enough, it might be of some assistance to me in the coming election."

"You'll need plenty," said Jim Nelson coldly. "Henderson will beat you so badly that you'll be ready to leave Wild Horse Valley."

"I am all a-twitter with apprehension," declared Henry soberly.

HOWEVER, JIM NELSON cooperated one hundred percent by closing the King's Castle and insisting that every employee go down to Doctor Bogart's place. The room was not very large, so the line formed out at the gate. It seemed that everybody in Tonto City was present. Henry stood inside the room, leaning against the wall, only a few feet from the casket, while through a slit in the portieres, Ferguson sat, where he could see the faces of everyone who halted to look at the dead man.

Then began the slow shuffle of feet, as cowboy, cattlemen, miners and townsfolk moved slowly past the open casket. The girls from the King's Castle were at the far end of the line. Henry, squint-eyed and thoughtful, watched the expression of their faces.

Suddenly a gunshot broke the quiet of the place. Glass tinkled, the portieres shuddered violently, and a heavy thud sounded. Henry whirled and yanked a portiere aside. The detective was flat on the floor, one hand still clutching the bottom of one portiere. One pane of glass in the window behind him was shattered.

Henry turned and looked at the shocked audience. Doctor Bogart came from another room, and Henry motioned him. Then he said:

"I shall have to excuse you, folks—at least for a while; we've got another one."

Judge tried to shoo them out, like a bunch of chickens, while Henry ran out, managed to get through the fence, and circle the place, but there was no one in sight. He shoved his way through the crowd outside, and joined Judge and the doctor.

"This man is dead, Henry," said the doctor. "My God, this is awful! In my house! Someone shot through the window. Did you see anyone?"

Henry shook his head. "They rarely wait for the law," he said. "Take care of things, Judge; I must look around a bit."

Some of the crowd were still in the yard, but the folks from the King's Castle had all gone back to the saloon. John Harper, the prosecutor, met Henry. Neither of them had anything to say, until Harper remarked:

"I guess you've got a job ahead of you, Henry."

"You mean—finding the murderers, John?"

"Henry, if you don't—you're sunk; you will have to leave them for Ed Henderson to solve."

"And then," replied Henry quietly, "*he* will be sunk."

"No doubt—but he will be the sheriff, Henry. He has said that when he is elected he will guarantee that crime will cease in Wild Horse Valley."

"Which, in my estimation, John, is the talk of a half-wit."

"True enough," agreed the lawyer, "but the masses love it."

"Perhaps. But John, I should hate to see crime abolished in Wild Horse Valley—and so would you. It's part of the place. And who wants to live in a milk and honey Utopia?

It doesn't fit, John. It would be like a cowboy wearing a silk topper."

The lawyer laughed. "Maybe you're right, Henry; but don't voice it to anyone else. They're all talking of a crime-less county, with Honest Ed Henderson for sheriff. They know better—but it sounds good."

Henry went back to the office, where this time he succeeded in getting his two feet up on the desk-top. Judge came in, tilted his accustomed chair against the wall and hooked his heels over the lower rung. Henry opened his eyes, looked at Judge, and closed them again.

"Of all the damn things to happen—now!" grunted Judge.

"What was that?" asked Henry.

"Why, that murder at Doc Bogart's—what else would I be speaking about?"

"Oh, I thought something new had happened, Judge."

"New? My God, Henry, that happened less than an hour ago. They are already criticizing you, although they do not know what that stranger was doing behind the curtain. They think it was your idea."

"It seems," said Henry quietly, "that this Mr. Ferguson followed the stranger here, possibly seeking someone else, whom the man might contact. The stranger died, and the one he wanted to find—didn't want to be found. As Oscar would say, he's a tough yigger."

"Two murders," sighed Judge. "And election in the offing."

"And," added Henry, "at odds of twenty to one. Why struggle, Judge? Even allowing for J.W.L. Pelly's malice and imagination, at two votes to our one, we are vanquished."

"You mean that you are not going to—er—make an effort?"

"Judge," replied Henry soberly, "when I came into the office the gamblers of Tonto were offering juicy odds that I would never be able to put my two feet on my own desktop. Did those odds deter me? They did not, sir. In spite of the odds, and in spite of my own—er—rotundity, I made it. Damme, Judge, I haven't even begun to fight!"

"When and how will you make this fight, as you term it, sir?"

"I have no tongue for oratory, Judge. My actions will speak for themselves. Is there any more of Frijole's distillation in the back room?"

"Enough," replied Judge, "to addle the brains and atrophy the muscles of an army."

"Good!" said Henry. "That will make a small drink for each of us."

JAMES WADSWORTH LONGFELLOW Pelly, editor and owner of the Scorpion Bend *Clarion*, came to Tonto City. Word of the first murder had reached him, and he came to Tonto immediately. He was not an impressive figure, being rather scrawny, near-sighted, and with a high-pitched voice, which usually broke badly under strain of excitement. Pelly thoroughly believed in himself as a crusader, and never lost an opportunity to wield a vitriolic pen against the regime of Henry Harrison Conroy. It was Pelly who coined the expression, "The Shame of Arizona," when speaking of Henry, Judge and Oscar.

Pelly found Jim Nelson and Ed Henderson in the King's Castle, and from them he learned about the latest killing. Nelson told him about Henry's orders to have all the employees of the saloon try to identify the corpse, and that someone shot through a rear window and killed another stranger, who was seated behind the drapes. No one had told Nelson who the stranger was, nor why he was there.

"Very puzzling," agreed Pelly. "Great story, of course, but puzzling."

"I'll buy a drink," offered Henderson, who had already drunk too much.

"I never drink," said Pelly. "Thank you just the same. I must try and get more information."

PELLY DIDN'T WANT to go down to the sheriff's office. He was just a bit afraid of Oscar Johnson, who always wanted to shake hands, and Pelly had never been able to use that hand for hours afterward. Pelly left the saloon and crossed the street, where he stood in front of the general store, trying to make up his mind, only to suddenly find himself surrounded with Oscar Johnson, Slim Pickins and Frijole Bill Cullison.

"Ay am delighted you are ha'ar," declared Oscar. "Shake."

James Wadsworth Longfellow Pelly put his hands behind him and tried to back against the wall, only to find that Slim was directly behind him. These three had fine teamwork.

"No use a-bein' onfriendly," said Frijole.

"Keep your hands off me," gritted Pelly impotently.

Jim Nelson and Ed Henderson saw this tableau from the King's Castle, and decided that one of their biggest political assets was in trouble. So they went over there. Oscar, Slim and Frijole saw them coming.

"Now ain't that a shame?" said Slim quietly. "A maiden in distress, and here comes a couple knights."

"Las' night and night before," said Frijole. Pelly didn't see them, until they stepped up on the sidewalk, and Nelson said:

"Need a little help, Pelly?"

"Yes, I—I do."

Oscar Johnson was not one to stand on the ceremony. Without any preliminary motions he hit Jim Nelson on the jaw. Nelson was a big man, solid built, and reputed a fighter, but the Swede had the kick of a work mule in either hand, and that blow knocked Nelson, not only off his feet, but off the two-foot-high sidewalk.

As quick as a cat Frijole dropped behind Ed Henderson, and a quick push by Slim Pickins sent Henderson upside down to join Nelson, who was still enjoying a constellation of some sort. Then Oscar took hold of Pelly's sleeve and said quietly:

"If you vant to see Hanry, we vill take you to him."

Pelly didn't say anything. His legs started functioning, and he went with them, while a crowd gathered around Nelson and Henderson.

Henry and Judge had just finished their second drink, and were in a very expansive mood. They looked in amazement at James Wadsworth Longfellow Pelly and his companions. Pelly blurted:

"I resent this, I tell you! I am a citizen of this country, and I am entitled to protection. The actions of these men are reprehensible!"

"Have they injured you mentally or physically?" asked Judge.

"They forced me here, I tell you! They—"

"Who forced yuh?" interrupted Slim, assuming an injured air.

"Well, damn it, I was afraid that if I didn't come—"

"Purely a mental case," said Henry soberly.

"I demand my rights!" shrilled Pelly.

"Well, we haven't got them," declared Slim.

"This situation," declared Judge, "is getting inane. Invite Mr. Pelly to have a drink, will you, Slim? I'm not speaking to him myself."

"I don't want any drink!" snapped Polly. "My friends come to assist me, and are beaten and slugged. A fine state of affairs, I must say."

"Your friends?" queried Henry.

"Mr. Nelson and Mr. Henderson," said Pelly hotly.

"Beaten and slugged?"

"Good heavens, what happened?" asked Judge quickly.

"Aw, it wasn't anythiu'," said Frijole. "Jim Nelson had a run-in with Oscar, and got his jaw cracked. Then Ed Henderson fell over me and landed in the street. They prob'ly ain't hurt much—I'm sorry to say."

"Oscar, why did you hit Jim Nelson?" asked Henry severely. Oscar grinned slowly.

"Va'al, he asked for it, Hanry," he replied.

HENRY NODDED, APPARENTLY satisfied with the reply.

"My God, Henry, do you condone such actions?" remarked Judge.

"I believe in service," replied Henry soberly. "Why, I believe it is mentioned in the Bible—ask and thou shalt receive. Possibly Mr. Nelson doesn't read his Bible."

Judge walked to the doorway and looked up the street. There were several men in front of the King's Castle, and the usual number on the street, but Nelson and Henderson were not in sight. Tommy Roper, a stuttering cowboy, who managed the livery stable, came up to the doorway, grinning.

"I sus-sus-sus—" he began.

"You saw it," finished Judge soberly. "Who was to blame, Tommy?"

"That bub-big Swede can huh-huh-huh—"

"Yes, he can hit," said Judge.

TOMMY WALKED AWAY, still grinning and unperturbed. He was used to having folks finish his sentences for him. John Harper, prosecutor, came from the King's Castle. If John had any sense of humor, it rarely came to the surface. He came into the office and looked at the assemblage.

"I did not see it," he stated, "but the folks over at the saloon say that Oscar made an unprovoked attack on Jim Nelson. And that what happened to Ed Henderson was also unprovoked and very embarrassing to their candidate."

"John, just what am I supposed to do about it?" queried Henry.

"You might appoint another jailer, Henry."

"Listen, John," said Henry quickly, "I am not toadying to the King's Castle. Oscar Johnson is still my choice as a jailer. You may carry that statement back to Jim Nelson, and in a little personal message from me, you can tell him to go to hell."

The lawyer flushed quickly. "I am not a messenger boy, Henry," he said.

"You came here as one, John. You brought a message from Jim Nelson."

"Did I? Yes, perhaps I did. Sorry. But if you have anything to tell Jim Nelson, you can tell it to him personally."

"Thank you, John; I shall."

The lawyer walked out and James Wadsworth Longfellow Pelly said:

"What about me?"

"We have wondered that same thing lots of times," said Judge.

"I've got a fresh jug out in the car, Henry," said Frijole. "It seems that this is the proper time to have a little drink."

"Mr. Pelly," said Henry, "you came here for information, I believe."

"I was forced to come here," declared Pelly warmly.

Oscar leaned over and looked into Pelly's face.

"You vars—what?" he asked.

Pelly blinked and drew back. "I—I could use some information," he said weakly.

"Pour some drinks, Judge," said Henry, "while I enlighten Mr. Pelly. You have cups for six, I believe."

"None for me,", said Pelly quickly. "I—I rarely drink."

"Only *six* drinks, Judge," said Henry. "Now, Mr. Pelly, just what do you wish to know?"

"Everything," replied Pelly, "and I don't drink."

"You want to know *everything*—and you do not drink," mused Henry.

"I mean I want to know all about those two murders," corrected Pelly.

"That is very simple," smiled Henry, "but, my dear man, you surely will be willing to wait until I know something about them myself. One man was shot on the porch of my ranch house. One was shot behind the curtains in Doctor

Bogart's home. Why and by whom, we do not know. The last death was a Mr. Ferguson, private detective. Where he came from and why he came here we do not know. The identity of the first murdered man is still a mystery."

"Do you expect me to believe all that?" asked Pelly.

"Here's yore drink, Pelly," said Slim, handing the tin cupful of Frijole's concoction to the newspaper editor.

"But I do not want it," insisted Pelly. "I told you—"

"Ay don't like to be snoo-tee," said Oscar, "but Ay t'ink you vill like it."

James Wadsworth Longfellow Pelly drank it. He shut his eyes, tilted the cup, and did not draw a breath, until the cup was empty. Then he almost didn't. He leaned on Henry's desk, wheezing, his eyes pouring tears down his lean cheeks, while Slim Pickins pounded him on the back. But he recovered, blinking through his tears, as he tried with unsteady hands to adjust his necktie. Finally he took a deep breath and turned to Henry.

"As you were saying," he remarked in a husky whisper, and then began to grin foolishly. The depth-bomb had busted.

DOCTOR BOGART WAS a very busy man, what with two corpses and his regular round of visits. With only one man identified, and no clue as to where either came from, it looks as though Wild Horse Valley would have to bury them both. There wasn't much money in that for Doctor Bogart.

He had just put on his coat, preparatory to going up to talk with Henry about the inquests, when there was a quiet knock on the back door. It was the entertainer from the King's Castle, known as the Slim Princess. She *was* slim, olive-skinned, dark·haired, and very pretty. Doctor Bogart had only seen her at a distance.

"This may seem like a queer request, Doctor," she said quietly, "but I should like to see the dead man."

"My dear lady, we have two," said the doctor.

"I—I mean the first one, Doctor," she said quickly.

"Why, yes, you may see him. Step this way, please."

He led her to the back room, where she looked fearfully at the two white-draped boxes, and did not come forward until he had uncovered one of them. Then she came timidly forward, her eyes wide. Suddenly she stopped, swaying forward, and it seemed to Doctor Bogart that there was an expression of horror in her eyes and on her face. She stepped back and stood there, lips tightly shut.

"Do you know him?" asked the doctor quietly.

"Know him?" she looked up quickly. "No, I—I—don't, Doctor. I thought—" she shook her head. "I thought I might," she finished, and turned back to the other room. Doctor Bogart followed her to the back door, where she stopped and opened her purse.

"Would the county have to bury him—them?" she asked.

"Unless some friend or relative could be located, Miss."

She handed him a roll of bills and turned away quickly.

"That might help a little," she said, and went across the yard.

Doctor Bogart was frankly puzzled. Why would this girl come down there alone, look at one of the dead men and then give him two hundred dollars to help pay funeral expenses? He put on his hat, pocketed the money and decided to talk it over with Henry Conroy.

Things had become very rosy at the sheriff's office. James Wadsworth Longfellow Pelly wanted to sing.

"I c'n do it, too," he declared owlishly. "I used to b'long to a quar't."

"A what?" asked Slim.

"A quar't," explained Pelly. "Four shingers. I wash the ten'r."

"What did you wash him with—soap?" asked Henry.

"I needa drink."

"My lad," said Judge patronizingly, "do not forget that you are the owner and editor of the *Clarion*."

James Wadsworth Longfellow Pelly cuffed his hat over one eye and leered at Judge.

"I am," he declared, "the mas'r of my own shoul, the cap'n of my own fate. I run 'er, or leave 'er alone. I wanna shing."

Henry took Slim aside and whispered that it would be a very bright idea to take Mr. Pelly out to the ranch and sober him up a little. Slim, nearly as cock-eyed as Pelly, agreed heartily.

So Slim explained that Pelly should be their honored guest at the JHC, where they had plenty more of that same brand of liquor. Pelly accepted the idea, cried over their hospitality, and was willing to ride Slim's horse, while Slim rode behind him. The horse had never borne a double burden, but nobody cared about that. Ed Henderson saw what was going on down at the office; so he came down there, possibly thinking that Pelly was being misused.

Pelly was already in the saddle, and Slim was about to mount behind him when Henderson arrived. Henderson stepped in beside the horse and said to Pelly:

"What in the devil is the matter with you, Pelly?"

Slowly the editor of the *Clarion* turned his head and looked down at the man he had dubbed "Honest Ed." He chuckled foolishly and pointed a bony forefinger at Henderson, as he said quickly:

"Now wouldn't you like to know?"

And almost at that same moment Slim Pickins leaped off the sidewalk, grasped the cantle of the saddle with his right hand and tried to make a fancy mount behind the saddle. He hit the animal's rump with one knee, and did a sort of swan dive over the rump and into the street.

NO HORSE WOULD stand for such actions behind its back, much less a half-broke animal such as Slim rode. With a snort of fright, it bogged down its head, reins flying, and headed down the street, pitching wickedly, while James Wadsworth Longfellow Pelly clung with both hands to the horn. There could be only one finale, although Pelly made a famous ride. Nearly against the big watering trough in front of the livery stable, the horse sun-fished to the left, and James Wadsworth Longfellow Pelly, describing a nearly perfect arc, went full length into the two feet of water.

Tommy Roper ran from the stable and pulled him over the edge, while the horse kept right on bucking, as it headed for the JHC. Doctor Bogart joined them in front of the office, wondering what it was all about. It was evident that Pelly was not badly injured, because he was on his feet, apparently arguing with Tommy Roper.

"It's a wonder the damn fool wasn't killed," said Henderson.

"We can't have everything," said Henry soberly, although

there were tears in his eyes. Henderson grunted and headed for the stable.

Doctor Bogart touched Henry on the arm, and indicated that they walk up the street.

"I don't know what this means, Henry," explained the doctor, "but perhaps you can figure some angle to it." And then he told Henry what had happened at his home.

"Do you think she knew the old man?" asked Henry.

"I do, Henry," declared the doctor. "Her actions indicated that she knew him. She didn't care to see the other body."

"And she gave you two hundred dollars. Hm-m-m-m. And she came and left by the back door, which would indicate that she didn't want anyone to see her."

"A very, very pretty woman, Henry," said the doctor.

"And rather hard around the edges, I might add," said Henry. "Still, she would be—the life she leads. And Jim Nelson watching her like a hawk. Doc, I feel that you have really dug up something for me. Did she ask you to keep this a secret?"

"No, she didn't, Henry."

"I see. Well, we will keep her secret—as long as possible, Doc. Thank you for telling me."

Ed Henderson had taken James Wadsworth Longfellow Pelly over to the King's Castle, fearing that he might have gone over to the enemy. Jim Nelson was mad. His prestige had been marred by a big, ignorant Swede, and he was ready to curse anyone, just to relieve his own feelings. He looked at Pelly, still wet and only partly sobered by his ride and dive.

"Well, you let Conroy and his gang make a first-class fool out of you," he said angrily.

"That," declared Pelly, "is none of your business. You didn't look so good, out there in the street a while ago yourself—nor did Henderson. Honest Ed—on the back of his neck in the dust. And you jump onto me! Take care of your own morals—I'll look after mine."

"Take it easy," said Al Horne, one of Nelson's gamblers, as he tried to make Pelly presentable, with the aid of a towel. "Jim didn't mean anything, Pelly. He has your interests at heart."

"That's right, Pelly," said Henderson. "We're all friends of yours."

"There's one thing I like about Conroy and his gang," said Pelly. "They don't like me, and they don't try to make me feel differently. At least they're honest. I've fought them ever since they were elected, and they've never tried to win me over to their side. Damned if I don't believe they like to fight me."

"Well, you won't have to fight them much longer," assured Henderson.

Al Horne gave Pelly a drink of liquor and he downed it at a gulp. The strong whiskey brought color back into his face. There were a lot of people standing around, watching them minister to the needs of Pelly, and listening to what was said. Someone said something about a new regime bringing peace and safety to Wild Horse Valley.

"That's a lot of bull, and you know it," said Pelly. "It sounds good in print. I've been thinking about it—lately. My fight against Conroy has made my paper popular. I realize that Conroy told me a little while ago that when he is defeated I won't have anything to write about; so I might as well come down and live with him at the JHC, and we'll both go to seed."

Jim Nelson shoved through the crowd to Pelly. "So that's the way you feel about it, eh?" he snarled. "Going to throw us down at the last moment, eh? How much is Conroy paying you to double-cross us?"

"Conroy," said Pelly firmly, "said that if I ever said anything good about him he'd come down and break my damned neck. I don't believe I like either of you. At least, I'm free and can do as I please. I'm not for sale, Mr. Nelson, and I'm too big a coward to be scared into anything."

"Have another drink and forget all this foolishness," said Al Horne.

"I'll have the drink—and pay for it," said Pelly. "And I've always prided myself on a first-class memory."

JIM NELSON AND Ed Henderson went to Scorpion Bend next day. Henry was of the opinion that they went to make peace with James Wadsworth Longfellow Pelly, and to do a little promoting for Ed Henderson.

Henry wanted a chance to talk with the Slim Princess.

He knew that her dressing room and living quarters were upstairs over the honkatonk in the King's Castle. The rest of the girls lived up there, too, and all used a rear stairway from the stage to reach their dressing room. Henry wanted this interview to be private, but just how to accomplish this he did not know. There was a main stairway leading up from the gambling parlor, but this was in full view of the public. Henry had never been too popular with Nelson, who seemed to resent even having the law come there for innocent pastime.

But Henry was resourceful. He had a private talk with Oscar Johnson that evening, and the big Swede, known as the "Vitrified Viking," was more than willing.

"Maybe it vill vork into somet'ing, Hanry," he said, grinning widely.

"Don't go too far," advised Henry.

"Ay vill yust go far enough," assured Oscar.

That evening, when things were beginning to warm up in the King's Castle, Henry sauntered into the saloon and made his way slowly back to the gambling room. Not over six people were in there, including Al Horne, who usually operated the roulette wheel. Henry stopped near the foot of the stairs, casually watching the play at the roulette.

Suddenly from the bar came the loud voice of Oscar Johnson:

"Ay can vip any damn man in de house, ay ta'al you that!"

"Oh-oh!" grunted one of the players. "The Swede's on the war-path again!"

"Ay vipped Yim Nelson, and Ay can vip him again!"

Al Horne stopped the wheel and headed for the arch-way, followed by the players. A few moments later Henry was up the stairs and safely in one of the halls, where the light was dim. There seemed to be an uproar from the barroom, but that was to be expected, where Oscar was concerned.

Not knowing the layout up there Henry was unable to determine just which rooms the Slim Princess occupied; so he took a chance and moved back to the stairway, leading to the stage. From there he could hear her singing one of her encores, and in a few moments she came up the stairway, with a swish of silken skirts.

He stepped out to meet her, and she stopped short, her face only a white blur in the dim light, For several moments they faced each other. Then she said, "What are you doing up here? Don't you know—"

"Yes, my dear, I know that Jim Nelson never allows men up here. But I am up here, and what I want is a private matter, which we may only discuss together. In a few moments there will be a chorus of girls up the stairs."

"Then you better get out of here," she said coldly. Henry laughed.

"After all, my dear," he said gently, "I am the law. Your beauty and grace do not appeal to me at all, and I am old enough to be your father. Please be sensible for the moment and take me into your room, where we may talk things over."

Only a dozen steps down the hallway she unlocked the door, and Henry followed her in. It was the living-room of their apartment. The Slim Princess sank down in a chair. There was no light in the room, except from a curtained window. The girl said quietly:

"What did you want to know, Mr. Conroy?"

"Did Nelson know that you gave two hundred dollars to Doctor Bogart?"

"No, no," she said quickly. "I—I don't know why—"

"What was your father's name?" asked Henry. It was a shot in the dark.

The girl jerked forward, staring at Henry.

"You knew?" she asked huskily.

Henry drew a deep breath and settled back in his chair.

"You see," he explained, trying to appear casual, "the other man was a detective named Ferguson. He told me part of the story. I'd like to have your part, my dear. But first your father's name."

"His name was Jack Winters," she said, "but I don't know any of the story. I don't know why he came here. I haven't heard from him for over ten years. Mr. Conroy, I thought he was dead."

"A strange story," said Henry quietly. "Did Jim Nelson know your father?"

"No. Oh, we must hurry. I have to be back there in a few minutes."

"One more question, if you do not mind," said Henry. "Were you among the girls who came down to Doctor Bogart's place to view the corpse?"

"No," she said quietly. "Jim said I didn't need to go."

"I see. You didn't happen to know Ferguson, the detective?"

"No, I did not, Mr. Conroy. I didn't even know what his name was, nor that he was a detective."

"I guess that is all and thank you very much, my dear. Perhaps you had better wait until I get downstairs. I shall hurry."

Henry closed the door quietly and went down the hallway to the railing near the stairway above the gambling room. None of the games were operating. It was a chance for him to gain the lower door, without being seen. But as he stepped over to the top of the stairs he saw Al Horne, the gambler, standing in the shadow near the top of the stairway, leaning against the wall.

"Looking for somebody?" he asked coldly.

"Not now, sir," replied Henry, and walked down into the gambling room.

Al Horne followed him down, but had nothing further to say. Henry went into the barroom. There were quite a number of men in there, and one of the swampers was sweeping up broken glass from behind the bar. John Harper, the prosecutor, was at the bar, and he followed Henry to the street.

"What happened, John?" asked Henry.

"That big Swede again, Henry. He came into the barroom and announced that he could whip any man in town, including Jim Nelson, I believe. Buck Faber and Dave North, the two bouncers, decided to throw him out."

"Did they?" asked Henry.

"I don't think so," replied Harper. "I didn't see it all. I saw Oscar throw Buck Faber halfway across the street, and then he went back. They say he threw North across the bar and smashed a hundred pieces of glassware. They had to take North down to have Doctor Bogart sew up some of his wounds. Henry, you'll have to get rid of that man; he is a menace to society."

"Buck Faber and Dave North are not society, John," said Henry.

"No, I—I guess that's right, too."

"Ergo, we keep Oscar, John. Really, he is a jewel. A bit rough, of course, but who would expect a jailer in Wild Horse Valley to be polished? I love every bone in his hard head."

"Well," sighed the lawyer, "I suppose it is up to you, Henry."

"Thank you, John."

He found Judge and Oscar in the office. As far as he could see Oscar had suffered no bodily harm.

"Of all the damnable things, Henry!" said Judge.

"Did Ay do oll right?" grinned Oscar.

"You did," stated Henry. "Possibly you overdid it a trifle, but that was to be expected."

"Just a moment!" exclaimed Judge. "Did you—er—have a part in this, Henry?"

"Oscar," replied Henry, "was working under my directions, Judge."

"Have you both gone crazy?" asked Judge.

"It vars a gu'ud fight, Hanry," declared Oscar. "Das North vill have seven year of hord luck. He broke de backbar mirror vit the seat of his pants."

"Henry," groaned Judge, "will you explain what this is all about?"

"Oscar," said Henry calmly, "merely started trouble to cover my actions."

"Ay am damn gu'ud yailer, eh?" grinned Oscar.

"The best in Tonto City," agreed Henry. "It worked rather well, I thought. Judge, if there is any more of Frijole's pain-killer on hand—I believe I could use about the full of a mule's ear."

"Am I to be kept in ignorance?" asked Judge peevishly.

"At present, you will remain normal, Judge. Suffice to say that Oscar's actions were at my suggestion, and meet with my approval. Of course, he wasn't instructed to wreck the saloon and hospitalize any of the inhabitants, but that, I suppose, was a normal conclusion. The jug, Judge."

JIM NELSON AND Ed Henderson got back from Scorpion Bend in time for the double inquest, and none too happy over James Wadsworth Longfellow Pelly's editorial in the *Clarion*. Judge read it, snorted a few times and called Henry.

"Listen to this," he said. "Mr. Pelly writes, 'No one can honestly say that Henry Harrison Conroy had not given us an efficient, although humorous and not too sober a regime. Crime and criminals do not dismay him. He laughs. In other words, Wild Horse Valley is the stage, on which a master comedian has held the spotlight for several years. What now'?"

Henry chuckled and shook his head. "J.W.L. Pelly is slipping," he said.

"And there is more," said Judge. "Listen to this: 'Honest Ed Henderson is an unknown quantity. This paper will not go on record as saying that Henderson will be a great sheriff. We will not even predict that he will be any better than the present incumbent. The worst we can say now about Henry Harrison Conroy is that he laughs at the world, drinks his whiskey raw, and has never done or said a word to influence the opinion of this paper. May the best man win.'"

"Nothing about the Shame of Arizona?" asked Henry.

"Not a word. James Wadsworth Longfellow Pelly has reformed."

"I hope not, Judge. Evidently he has fallen out with the other faction, and—How do you do, Mr. Nelson."

Henry turned his head and saw Jim Nelson standing in the office doorway. Nelson scowled. Evidently he had heard Henry's comment.

"I want to talk with you about that damned Swede, Conroy," said Nelson. "I've stood about all I'm going to from him."

"Have you mentioned the matter to Oscar?" queried Henry blandly.

"He is employed by you," snarled Nelson. "I'm not going to have my place wrecked by that ignorant bum."

"Bum?" queried Henry. "Oscar will not like that appellation, Mr. Nelson."

"I don't care what he likes! The next time he starts trouble for me, he'll get filled with lead. The boys have their instructions. I've warned you, Conroy, and I never warn twice. Good day, sir!"

"My gracious!" exclaimed Henry as Nelson went back across the street.

"If I were you, I'd fire Oscar," said Judge.

"Fire him? Why, Judge!"

"Do you want him filled with lead?"

"Hm-m-m-m, no, I wouldn't like that. I'll tell Oscar what sort of a reception to expect."

"I don't know," sighed Judge. "Sometimes I wonder which of you has the fewer brains."

"Had you average intelligence, Judge, you could look at us and determine that."

"Oscar, I presume, sir."

"Wrong again. Well, I presume we must prepare for the inquest. Doctor Bogart said it would be at two of the clock, and it is nearly that time."

THE INQUEST BROUGHT out no startling evidence, nor was any expected. Henry told them what he knew about the murder of the old man on the porch of the JHC ranch house. The stage driver testified that he brought the man to Tonto City from Scorpion Bend, while Russ Haley, the cowboy, testified that he had directed the man to the JHC, after which the man stole his horse.

Doctor Bogart and John Harper testified that the detective, named Ferguson, after swearing them to secrecy, asked them to help him view the folks of Tonto City, as they came to try and identify the corpse. They did not know where he was from, nor who he was looking for. Henry had asked Doctor Bogart to not mention the money given him by the Slim Princess.

Henry wanted another talk with the Slim Princess, but he knew that his chances were almost nil. He went to the King's Castle that night, but she was not on the program. The crowd was disappointed, but Jim Nelson made no explanation. During an intermission Henry drew "Doc," the piano player aside and questioned him. Doc was reputed a marijuana addict, but a good honkatonk piano player.

"Hell, I dunno what happened," said Doc, "One of the girls told me that her and Nelson had a hell of a fight about somethin', and he locked the door, when he came out. He's been grouchin' around all evenin'. He's crazy, if yuh ask me; she's the only trouper he's got, even if she ain't no Nellie Melba on the pipes."

"Do you know what her right name is, Doc?" asked Henry.

"You, too, eh?" grinned Doc. "No, I dunno any other name for her, unless yuh want to call her Mrs. Nelson, which I doubt like hell."

Henry doubted it, too, but he didn't say so. After a while he went back to the office. The house was dark, but Judge met him outside the door.

"What is going on around here, Henry?" asked Judge severely.

"I just came, sir," replied Henry soberly. "Suppose *you* tell me."

"The Slim Princess is in the office," whispered Judge. "She came a moment ago and insisted on going in and waiting for you. She didn't want any lights. As a matter of fact, I was going to look for you."

"My goodness!" exclaimed Henry quietly.

"You might find a less prominent place to hold a tryst," suggested Judge.

"Possibly, Judge, I had nothing to do with it. Will you come in with me?"

"I, sir," replied Judge, "am no damn cupid. Do not drag me into it."

"Very well, sir—stay out."

Henry walked into the dark room, closed the door and lighted the lamp on his desk. The Slim Princess was seated against the wall, one of her beautiful eyes well blacked. It was the first time Henry had ever seen her, except in her stage finery, and she looked like a very weary young lady. Even the rouge and mascara was missing.

"I suppose you are surprised to see me here," she said.

"Life is ever a surprise to me, my dear lady," he replied. "I suppose that Mr. Nelson would also be surprised. Your eye looks very bad."

"It should," she replied coldly. "He hit me. Then he locked me in the room, and I climbed out on a blanket, dropped a few feet and almost broke a leg."

"My goodness! You have had troubles. What happened?"

"He found out about the two hundred dollars I gave the

doctor. It was his money. I had to tell him. Then he accused me of entertaining you in my room, and I had to tell him what our conversation was about."

"I suppose Al Horne told him," said Henry. "After I left your room I met him at the head of the stairs. Is he your keeper?"

"Possibly," she said slowly.

"You are not married to Jim Nelson?" queried Henry.

She looked up quickly. "All right, we're not married," she said.

"Did Jim Nelson kill your father?"

"No!" she said quickly. "Jim wasn't away from the King's Castle that night. Why should he kill my father?"

"I'm sure, I do not know, my dear—I merely wondered. Tell me something about yourself."

"There isn't much that I'd care to tell," she said. "I believe I was born near New York. My mother died while I was still young. I never did know what my father did for a living. When I was twelve years of age, I was sent to a private school in New Orleans, I was eighteen, when I learned that there was no money for further schooling. I didn't know where to find my father.

"Then I met Jim Nelson. I suppose it was the same old story. It would fit most of the girls over in the honkatonk. Jim taught me to deal faro. I had studied music a little. We knocked around over the country, until Jim heard about this place being for sale. That's about all, Mr. Conroy."

"And after all those years you recognized your father?"

"Yes," she said quietly. "They say that death wipes away the years."

"Why did you even think that it might be your father?" asked Henry.

"I saw him that night at the show, Mr. Conroy. It was only a flash, but something told me that I knew that man. Then I heard he was killed, and I—I wanted to be sure. It was my father—older and more gray. His hands were gnarled and hard, as though he had worked hard."

"He wasn't that way the last time you knew him?" asked Henry.

"No, he wasn't. Dad dressed well, and he had wonderful hands."

"How on earth will you ever get back to your rooms?" asked Henry.

"I'm not going back," she said firmly. "I'm through. I told him over a year ago that if he ever struck me again, I'd leave him. I'm leaving."

"But, my dear, where are you going?"

"To Scorpion Bend. I've got money—my money. I won't go back to Jim Nelson. I'll hire a livery-rig and go alone. If I can ever get to a railroad, he'll never find me."

"Did you ever drive a horse?" he asked curiously.

"Never in my life—but I'd take that chance."

"Hm-m-m-m." Henry squinted thoughtfully. Finally he made up his mind. He took a sheet of paper and pencil, wrote a note and left it on the desk. He took a six-shooter from a desk drawer, put it in his coat pocket and got to his feet.

"What are you going to do?" she asked anxiously.

"We are going to Scorpion Bend, my dear lady," he said. "I shall get a horse and buggy, and drive you there myself."

"Do you really mean—you'll take me to Scorpion Bend?"

"Certainly. It is a small matter for a man like me. Come."

They went outside. No one was in sight. Henry told her to wait in the darkness, until he could secure the vehicle. Judge Van Treece, hunched in the darkness of an alley just above the office, watched Henry drive from the stable, pick her up near the office, and then go on toward Scorpion Bend.

"And just when the *Clarion* was in our favor!" groaned Judge. "Only three weeks before election—and he runs away with another man's wife. And I thought that Oscar was the brainless one."

JUDGE WENT INTO the office and lighted the lamp. There was a faint odor of perfume in there, and Judge snorted disgustedly. Suddenly the door was banged open and in came Jim Nelson and Al Horne. Nelson glared at Judge, and looked around the office.

"Where's Conroy?" he asked harshly.

"My dear man," replied Judge, "I have no idea where he is. I presume he is around town."

Jim Nelson sniffed audibly. "Around town, eh? What's this?"

He leaned over and read the penciled note which Henry had left for Judge. It read:

HAVE GONE TO SCORPION BEND ON BUSINESS.

"He's gone to Scorpion Bend, Al," said Nelson. He whirled on Judge who came over to see the note.

"How long since you saw him, Van Treece?" he demanded.

"I do not like your attitude, sir," declared Judge stiffly. "After all, you haven't any right to talk—"

"Oh, go to hell!" snapped Nelson. "Come on, Al; we'll find out at the livery stable."

They slammed the door and headed across the street. Judge didn't know what to do. Evidently they had found out that the Slim Princess was gone, and in some way they knew she had gone with Henry. As he started out of the office, he almost ran into Slim Pickins and Frijole Bill. Frijole had a gallon demijohn in his hand.

"We kinda thought yuh might be runnin' low," said Frijole.

Jim Nelson came from the livery stable doorway, calling back to Horne, "Pick me up at the saloon, Al—and make it fast."

Judge said, "Frijole, did you two come in the buckboard?"

"Shore did, Judge," answered Slim, before Frijole could reply.

"Come with me," ordered Judge. "Henry ran away with the Slim Princess tonight, and Jim Nelson is going to try and catch them. We've got to get out of here ahead of Nelson, or Henry might get hurt."

"My Gawd!" blurted Slim. "Henry Harrison Conroy!"

"Do your marveling on the road!" snapped Judge. "Hurry! Bring that jug along, Frijole—we may need it."

And as Al Horne drove a horse and buggy out of the wide doorway of the livery stable, the JHC buckboard team lurched away from the hitch-rack in front of the general store, and went out of town at a swift gallop.

"You'll kill this team at that pace!" said Judge anxiously.

"Maybe," replied Slim, "but all we've got to do is beat 'em to the Lobo Grade, Judge; they can't pass us after that."

"Speaking of passing," said Judge, "where is that jug, Frijole?"

"Right here on m' lap, Judge. But we better wait for a smooth stretch."

"Yo're right!" yelled Slim. "I spilled some on my red necktie at the ranch, and turned the danged thing to a pea-green. But I can't git over Henry runnin' away with the Slim Princess, Judge."

"She's another man's wife!" exclaimed Judge. "You can't get away from that, Slim."

"I wouldn't want to," replied Slim. "How the hell did he ever git a chance to court her?"

"Must have been love at first sight," said Frijole. "And if you don't pay more attention to drivin' and less to love, we'll all be in the ditch. Don't forget that we've got four wheels on this here hack."

"I'm too sober, I reckon," said Slim. "When we hit the mesa we'll all have a snifter. Well, well! Ol' Henry fell in love! Viva la Hank!"

"And election only a short time away," said Judge. "We're sunk."

"What was it Henry used to say, 'Live, laugh and love, 'cause there'll come a time when yuh can't?' I reckon the old boy met his Waterloo."

"We might be able to save him, Slim," said Judge.

"Gawd, I'd shore resent that idea, if I was with her," said Slim.

"But he can't love her," said Judge. "It must be a passing fancy."

"Can't, huh?" queried Frijole. "Well, if he can't love her—what about her lovin' him? Is her eyesight all right, Judge?"

"I have never tested them, Frijole."

"I've looked into 'em—from a distance, and they shore looked all right to me," said Slim. "If I thought she'd fall in love with a feller like Henry—I'd shore got closer to her. Yuh never can tell what might have happened. But that's me—allus a shrinkin' vi'let."

At the top of the mesa, Slim drew the team to a stop, while they uncorked the jug and had a big drink.

"That team is pretty tired, Slim," remarked Judge, after he recovered his breath. "Better take it easy."

"Tie down the cork, Frijole," ordered Slim, " 'cause we're goin' to kick the tails off them two broncs, until we hit the grades. After that, we'll let Jim Nelson do the frettin'. Hang onto yore hat, Judge."

JIM NELSON AND Al Horne tried once to pass them, but that buckboard team put on extra speed, and almost buried them in a cloud of dust. Nelson didn't know that this was the JHC buckboard, and that they had had their last chance to pass it until the end of the Lobo Grades.

Those narrow, dangerous grades far above Lobo Canyon had places where two vehicles might pass, but not unless the team in front permitted—and this the JHC buckboard would not permit. In fact, the buckboard made a number of stops, while the three men lowered the liquid content of that jug, and the two men in the buggy had to wait.

"I ain't never been cussed so hard before in m' life," declared Slim. "Every time we stop it gits worse."

Their final stop was not over two hundred yards from the end of the grade, and it seemed that Jim Nelson could not contain himself any longer. The moonlight was bright, but the dust from the buckboard had never given Nelson and Horne a clear view of who was head of them. But now he got out of his buggy and came up to the buckboard.

"This is insufferable!" he snapped. "You've deliberately kept us back all the way. You wouldn't let us pass, and now you stop—oh!"

He got a full view of the bareheaded Judge in the moon-light.

"You!" he snorted. "Damn you, Van Treece, I'll—"

"You'll do what?" asked Slim Pickins coldly, and the click of his six-shooter caused Nelson to hesitate.

"So you're in with Conroy on this deal, eh?" he snarled.

"Henry," said Frijole, "is part of our outfit, Mr. Nelson. Have a drink?"

"I might have known it," said Nelson, and went back to his buggy.

"Aw, yuh scared him, Slim," said Frijole.

"I can shore make that upper plate of mine sound jist like cockin' a six-gun," chuckled Slim. "All set, gents? Let's go. If Henry ain't halfway on his honeymoon, it ain't our fault."

In less than a mile from there the buggy passed them, the horse on a gallop, but the buckboard team kept at a sedate pace—their work was over.

It was about two o'clock in the morning, when they arrived at Scorpion Bend. Slim tied the team in front of the Scorpion Bend Hotel, where Henry and Judge always stayed when in that city. There was no sign of Jim Nelson and his horse and buggy along the street.

The sleepy-eyed hotel keeper recognized Judge.

"Did Henry Conroy and his bride register here, Mose?" asked Judge.

"Bride? F'r Gaw's sake, when did he git hitched, Judge? No, he didn't have no woman with him. He's in yore regular room—but he's alone—'s far as I know."

THE THREE MEN plodded up the stairs, none too steady on their feet, and opened the door of the room. Slim Pickins scratched a match and lighted the lamp. Henry sat up, blinking at the lamp and at the three men.

"A cheese sandwich late at night always does this to me," said Henry. "I don't know why I indulge."

"Where-at's yore woman, Henry?" asked Slim soberly.

"My—my what?" gasped Henry. "Is that really you, Slim?"

"I dunno," replied Slim. "Frijole's whiskey does things to me."

"Hm-m-m-m," muttered Henry. He brushed a hand across his eyes and looked questioningly at Judge.

"I—I found your note, Henry," said Judge. "Jim Nelson and Al Horne came and saw it, too. They were going to try and catch you; so we blocked them on the grades. We had to do something, you know."

"I see," nodded Henry. "Friends in need. Well, well! My gracious!"

"We didn't blame yuh," said Slim. "I'd have done the same thing."

Henry wiped his moist eyes and tried to think of something to say.

"You are going to marry her, Henry?" queried Judge. "But you must remember that she already has a husband"

"I thought of that, too," said Henry huskily. "Frijole, is that a jug you have in your hand—or is it still a dream?"

"The fix you are in—and you jest," sighed Judge.

"Am I in a fix, Judge?"

"Are you in a fix? You run away with another man's wife—and he is right here in Scorpion Bend, wild-eyed and ready to do murder."

"My goodness! Frijole, will you hand me that glass on the table? Thank you. Now—the jug."

They all drank from the same glass. Henry said:

"Slim, you and Frijole go downstairs and register for a room. There is no use wastin' all the night. Judge, you will sleep here. I am afraid we have things to talk over."

"I should think that some explanation is forthcoming, sir," replied Judge.

After Frijole and Slim had left the room, Henry locked the door and blocked it with a chair-back placed under the knob.

"Just in case," he smiled.

"Now, sir," said Judge severely, "suppose you explain this peculiar action on your part."

Henry sat down on the edge of the bed, motioned for Judge to move his chair closer, and lowered his voice.

"The lady," he said, "is not a very good actress. In fact, it is easy to see why she never went higher than a honka-tonk, Judge. Her histronic ability is very poor. She set the stage, but her props were bad. For instance, that black eye, suffered from the fist of Jim Nelson, was badly made. Close inspection revealed grease-paint, no swelling, no injury to a very pretty eye."

"But why on earth did you bring her here, Henry?"

"Oh, yes, of course—you were not present. For your information, when Oscar started that trouble in the King's Castle, I went upstairs, managed to get an interview with the Slim Princess, who admitted that the man who was killed on our ranch house porch was her father. She gave me the usual line about innocent childhood and all that.

"Then she has a fight with Jim Nelson, who gave her a grease-paint black eye. She is supposed to have crawled out a window and swung to the ground on a blanket-rope. She wanted to get away at once. She was through with Jim Nelson. She played on my heart-strings, Judge; so I hired a rig from the livery stable and brought her here. When we arrived she told me she couldn't go through with it. She was afraid he'd find her, no matter where she went. I knew she'd say that, before we left Tonto City."

"But, Henry, I don't believe Jim Nelson was acting," said Judge.

Henry laughed quietly, "Judge, why did they come straight to the office? And so soon after she left."

"Well, I am amazed," declared Judge. "But what good has it done?"

"I do not know—yet," confessed Henry. "It was a shot in the dark when I asked her how long her father lived in Chicago, and she replied that she wasn't sure how long, but it was several years. I left her here at the hotel, and went to the depot, where I wired the Chicago police, asking information on both Winters and Ferguson. I hope they can tell us something."

"But why should she do all this acting, Henry, and get you to drive her all the way up here? It doesn't make sense."

"Judge, she wanted to find out how much Ferguson told me."

"But Ferguson didn't tell you anything, Henry."

"Judge, when you deal with liars—do a little lying yourself. It might pay dividends."

"Sometimes you amaze me, Henry."

"Sometimes I amaze myself, Judge."

"Did—did the Slim Princess take a room at this hotel?"

"She did not. I asked the clerk when I came back from the depot. She is probably waiting for Jim Nelson to reach here, and they will go back to Tonto together. But she never got any information from me, I can assure you of that. And what misinformation she got will not make them feel any better. Take off your clothes, Judge, and get into bed."

"But, Henry, do you suspect Jim Nelson of wrong-doing?"

"Somebody did wrong, Judge, and I cannot believe that the Slim Princess would do all that acting for anyone but Jim Nelson."

JAMES WADSWORTH LONGFELLOW PELLY was up fairly early next morning. He didn't wait to open the *Clarion* office, but headed directly to the Scorpion Bend Hotel. Henry, Judge, Frijole and Slim were in the dining-room eating breakfast when Pelly came in.

"The despoiler of appetites," groaned Judge, shoving his plate aside.

Pelly came straight to the table, ignored a proffered chair, and glared at Henry.

"What is your defense, sir?" he asked severely.

"My ability to laugh at the world, I suppose, Mr. Pelly.

I am not fleet of foot, have little ability as a boxer, and my shooting is vile."

"What in the devil is wrong with you, Pelly?" queried Judge.

"I am not talking to you, sir," replied Pelly. "For the first time in my life I relented and gave Henry Harrison Conroy an even break in my editorial. I gave him the benefit of all doubt—put him on a par with Ed Henderson. Now what? Jim Nelson awoke me at an early hour and told of your perfidy, Conroy. Last night you deliberately ran away with his wife, brought her to Scorpion Bend, and while you arranged for transportation at the depot, Jim Nelson arrived from Tonto City and saved her from disgrace."

"He did?" asked Henry in amazement. "My goodness!"

"You cannot shrug that off, Conroy," said Pelly.

"I am not shrugging, sir," replied Henry soberly. "But doesn't it sound rather humorous that a performer at the King's Castle should be saved from disgrace. It is really a miracle, Pelly."

"He is her husband," said Pelly doggedly.

"You have, I presume, looked at their marriage certificate."

"I am willing to take the lady's word for it."

"Oh! So she visited you with Jim Nelson, eh?"

"She admitted to me that you urged her to accompany you."

"Did she exhibit her black eye, Pelly?"

"I saw no black eye."

"I told her she might as well wipe it off," smiled Henry. "Did she tell you that she had a fight with Jim Nelson, who locked her in her room, and then slid from a window to the ground on a blanket?"

"She did not," replied Pelly.

"At least, she was honest in that respect, Pelly. But, in my opinion, she is one of the most prolific and least impressive liars I have ever met. As an actress, Pelly, she isn't worthy of carrying the make-up kit of one of the Cherry Sisters. Pelly, have you ever seen the Cherry Sisters?"

"I have not, Conroy. But isn't it rather ungentlemanly to say that a lady is il liar?"

"A lady—yes, indeed."

"Oh! I see. Well, do you deny that you eloped with her, Conroy?"

Henry chuckled. "Pelly, you amaze me. A man of my age and girth, not to mention my financial disability, eloping with a beautiful, young thing like the Slim Princess. I may be nearly everything you have called me in your newspaper, but down deep in my heart, Pelly, I am not that big a damn fool!"

James Wadsworth Longfellow Pelly was a bit puzzled. The story seemed plausible last night, or rather, early this morning, but just now it had new angles.

"Why on earth would Jim Nelson tell me what he did, if it was not true?" he asked.

"My dear Pelly," said Henry, "haven't you noted the political angle? They felt that they were losing the support of the *Clarion*, due to your last editorial. Without you and the *Clarion*, they are lost. Ergo, they try to frame me, kill my reputation, sink me in my own iniquity."

"I see-e-e," muttered Pelly. "That is possible. Well," Pelly shrugged his shoulders, "I shall wait for developments.

Perhaps you are right. But if you are wrong I'll never let up on you, be sure of that."

"Oh, I am, Pelly; I really am," said Henry soberly.

"How about a little ham 'n' aigs?" asked Slim. "They're good."

"Thank you, I have had my breakfast," replied Pelly, and walked out.

"Mr. Nelson," said Judge gravely, "almost scuttled our ship."

"It is still leaking," smiled Henry, "but we may make port."

FINISHED BREAKFAST AND went to the depot, but there was no answer to Henry's telegram. He decided to send Frijole and Slim back, and he and Judge would either take the morning stage or wait for the night stage.

It was four o'clock in the afternoon when the telegram came. It was from the detective bureau at Chicago, and read:

> WINTERS RECENTLY PAROLED FROM JOLIOT AFTER TEN YEARS FOR BIG PAY ROLL ROBBERY. REST OF GANG NEVER KNOWN. ANY INFORMATION WILL BE APPRECIATED. FERGUSON OUSTED THIS CITY FOR BLACKMAIL, NO RECORD HIS PRESENT CONNECTIONS.

"I told you that he wore prison clothes," said Judge.

"Blackmail, eh?" muttered Henry. "The plot grows thicker, Judge."

"Too thick, I am afraid, Henry."

"At least," smiled Henry, "we know more than we did."

"Yes," agreed Judge soberly, "and the same applies to our friend James Wadsworth Longfellow Pelly—but he isn't sure."

The day passed without event. Few people mentioned the election to either of them. The night stage left at eight o'clock. Henry and Judge were the only passengers, and they rode inside. Judge, still tired from his ride to Scorpion Bend, was snoring shortly after they left town.

Jimmy Sears was a good driver, and Henry felt perfectly safe. There was a big moon across the Lobo Canyon, making conditions good for the driver, because it illuminated most of the hair-pin curves. He was dozing, listening to Judge's snores, when the stage jerked up sharply. Then it lurched ahead, and Henry heard the sharp pop of Jimmy's whip.

He heard a voice yell a command of some sort, followed by the crack of a gun-shot.

But the four horses were running now, traveling down a dark stretch of the narrow grade. Henry yelled at Sears, but knew that the driver would not hear him. Judge was awake, trying to get somebody to tell him what had gone wrong, when the stage suddenly sideswiped the rocky wall on the inside of the grade. Sparks flew, as the iron tires bit into the solid rock of the roadbed. As it bounded back the door flew open and Henry fairly tumbled out.

He clawed his way to the front of the stage. In the moonlight he saw the driver, slumped in his seat, but still clinging to the lines. As Henry managed to climb over the wheel and reach the seat, a bullet went past his head and riccocheted off the rocks with a high-pitched whine, like the breaking of a guitar string.

But Henry didn't hesitate. He tore the lines from Jimmy's hands and swung the team into line. Luckily the harness was intact. Another bullet whined past him, causing him to duck low. He was on the wrong side of the seat, and could not control the brake, but he was in no position to bother with small details. With one arm around Jimmy Sears, hunched forward, doing all the driving with one hand, he yelled at that frantic team, and they responded.

There was more shooting, but Henry didn't mind. He couldn't stop that team, anyway, That side of the grade was all downhill, and it was only a question of keeping the team ahead of the heavy stage, and keeping them all on the grade. He realized that if the lead team ever sagged back and allowed the wheelers to get their legs over the stretchers, there would be a grand wreck on Lobo Grade, in which none of them would be likely to live longer than it took to fall all the way to the bottom of the canyon. Praying that there would be no north travel on the road, Henry drove around narrow curves, until he became dizzy.

And this nightmare driving was not over until they came down the last stretch, wheels smoking, and headed for the upgrade to the top of the mesa above Wild Horse Valley. Henry stopped the exhausted team and got down, his legs so trembly that he could hardly walk. Both doors of the stage were closed, but Judge was missing. He had no idea what happened to Judge. Had Judge fallen out, or did he get out when Henry took charge, and failed to get aboard again, he wondered? There was nothing to do about it at present. He had to get Jimmy Sears to the doctor, regardless of anything and then come back for Judge.

Jimmy Sears had been shot through the right shoulder, and Doctor Bogart was optimistic over his chances. Henry found Oscar asleep on the office cot, and ordered him to saddle his own horse, along with Judge's animal, and go back to Lobo Grades to pick up Judge. Oscar was not the one to ask questions, especially when he was still half-asleep. Then Henry kicked off his shoes and went to sleep on the cot.

AND HENRY SLEPT right there until ten o'clock, when Oscar returned without Judge.

"Ay can't find Yudge," he declared.

Henry was puzzled. Had Judge fallen off the grade, he wondered? Or had the men who were shooting at him— Henry scowled thoughtfully. Had Judge left the stage, following him out, those men might have found him. They had followed the stage a little while. Henry was trying to visualize what might have happened, when a man came in. He was a small, thin, grizzled person, badly in need of front teeth.

"Hyah, Sheriff," he grinned widely.

"Len Buckley!" exclaimed Henry. "We haven't seen you since—"

"Since you sobered me up in yore jail three months ago," finished Buckley. "Well, sir, I'm out of a job, Henry. Got fired right after breakfast this mornin'. Ed jist said, 'I'm goin' to git a new cook, Len; so yuh can pack yore warbag and I'll have Dell Cates take yuh to Tonto.'"

"I thought the Circle H assessed you as personal property, Len."

"Yeah? Well, I reckon not. Yuh don't know where I can git me a job, do yuh?"

"No, I don't, Len. But you should be able to find a job.

Ed Henderson always swore you were the best cook in the valley."

"Oh, I'll get a job all right," said Len. "Ain't been to town for three months; so I reckon I've got to get drunk. And how I hate it."

Len walked to the doorway, but turned and said, "And I ain't votin' for Honest Ed Henderson."

Oscar came back from breakfast, picking his teeth with the pointed blade of his pocket-knife.

"Yudge ain't come yet?" he asked.

"Not yet, Oscar."

Oscar wandered back into the corridor of the jail, just as Jim Nelson came. The big gambler was either mad, or doing a good job of acting.

"Conroy," he said harshly, "I've stood all I'm going to stand from you. Last night was the last straw."

"That was queer, wasn't it?" smiled Henry. "All that fuss, just to try and pry some information from me. Nelson, you rained on your own parade, and now you try to blame me because everything got wet."

"What do you mean, Conroy?" rasped Nelson, leaning across the desk.

"For instance, the lady with the black eye," said Henry calmly, "I realized that it was a fake, long before I agreed to take her to Scorpion Bend. I knew she wanted information, Nelson, but I was the one who got it. And the injured husband, trying to turn a *faux pas* into political profit, went to the newspaper editor. I thought you had more brains than that."

"Why, you damn red-nosed monkey!" roared Nelson.

"I'll break every bone in your damned fat carcass, and throw—"

JIM NELSON STOPPED, because he was out of breath. Oscar Johnson had stepped in behind him, hooked his left elbow around Nelson's throat, and put his right knee into Nelson's back.

"Say de vord, Henry," said Oscar tensely, "and Ay vill yerk just vonce."

That one jerk by the giant Swede would break Nelson's back; so Henry did not give the word. He got up, removed a revolver from Nelson's coat pocket, and motioned Oscar to release him. The big gambler wheezed breath back into his lungs, as he stood unsteadily against the desk.

"If you vant any more, Ay vill give it to you," said Oscar.

Nelson didn't. That grizzly-like strangle-hold had taken all the fight out of him.

"This won't end here," he whispered. "You still owe me a debt, Conroy, and when a man owes Jim Nelson a debt—he pays, sooner or later."

"I am usually available, Nelson," said Henry. "Call again."

Nelson went on. His legs were none too steady.

"You must have squeezed hard, Oscar," said Henry.

"Yah, su-ure," grinned Oscar. "Ay don't like him."

"I wish I knew where Judge is," said Henry. "Stay here, Oscar, while I get the mail."

Henry walked up to the post office and got the office mail, which consisted of two papers and one letter. The letter, strangely enough, had been posted in Tonto City, and consisted of one sheet of none-too-clean note paper, on which had been written in sprawling characters:

We hav yur depity. Unles you resin and leeve this valley inside of twenty for hours we will kill him. Then yu wil be next. We meen bisiness.

There was no signature. Henry read it twice and put it in his pocket, after which he opened one of the newspapers, reading it as he walked back to the office. If anyone was watching for his reactions to the receipt of that letter, they must have been disappointed. He sat down at his desk and stared thoughtfully at the opposite wall.

"Any mail, Hanry?" asked Oscar.

"Nothing of importance, Oscar," he replied. "And, Oscar, please do not mention the fact that Judge is missing."

"Ay vill not," declared Oscar. "Yudge vill be along. He is tough old yigger—but Ay like him, Hanry."

"I guess we all do, Oscar," said Henry sadly. "I don't know what I'd do without him—and I can't do anything *with* him."

Time seemed to stand still for Henry. James Wadsworth Longfellow Pelly came to Tonto City driving the livery rig, which Henry had used to take the Slim Princess to Scorpion Bend. The same man owned both the Tonto City and Scorpion Bend stables.

But Pelly did not come near the office. John Harper dropped in for a short chat, and informed Henry that Jim Nelson was putting on a little election rally at the honka-tonk that night.

"I suppose he will have Ed Henderson make a speech," smiled the lawyer. "That last editorial in the *Clarion* has them worried. Folks are wondering if Pelly is going over to your side."

"I do not believe it," said Henry. "I saw Pelly arrive a while ago, and he is still at the King's Castle. Perhaps he was invited to make a speech on behalf of Ed Henderson."

"I must be there," laughed the lawyer. "That *would* be worth hearing."

Slim Pickins, Frijole Bill, Thunder and Lightning Mendoza came in from the ranch. The two Mexican brothers were short, squat, more Indian than Mexican, and with the ability to tear the King's English to shreds.

"Buenas dias, padron," grinned Lightning. "And how am I, you hope? *Mucho gracias,* we are better than you could be expected."

"The same to you, and much of eet," added Thunder expansively. "Those corrals post ees all dugs up, and those hole ees ready for sitting."

Henry gave each of them a silver dollar, and they waddled away to a *cantina*, where they could secure tequila at rock-bottom prices.

"Where's Judge?" asked Slim. Henry closed the office door, and told them what happened on the stage. He let them read the note, too, but cautioned them to not mention a word of it.

"But we've got to do somethin', Henry," said Slim anxiously. "My Gawd, he's one of our set! Don'tcha realize we can't let 'em hurt him?"

"If we only knowed who to kill," sighed Frijole. "What'll we do?"

"Nothing," said Henry. "You and Slim stay around town, where I can get you—if I need you. Stay sober, if possible, too."

"My Gawd, we ain't drinkin' now, Henry!" exclaimed

Frijole. "Maybe we'll have a couple—after we find Judge. Henry, I came away without m' gun. If you've got a extra hawg-leg—"

Henry had. Frijole shoved it inside the waistband of his overalls.

"I feel plumb dressed now," he said. "See yuh later, Henry. Me and Slim will do a lot of listenin', but no talkin'."

SUPPERTIME CAME. IN the restaurant Henry heard men talking about the political meeting at the King's Castle. It was to be held after the first show at the honkatonk. That would make it about ten o'clock. Henry went back to his office and lighted the lamp. From an old wardrobe he took his clothes and made a complete change to overalls, old flannel shirt, high-heel boots and a slightly battered sombrero. Then he belted a heavy gun around his expansive waist, locked the front, went out through the jail corridor and mounted his horse.

About four miles out of town he turned to the left on a side road, which led to the Circle H ranch. He rode more cautiously now, not wanting to meet anyone. An overcast sky was to his liking tonight. The Circle H ranch house had been built on a slight raise, partly screened in a sycamore grove. South of the house was the big stable and a series of corrals. Directly back of the house, and about fifty feet away, was a big storage shed.

There was a faint light through the curtains in the main room, as Henry dismounted in the heavy shade of a syca-more at the east end of the corrals. He walked quietly up to the old shed. The door was partly open, and the rear window was only a hole in the wall. He went inside, shielded a lighted match carefully and looked around. On the floor, near the doorway, were two ten-gallon cans of kerosene.

Henry carried them to the rear of the shed, and quickly slashed the sides of them with his pocket-knife. Kerosene gushed out over everything. Then he went quietly around to the rear of the shed and leaned against the wall at the open window. There was not a sound.

From his overalls pocket he took the letter he had received from the kidnapers, crumpled it in his fingers, and reached for a match. The air reeked of kerosene. Then he tossed the lighted piece of paper through the open window and went running for the corner of the house.

He was nearly there before the flame caught in the kerosene, and the explosion lighted the surroundings. Yellow flame gushed from the doorway, and in a few moments the whole shed was blazing. Someone inside the house yelled, and the kitchen door banged open.

"That damn shed's on fire, Ab! Get a bucket!" he heard Dell Cates yell.

Henry heard them banging buckets, as they raced for the watering-trough, swearing, stumbling. Then he twisted around the corner and quickly entered the kitchen. Henry did not hesitate, as he ran into the main room and up the stairs. The room at the corner was his objective. The door was locked, but he stepped back and crashed it loose.

Roped to a chair was Judge Van Treece, his features plainly visible, as he craned his long neck, trying to see what was causing the glow through the partly-covered window.

"It's me—Henry!" panted the sheriff, as he fumbled with his knife.

"Ungrammatical, but welcome," said Judge huskily, as Henry cut away the ropes that bound him to the chair.

"Can you walk?" asked Henry.

"I—I hope so," groaned Judge, as Henry helped him to his feet. "But where on earth did you come from?"

"A debate is out of order right now, Judge. Follow me!"

They reached the stairs. Judge was having difficulty, because of being tied in one position for so long. It had not helped his rheumatism. They were halfway down the short flight of stairs, when the two men, panting, came into the kitchen.

"Let the damn thing burn!" panted Cats. "It can't hurt anythin' else, now. I told Ed that we hadn't ort to store that—"

They had entered the main room and saw the two men on the stairs.

"Well, my Gawd, where did you—" exploded Cates, and streaked for his gun.

BUT HENRY HAD his .45 muzzle across the stair railing, and he squeezed the trigger. The heavy bullet drove Cates back into Ab Rader, who threw both hands into the air, and went sliding along the wall. Cates went down and his half-drawn gun clattered on the floor.

"I quit!" yelled Rader. "To hell with it! Never liked the deal, anyway."

Henry and Judge came slowly down the stairs. Rader wasn't wearing a gun.

"I'll be a liar!" he said. "Didn't recognize yuh in them clothes. And they said you was dumb—and couldn't shoot. Huh!"

"So this is the Circle H," marveled Judge. "Of all things!"

Henry managed to dig a pair of handcuffs from his hip-pocket. He snapped one end on Rader's right wrist, and the other around the door-knob.

"You will not go far, dragging the house," he said quietly. "Will you tell me which horse in the stable is gentle?"

"The gray one," said Rader wearily.

"You would not play a joke on two elderly men, would you?"

"Not in my present position, Conroy; he's gentle."

They looked at Cates as they went out.

"He is tied to something bigger than a door-knob," said Judge.

THE KING'S CASTLE was crowded that night. Word had gone out that Jim Nelson was holding a political rally, and the honkatonk was jammed. The Slim Princess had finished her last encore amid deafening applause, as Jim Nelson, Ed Henderson and James Wadsworth Longfellow Pelly came out on the stage. Henderson, Pelly and the Slim Princess sat down on chairs quickly arranged near the footlights.

Oscar Johnson shoved his way down the center aisle, stopped at a front seat and tapped the man on the shoulder. When the man looked up, Oscar said something. The man scowled and replied, but Oscar took him by the shoulder, and the man got up quickly. Then the big Swede slid into the chair.

Jim Nelson saw the tableau, but did not hear what was said. However, he realized that Oscar had forced the man to relinquish the seat. He wondered why the Swede had done this. If it was to heckle any of the speakers, he would find a quick way to silence the Swede. This was one time that Oscar better stay where he was and behave himself.

Then Jim Nelson, smiling widely, walked close to the footlights and motioned for silence.

"Gentlemen," he said, "this is just a little innovation from our regular show. You all realize that it is only a few days until election. You probably know that I am backing certain candidates, because you are all sick and tired of the present incumbents.

"Gentlemen, I feel that Wild Horse Valley is entitled to the best, and at this coming election, you may be sure we will have the best."

The applause was deafening. Nelson smiled with satisfaction. If they could only go and cast their votes right now. When the applause died down, he continued:

"For instance, you all realize the inefficiency of the sheriff's office. They have made Wild Horse Valley the laughing stock of Arizona long enough. Gentlemen, I want you to meet the man we feel is our best choice for sheriff; a friend to all of you, and a man you can be proud to vote into the office as the sheriff of Wild Horse Valley—Honest Ed Henderson!"

The audience, most of them at least partly drunk, got to their feet and gave Ed Henderson a great ovation. Jim Nelson waved them to silence, and they gradually sat down, the room roaring with conversation. Nelson held up his hand, until the noise subsided. Then he said:

"Honest Ed Henderson, next sheriff of Wild Horse Valley, will say a few words to you. Ed is not an orator, but his words to you are honest."

Henderson stepped forward awkwardly and looked

down at the crowd. He started to speak, but the words stuck in his throat. Coming down the center aisle, bareheaded, walking slowly, was Judge Van Treece, his eyes on Henderson.

JIM NELSON HAD started to sit down, but merely hunched there, holding to the back of the chair with his left hand, his eyes glued on the tall, old man, coming down toward them.

"Hyah, Henry! Comin' to yore own funeral?" yelled somebody in the crowd.

Nelson jerked around. Behind them on the stage was Henry Conroy. He had come in from the wings. The Slim Princess screamed, jerked to her feet, and suddenly put both hands over her face. No one in the audience, except Oscar Johnson, knew what was going on.

"Henderson," said Henry, and his quiet voice carried to everyone, "Cates is dead, and Rader is handcuffed to the front door. Your campaign is over."

But Honest Ed didn't have the nerve to face the music. He yanked a gun from under his coat and leaped for the center aisle, intending to try and force his escape through the saloon, but he reckoned without Oscar Johnson, who raised up to meet him.

The gun went flying, and the candidate for the sheriff's office went down in a crumpled heap, with the giant Swede on top of him.

Jim Nelson had a gun, and he whirled, shooting at Henry, but his aim was bad. Henry shot once, twice, as calmly as he usually did everything, and Jim Nelson almost did a top-spin on his left heel, before he went down, crashing into the vacant chairs.

It was too much for the nerves of James Wadsworth Longfellow Pelly. He went out of his chair, slipped, when he tried to jump, and dived headfirst right over the top of the upright piano, taking Doc, the piano maestro, right along with him. The crowd was starting to stampede, but Henry, with one hand holding the arm of the Slim Princess, yelled:

"It is all over, men! Take it easy! We have just smashed the worst gang that ever operated in Tonto City. No time to explain now. Will somebody call Doctor Bogart? Oh, there you are, Doc! You know what to do. Are you all right, Oscar?"

"Yah, su-ure!" called Oscar. "Das von is not going to run for anyt'ing."

Someone yelled, "Henry!"

"Yes, Frijole."

"Al Horne tried to escape," said Frijole. "Slim had to shoot him."

"Good work, Frijole. Help Oscar put Henderson in jail."

"He don' need a yail, Hanry," said Oscar. "He is yust a remain now."

The Slim Princess was on the verge of collapse, as Henry led her backstage, where they met John Harper, the prosecutor. Without a word, they helped her up the stairs and down the hall to her room, where she almost fell into a chair.

"My dear lady," said Henry kindly, "as you probably know, the law is always lenient to those who assist the law. Your confession might make things a lot easier for you."

"What can I say?" she whispered. "You knew—"

"But we would rather have you tell it," interrupted

Henry. "After all, what I know wouldn't help you in the least—before a judge."

"I—I don't care now," she said huskily. "Jim's gone—they got Al. I'll tell you what you want to know."

The door opened and the disheveled James Wadssvorth Longfellow Pelly came in. He had a long scratch down his thin nose, one eye was swollen, and he had lost his collar. The Slim Princess did not even look at him, as she said wearily:

"Ten years ago Jim Nelson and his gang robbed that payroll. We got enough to last us—always. They got Jack Winter, but he never talked. There was only Jim, Al Horne, Henderson and Winters. Winters took the rap. Henderson bought that cattle ranch, but the rest of us moved from place to place. What we did don't matter now. Jim kept in touch with Henderson, and it was through him that we came here.

"Jim wanted to boss the valley. I told him it was a mistake, but he was bull-headed. Then Winters came. Jim spotted him right away. Winters wanted money—his share. Jim laughed at him. I guess Winters lost his nerve and was going to tell on us. Henderson beat him to your ranch and shot him. We were sure that none of us would be suspected, when Ferguson showed up. Jim knew him. Ferguson was a blackmailer. He wanted to know who Winters came to find. Henderson killed Ferguson. They said you didn't have any brains.

"You were right, when you said I lied about my trouble with Jim. I did it to find out what you knew. We came back from Scorpion Bend and saw Henderson's two men. The idea was to kill you. But I guess that fell through, but they got Van Treece. How you knew where to find him, I do not know. I guess that is the story."

"Not a bad story, John," said Henry. "But my dear, Winters wasn't your father."

She shook her head. "No, I lied to you. I liked Jack Winters, and I was fool enough to show it. Now you can take me to jail."

THEY DID. AL Horne was dead, and Jim Nelson only had a small chance to live. Henderson had a broken shoulder and a fractured arm. Men came and congratulated Henry; the same men who roared applause at Ed Henderson. But Henry was too tired to enjoy it. He and Judge went up to their room at the hotel, where they undressed in silence. Finally Judge said:

"Henry, I do not know how you discovered all this. I retract everything I ever said about your mental processes. You are a great officer; the greatest I have ever known. Tonight you saved my life. I appreciate that. It isn't much— but it is all I had."

Henry sat on the edge of the bed, which buckled under his weight. He was not impressive in his full-length, bulging underwear. His eyes blinked wearily. Finally he replied:

"I appreciate that, Judge. A great officer of the law. Almost single-handed I smashed a gang of cold-blooded killers. None got away. I wove a web that caught them all."

"You did, my friend, and I appreciate every action. But, Henry, now that we can be honest with each other, and leave all the bull behind—just what *did* you know?"

Henry's face twisted into the first hearty laugh he had had since Winters had been murdered.

"For your ears alone, Judge," he chuckled, "I didn't know

a damn thing. If it hadn't been for the Slim Princess' confession, I could have been made the biggest fool in Arizona. All I knew, Judge, was that Ed Henderson fired his cook on short notice. That cook is an honest man, and they had to get rid of him, in order to keep you there at the Circle H."

"Is that all you had, Henry?"

"Except deep and dark suspicion, which never convicted anybody."

Judge reached under the bed and drew out a gallon jug. Henry blinked at it thoughtfully.

"Ambrosia," he whispered. "Nectar of the gods—fit for the palate of a king."

"Or the palate of a fool," amended Judge.

"Two fools," whispered Henry. "Get the glasses, Judge."

www.ingramcontent.com/pod-product-compliance
Lightning Source LLC
Chambersburg PA
CBHW051143030726
47504CB00004B/1011